The Epidemic

The Epidemic

Darrell Nkholoma Phiri

First Edition

Hidden Brook Press
www.HiddenBrookPress.com
HiddenBrookPress@gmail.com
EST. 1994

The Epidemic
by Darrell Nkholoma Phiri

Editor – Richard M. Grove
Cover Design – Henri Papier
Layout and Design – Richard M. Grove
Cover Images:
    – "The Child" and "The Mask" – Shutterstock
    – The man behind the mask – Pexels
    – Army Dudes in the Front – pexels-art-guzman-8079183
    – Generals Face(well chin) – pexels-ryutaro-tsukata-6249093
    – Generals Attire – pexels-carmen-attal-2859054

Typeset in Garamond
Printed and bound in Canada

Distributed in USA by Ingram,
        in Canada by Hidden Brook Distribution

Library and Archives Canada Cataloguing in Publication

Title: The epidemic / Darrell Nkholoma Phiri.
Names: Phiri, Darrell Nkholoma, 1992– author.
Identifiers: Canadiana 2021024397X |
        ISBN 9781989786482 (softcover)
Classification: LCC PR9639.4.P55 E65 2021 |
        DDC 823/.92—dc23

Dedicated to my late grandmother

Mrs. Mary Kalikeka.

1934 - 2021

Table of Contents

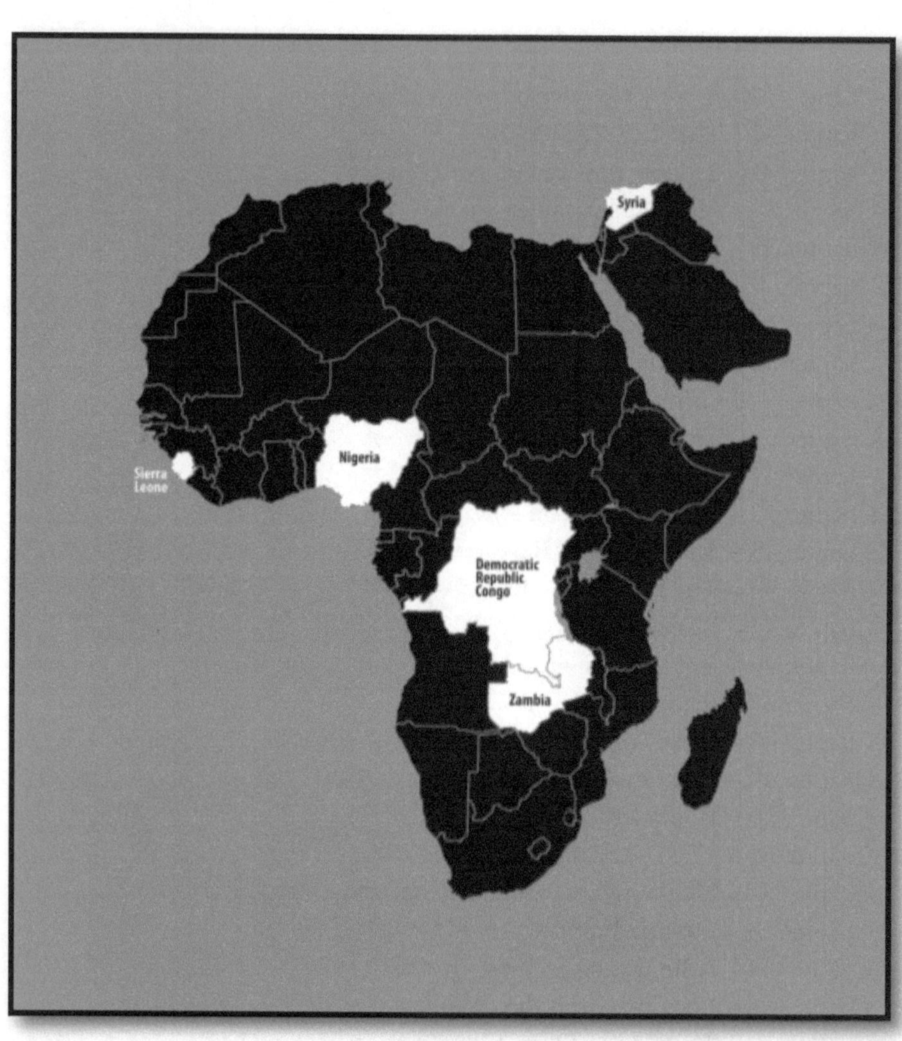

Syria
Sierra Leone
Nigeria
Democratic Republic Congo
Zambia

Prologue

THE SAINT MARGRET Hospital's receptionist noticed an unexpected surge in the number of patients who were walking through the facility's swinging doors. Even during peak periods, they had never had more than ten patients at once; after all, it was a small community. The patients kept pouring in. By the third day the influx had reached unsustainable proportions such that the hospital staff were left with no choice other than to lock those same swinging doors and leave desperately sick people outside on the porch.

The hospital was in the middle of the Yambuku Village which was situated in Zaire, approximately one thousand kilometers northeast of the capital Kinshasa. The year was 1976. The building had been constructed by the Catholic Church in the late 1960's. It was a new structure for that region but was only able to accommodate twenty patients in the general ward and some ten patients in the waiting room. It was in no way equipped to accommodate such a surge.

When the hospital was being constructed the size seemed to be very reasonable for a small village district but now, since the first week of August the patients were pouring in at an alarming rate. The existing patients only seemed to be getting worse. Initially the patients complained about suffering from the symptoms of influenza and joint pains. This became the growing consensus amongst the medical staff. Little did they know these were only the first cases of a brewing epidemic.

The second batch of villagers came in a few days after that lot with complaints about suffering from severe headaches. Almost like clockwork the first lot went on to experience a metamorphosis with their symptoms transforming to diarrhea and chest pains within moments of each other. The first patient who died from this unknown disease spent his last moment on this earth coughing and vomiting blood. After the villagers buried "patient one", as the staff began to call him, there was another extreme surge of patients; making this situation move from being difficult, to almost impossible to manage.

At this point the lead doctor instructed that the hospital's front door should be locked. As the receptionist sat at her desk, trying by all means to do the paperwork, she listened to the everlasting crying and screaming of the patients who were camped outside as their voices echoed throughout the area. There was a gloomy cloud that hovered over the people of Yambuku, such that everyone in the region was anticipating the end of their lives. The entire society was living with fear of death, both those who were healthy and those who were unwell.

The nuns were nurses and most of the doctors were priests, however none of them knew what to make out of the common symptoms that their patients were suffering from. Doctor Daniel Clancy initially suspected that it was some form of severe flu, but the weather in Zaire was so warm in that moment that he thought this to be an unlikely source. Several of the patients had arrived sick after burying one of their fellow villagers.

Doctor Clancy pondered about this in his office as he took a five-minute break. Was it possible that the living could catch a disease from the dead and if so, how was it spreading? Was it through the exchange of fluids, physical contact or worse? Was this dreaded virus airborne and if that was the case, how could they contain it? He had never seen anything like this but ensured that his staff wore face masks and gloves at all times.

Doctor Daniel Clancy knew that he had wanted to be a doctor from the time that he was a ten-year-old boy. He was dedicated academically and although he wasn't the brightest in the class in middle school, he was number one at the end of high school. His family had hoped that when their son became a doctor, he would go on to make a lot of money, yet he disappointed them when he decided to become a missionary. They sacrificed for him with the expectation that he could have given some of his years to obtaining wealth, however their son was adamant about being a missionary doctor working with the poor. He moved from mission to mission sharing the word of God and healing the poor with the limited medical resources that were at his disposal. Daniel was an expert at using little to heal a lot. He had faced many challenges during the course of his career, but now at sixty-five years old, he was faced with the greatest trial of them all.

Daniel was a devoted Christian and felt that he was in Yambuku in 1976 for a divine purpose. He imagined what would have happened if there had been no hospital in this village. Without the missionaries, the outbreak would have wiped out the entire district and no one in the international community would have even heard about it. He was often scared for his own life and dreaded caring for patients who were crying out to him in agony because he knew that eventually one of them could transmit the disease to him and he could soon share their fate. His mind drifted into scripture as he reminisced on Luke chapter twenty-two verse forty-two when Jesus was at the Mount of Olives and the scripture said "Father, if you are willing, take this cup from me; yet not my will, but yours be done." So as Jesus concluded by telling the Lord to let his will be done then Daniel would do the same. He was afraid, yes, but knew that moments like these were there to strengthen his faith.

His prayerful thoughts were suddenly interrupted. The door swung open ferociously as one of his nurses stormed into his office. She was shaking frantically and struggling to articulate herself for several moments until he rose to comfort her. He knew that it was time to return to reality, he couldn't hide away in prayer forever. He ushered her to a chair with a gentle hand. Her face displayed total horror. Before sitting down, she began to report to him, but she stammered so much that it was difficult for him to understand.

Pulling her mask from her face she stammered, "Doctor Clancy, its Martha. She is sick, just in the same way that all the patients are. I am scared to go back out there." With this quaking declaration she finally stepped out of her trance and placed her shaking hands over her face. She sat down hesitantly, as if she didn't trust herself not to fall. Isabelle was much younger than the other nuns and it must have been an inner calling for her to come to Zaire. Most young girls wouldn't have been as courageous because they knew all about the dangers which were ever present in that nation.

Zaire was a country that had been engulfed by internal fighting for many years, most of which was politically motivated as nations around the world were interested in their resources. Doctor Clancy ensured that all the foreign staff in the hospital were familiar with Zaire's recent history. His inductions always commenced with a history lesson on the Congo crisis which occurred from 1960 to 1965.

As far as Doctor Clancy was concerned "The Congo Crisis" began after the vicious riots in Stanleyville on October 1959 as this led the Belgians to realize that they would no longer be able to keep control of the vast and highly complicated country. A round table conference was held in Brussels in January 1960 which paved the way for independence, which was finally granted 30th June 1960 and thus Congo-Brazzaville was born.

After the finalization of parliamentary elections Patrice Lumumba emerged as the nation's prime minister and Joseph Kasavubu was named President. Following the secession of Katanga, Congo's richest province and Kasai, the second richest province from the rest of Congo, thereby creating two separate states. Patrice Lumumba looked to the Soviet Union for military assistance. The United States saw this as an attempt by the USSR to extend their communist agenda to central Africa. The US sent weapons and CIA support to Colonel Joseph Mobutu who had Patrice Lumumba arrested, tortured and killed in January 1961 in the capital of Katanga. The word was that his body was placed in acid and that was why it was never recovered.

The nation continued to experience war and infighting until November 1965 when General Mobutu seized power and declared himself as the country's president. In 1966 they changed the country's name to Zaire, which was translated as "the river that swallows all rivers". Ten years later here they were, in a one-party state and a dictatorship. Doctor Clancy wanted all his staff members to appreciate the situation as they conducted themselves and spoke because the wrong words, in the company of the wrong people could be the difference between life and death.

The church also went to great lengths to ensure that individuals who decided to volunteer in the Saint Margret hospital were aware of this before they even filled in the paperwork. When Daniel saw Isabelle arrive at the mission, he was deeply moved by her sacrifice and courage so early in her young life.

The church had been encouraged to build the hospital following the violence that surrounded demands for independence from Belgium. The early years of independence not only brought internal fighting, but also external fighting with regards to the Soviet Union and the United States of America conducting their Cold War in the rich Sub-Saharan African country.

Para-militants and mercenaries were pouring in to preserve mining interests for those fearful of losing their assets to the state with the communist influence. The church wanted hospitals to deal with those who had suffered from violence and they wanted priests to teach the people Christian values that could help to change the hearts of the people from thinking thoughts of hatred to thoughts of love and peace.

The country was enriched with almost every mineral resource that this planet valued. Sadly, its citizens were prepared to kill each other for them. It was for this reason that Daniel came here to spread the word and to heal those who were caught in the crossfire, but he made this choice after he had lived a long life, yet Isabelle was still so young.

Isabelle was an attractive, short, brunette girl who now had tanned skin and green eyes. Today, however, she had never looked worse and whatever little make up she applied had been smeared by her tears. She looked at Daniel hopelessly as if she expected him to whisk her out of that hospital and return her to the United Kingdom. He had to calm her down as quickly as possible because he needed her, they were completely understaffed. If he granted her permission to return to her dormitory, then he would be doing a disservice to himself and the other staff members.

"Isabelle, my dear, we made a decision to spread the word of the Lord and to provide health care for the most disadvantaged of his children. This moment of chaos and difficulty is exactly why we are here right now. If we weren't in Yambuku then there would be no hope for all these people, so even if death awaits us then we still have a duty to fulfill. We will do it for them, for us and for our heavenly father who blessed us with the ability to preserve life." He walked towards her and opened his arms widely to offer her a hug. She rose and placed her head on his chest for comfort. He responded by rubbing her back. He didn't know if this was helping but felt that he had to do something. He thought himself to be like a general who was sending his soldiers into a battle, all the while not knowing if they would make it out of the war alive.

Daniel's heart was racing as he thought about how he was going to treat people who were more than likely going to infect him. He opened the door and decided not to fear death, after all death was only the beginning of life in paradise. Isabelle was re-energized by their discussion; she immediately tried to restore order in the corridor to make room for him to pass. Some of the patients who didn't have beds were lying on the floor, but Isabelle leaned them against the wall to open up a pathway for Doctor Clancy. This required a lot from her because these people were wailing and crying profusely, most were holding onto her tightly.

The hospital had run out of painkillers; however, Daniel was optimistic that they would receive new supplies by the end of the day; at least this was the promise made by the ministry of health. Daniel couldn't stop to assist the people in the corridor because he decided to go straight into the ward and prioritize those patients. For people to have access to a bed then he knew that they had been there the longest and would be in the most pain.

The only way to cater for the majority was if he was going to run his hospital like an assembly line. If anyone was too far gone, he would ensure that his nurses were ready to dispose of the bodies. In a faithless moment of weakness, he even contemplated giving these hopeless cases a unique naturally grown drug to help them enter the afterlife. It would make them drowsy and before long they would make a more peaceful transition then what he was witnessing.

He was quick to dismiss this conjecture because no matter how dire the situation was only God was the giver and taker of life. During his career Daniel had seen patients who he was certain would die find a way to fight back so even though there was nothing much that he could do he had to try. If people wanted to die, then they would have stayed home instead of going to the hospital.

The corridor was filthy; there was feces and urine on the floors. Not to mention all the blood that was smeared onto the floor tiles. He stepped into a pile of vomit at the end of the corridor and saw the cleaner helping some patients to the ground. Obviously, the gentleman had decided to abandon his cleaning responsibilities to help the staff, Daniel concurred with this notion. They were understaffed and why should the man bother to clean when the place would become dirty again moments later.

Once in the ward he walked to the bedside of a young woman. From a distance she appeared to be reaching the end of the line, the woman had already developed a visible maculopapular rash which was a skin disease that left red dots all along the body. Daniel had seen this before and in accordance with his calculations, over seventy percent of patients that got that rash ended up dead shortly after its emergence.

The woman was sweating profusely, and the nurse immediately informed him that she had had diarrhea and had been regurgitating throughout the night. There was absolutely no food left in her system and her blood was not clotting. The woman, with a weak and shallow voice tried to speak to him. He leaned forward, ignoring his reservations.

She was mumbling words about having small children outside. Doctor Clancy had learnt how to speak the local vernacular however he was at a very basic level. Daniel asked the lady how many children she had and where they were. The nameless woman pointed toward the direction of the yard and whispered that she had a boy and girl before she took her last breath. Doctor Clancy placed his hand on her neck. There was no pulse, she had passed.

He signaled to Isabelle to move the body off the bed, he told the cleaner to help her. There were no clean bed sheets with which to change the bed, he informed the other nurse to help the next patient onto the bed. The bed sheets were dripping with blood, but the new patient was only happy to be on a bed after spending the night on a cold, hard floor.

Instead of attending to the next bed Daniel decided to find the children. The patient who he should have assisted screamed insults at him as he exited the ward. He understood the anger, but something within him sent Daniel in search of these kids. Doctor Clancy was determined to find the little boy and girl who had just lost their mother and had probably been out in the cold for two days. There were no good Samaritans in these times, those children would starve to death if he didn't step in.

Daniel walked out of the main hospital doors and was immediately confronted by a wave of desperate people who were clinging to his coat. Some of those villagers had been camped outside of Saint Margret's all night long and were tired of being told that the hospital was full. He tried his best to move through the crowd as people held onto him until one man grabbed hold of his trousers firmly. The slim gentleman pleaded for him to help them, but there was simply no room in the hospital. The lady who had died would only provide one bed yet there were over fifty villagers who were waiting outside on the porch. He sympathized with them and was heartbroken, but there was nothing that he could do. Whether they were inside or outside he had no medicine to treat them with.

Daniel didn't know where he was walking to, but the cries of a child somewhat guided him. He eventually found himself on the grounds looking at a small boy who was weeping in despair. The villagers eventually lost interest in Daniel as most were reluctant to lose their places in the queue, so none opted to follow him. There were no other children there, but a young boy who was pointing along the path that led away from the hospital. Daniel stared intensely but couldn't make out what he was being told to look at. Daniel walked up to the boy hesitantly. He didn't want to scare him away and was also unsure of how the child would react. The boy just continued to gawp at the path, but he didn't say a word. Daniel decided to pick him up and the child seemed to be okay with it.

Daniel didn't have any children of his own. He had been married once upon a time when he was very young, but his wife grew weary of moving around from country to country living in mediocracy. They remained married for a few years and stayed in contact through letters until she sent a letter requesting a divorce. The divorce didn't surprise him; they had only been seeing each other for a few weeks each year. After the marriage was dissolved, they remained friends even after she had remarried and went on to have her own family.

With the frail little boy in his arms Daniel knew in that moment that he would look after this boy and his sister when she eventually surfaced. The world was no place for an orphan, especially in a small African village where people were struggling to feed their own families. No one would be willing to take in more mouths. Daniel decided that this would be his last assignment; he would return home and raise these children as his own. He was satisfied with his contribution to this nation and believed that if he survived this crisis then he could walk away with a sense of completion.

Out of nowhere the boy started to panic and pushed Daniel off before he bolted along the dusty path. Daniel was in no shape but tried his best to keep up. He didn't know what he did to trigger this reaction from the child but was resolved to save this boy. When he eventually caught up to the child, Daniel found the boy staring at the Ebola River. It was almost as if the child expected something to emerge from it.

Daniel lifted him up once more and started to walk back to the hospital which was near his small home. As they hiked back Daniel told the boy not to do that again and he seemed to understand this. He was obviously scared and confused. The boy also looked dehydrated and hungry and these initial issues needed to be addressed immediately.

Daniel knew that a team of physicians was being sent by the World Health Organization. He was also expecting an independent research team to come from Belgium. This was extremely essential. They needed to understand this unnamed virus that originated near the mighty Ebola River. If the international community didn't step in, then it would not be long until this thing got totally out of control. The Zairians also needed programs in place to cater for the children who would be left on the streets after this situation was eventually contained.

Daniel could only take care of one or two orphans yet there were going to be hundreds. He knew that if his staff continued to get sick than he would be forced to leave Yambuku very soon regardless of how valiant he wanted to be. The church was going to pull them all out even though he tried to downplay the need for them to evacuate. He had a small home near the hospital, he took the boy there. The home had a bedroom, a kitchen, lounge area and a toilet and bathroom. Prior to this Daniel quite enjoyed his time in Yambuku. He grew vegetables in his tiny garden and read novels that the drivers would bring for him from the main cities whenever they brought in medicine.

He was a vegetarian so prepared a meal that most children where he was from would refuse to eat, but this child ate and finished it within moments of the plate being placed in front of him. Daniel fed the boy once more while reiterating to him not to leave. Daniel grabbed a thick blanket from the wardrobe and wrapped it around him when the boy finished eating his second portion of lunch. When asked if he was full, the boy smiled with gratitude. No words were needed. His bloated belly was all the confirmation that was needed. Daniel put the child on his bed and waited until the boy was asleep before making his way back to the clinic.

When the girl returned, he vowed to take her in also. For now, he had patients to treat while he awaited help from the local government and the World Health Organization. He took a deep breath before strutting back towards the hospital. His mind and body were mentally prepared to survive the day.

Daniel was tempted to give the boy an English name however something within him knew that this child could have a major role to play in Zaire. He decided that when he adopted him, the boy would be called Olivier and his sister would also be given a French name. Daniel looked around the grounds and the girl hadn't returned yet, so he proceeded into the hospital. He knew that the fact that the government required their citizens to change their French names to African ones meant that Daniel would only name the boy when he was out of the country.

The Yambuku village had one basic school which had subsequently become an abandoned building. It was hard to convince villagers of the importance of school when there was land and animals to care for. However, there were a small number that had faith that if their children could take in what was written in these books then they could be emancipated from their struggle. The villagers didn't know that they were struggling until people from outside of the community came in and exposed them to things that they didn't know existed. Cattle were the most precious asset in this society and the wealthiest man was always the one who could boast of the most livestock.

The Ebola River was a mighty river that meandered in a majestic manner. The villagers relied on it to provide all their water for bathing and in most cases, it was used for drinking but of course the main blessing from the river was the fishing. Most of them had built up their immune systems so their bodies could withstand the salty water and the parasites that came with it, but outsiders would be wise to boil the water first. They did most of their fishing along the banks of this river and most boys were fishermen before they even knew how to count. The village life almost prepared a person for how they could survive from the ground if they lost everything. It was almost as if those who made it out of there could be fearless because they knew that even if they reached their lowest point, they could survive anything that this world threw at them.

Chapter 1

Olivier's Return to the Past

OLIVIER DROVE into Saint Margret's hospital for the first time in a decade; ever since the missionaries had left no one bothered to maintain the place. Not a single renovation had been performed on the structure except for the random patch-up job here and there which looked tacky. When he walked through the hospital the doctors were almost embarrassed to show him what had become of the place. The wards consisted of three beds; each of them was occupied when he peeped inside.

The place stank and the open windows ensured that these poor patients lay with flies hovering above them. They had clearly lost the energy to chase them away. Olivier decided to walk out of the hospital quickly; he felt that he had seen enough. Although he didn't show it, he was slightly concerned about the number of people who had forced a handshake or a hug on him. This was to be expected since he was the village's "golden boy" nonetheless; he would have preferred to conduct physical greetings outside of the medical facility with less physical contact. He stood there for a moment, pondering on what his life would have been like if that man had decided to leave him there. He had grown up calling Doctor Daniel Clancy his father and he only realized that he wasn't when people pressed him about his biological parents. As the years went by Olivier thought more and more about Congo and his real family.

Doctor Clancy had never tried to reinvent the past. He treated Olivier like a son but educated him on Congolese history and expressed his desire that Olivier would return and not live in diaspora. He told him that he was there to gain exposure but should go and use all that he learnt to develop his own country. He made sure that Olivier was politically aware about all the violence that had taken place in the Congo and told Olivier to protect himself and his family before he even considered entering the fray. Olivier knew from the very beginning that he was being groomed for politics.

Doctor Clancy insisted that Olivier played chess. He told him that the direction he wished his son to take would require knowledge on how to anticipate the moves of his opponents and to read people's thoughts even when they weren't speaking. It was only in hindsight that Olivier realized the importance of this, he could look a person in the eyes and almost hear their thoughts. Doctor Clancy also encouraged Olivier to take public speaking training at a tender age, he ensured his son spoke at every type of occasion until Olivier craved the podium.

He decided to revisit his village as it was his mother's memorial that weekend. He could barely remember her, but her grave site was the only thing that gave him a sense of his origins. His driver politely ushered him towards the land cruiser that was parked a few meters from the field where he was standing. They had already spent longer there then was planned and as always, he was pressed for time. He could barely remember when last he had a free day.

The four by four moved along the dirt road at a sluggish pace. Every time that he had been there in the past, he promised the villagers that he would solve all their infrastructure problems, but the truth was that he couldn't. Roads were only built in regions that lead to economic activity and this little village offered little to the national GDP. The most that he did was pave the way from his mother's grave site back to St Margret's. He knew that whether or not he fulfilled his promises the villagers would support him politically. They truly saw him as an inspiration. Not to mention that African politics was heavily dependent on tribal lines.

His wife had decided to accompany him on his visit to Yambuku, but he would have preferred to go alone. He knew that she would want to talk to him along the way about things that he was not particularly interested in and she did just that. He had hoped to use the trip as an opportunity to think about a combination of state affairs and internal party issues. Instead, he had to listen to how she wanted to renovate the kitchen after he had just spent so much money buying the house.

She went on non-stop about all the many financial needs that her relatives had. Once this was over, she finally spoke about going on holiday with her best friend; this friend was a vulture, so he knew that both women's expenses were to be paid out of his pocket. Unfortunately, Olivier realized too late that he had married one of the most materialistic women in the entire Congo. He had no confidence in placing her in any of his businesses because she would deplete his resources, and this would only encourage her to hound him more over finances. It was better that she didn't know the full extent of the wealth that he had amassed.

Fortunately for Olivier he had two children who had taken after him instead of their mother. He intended to mentor his son to take over all his business interests, but for now he had to wait until the boy came of age. His daughter was in university in Paris and she was performing very well academically. He would encourage her to settle abroad, and she would listen because she was her father's little girl.

Olivier knew that his wife wouldn't shut up by herself and he just wasn't in the mood for her that day. He told her that he had a headache before pretending to be asleep for the rest of their journey. They didn't have long to go before they reached the grave site, but he just couldn't take any more of it. Pretending to be asleep didn't help him unfortunately, his wife turned her attention to the driver and bombarded him with hundreds of stories that he seemed to enjoy, even if he didn't the man would carry on as if he did.

His wife genuinely thought that the people in her life liked her, she couldn't comprehend that it was simply a result of Olivier's prominent position in society. Fortunately for Olivier he had been poor before so the people who helped him then were the ones that he kept close to his heart. His wife's father was an accountant and her mother a doctor, she had no idea what it felt like to struggle, and it was struggle that established who one's true friends were. He loved his wife deep inside, however he realized that he didn't respect her. There was nothing that she did during her day which inspired him to improve himself. He was working hard for his children, not so that he could buy his wife more shoes and outfits.

The car eventually came to a halt. While his spoilt wife waited for the driver to open her door Olivier simply jumped out to the dusty ground. Even though he was young at the time he couldn't forget that day when he lost his mother to the Ebola virus and his older sister went missing. The week had begun with his mother telling his sister to look after him before she walked towards the hospital doors and begged them to take her in. Olivier and his sister, whose name he couldn't remember exactly but knew that it had to do with the sun or dawn, waited on the field that was next to the hospital. During the night they realized that their mother was let into the hospital doors so they were happy that she would soon be okay. They were both extremely exhausted, so they cuddled together and feel asleep under a tree on the field. When he awoke his sister was gone and he was alone until Doctor Daniel Clancy took him in.

He had hoped that his sister had experienced a similar fate and had been rescued by good people although he knew the reality of that crisis. Villagers were scared to interact with any children who lost a parent to the virus; for fear that they would be carrying it. Many international organizations evacuated their citizens and every day after they left the country, Doctor Daniel Clancy sent letters to the relevant authorities asking if a Congolese girl was also found without a mother. He was told that there were hundreds and since he never met her it became difficult for him to describe her. Doctor Clancy changed the topic whenever young Olivier asked about her until he started to forget.

His thoughts were interrupted by his wife as she eventually caught up to him and pulled Olivier out of his daydream by saying "You will always have my mother now and my family. You are not alone". He smiled at her as if what she said was reasonable but felt the complete opposite.

He knew that she meant well, but he didn't want to be comforted. His mother-in-law had once told her daughter that she shouldn't marry a man who didn't have a family or money. After that advice from her mother his wife broke up with him until he got a very good job and drove past her in his new car. Once his career started to progress suddenly Vivienne and her mother loved him, yet they couldn't see the potential when he was just starting. It didn't matter that he was one of the brightest graduates. Most materialistic people only respect money and not a person's emotional or spiritual capacity. He ignored his instincts but now wished he realized this early on instead of when he settled down with a family.

Olivier had come a long way since he was a helpless boy from the village. Once the first outbreak was put under control Doctor Clancy decided to return to Ireland and take Olivier with him. Olivier lived abroad most of his childhood. In primary school he was very reserved and found solace in books that were written both in French and English. "His father", Doctor Clancy insisted on him continuing to speak French and his vernacular was spoken in the house.

The loneliness led him to be a prolific academic and as he entered High School it was discovered that he was very articulate. He joined the Debate Club and represented the United States of America on the Security Council at his school's

Model United Nations conference. He was a prefect, head boy and an all-rounder by the time that he was accepted into University. The year that he was accepted was also the year that Doctor Clancy died, the only family that he had.

Doctor Clancy didn't have much money but had transferred the tuition money for Olivier's entire degree program. The University offered a discount for parents who paid the tuition in full, this was beneficial to the parents who wanted to be protected from inflation and Doctor Clancy must have been preparing for this. During his tertiary education he worked part time with the sole purpose of saving his money however by the third year Doctor Clancy's money had run out, so he worked to survive.

Each year Olivier took a trip to Congo because Ireland didn't feel like home anymore. During his holidays in Congo, he went from business to business trying to apply for an internship, but he immediately got the impression that it wasn't what you knew, but who you knew. Each year he cut his holidays short because he was running out of money and had to get back to all his part time jobs before University recommenced.

When he graduated, he decided to return to Congo because he felt that if he was there longer, he could push his way into the job market. Unfortunately, this was not the case and two weeks after he got there for good, he had run out of money. Desperation forced him to buy a sack of rice from a farmer. He used some of it to eat but packaged the rest of it in small packages and took them to the market. The rice sold out that morning, so he was able to pay for a small room in a backyard of a shanty house. During the mornings he traded in the market selling rice, t-shirts, secondhand tires and other small things. He only spoke French in the market, so his English was completely dormant during this stage in his life.

In the afternoons when he was done trading in the market he would walk from business to business with his curriculum vitae while another marketer took care of his stall until one day, he was accepted to be a teller in one of the local banks. It took over a year before he entered formal employment, so he really cherished the opportunity. The bank didn't pay very well, but he was armed with an economics degree which gave him an advantage over the other tellers who only had diplomas.

His business partner in the market, Jean Claude, continued to run the day-to-day operations at the stall. Eventually they expanded and started to have many stalls, Olivier eventually reached a point when he put Jean Claude on a monthly salary and conducted stock taking with him every day after work. At the bank his first promotion came after seven months of him being there and he went out with his work colleagues and Jean Claude to celebrate.

Chapter 2

Discontent with Vivienne

THAT NIGHT was when he first met Vivienne, the woman that he would go on to marry. She saw him on a night when he looked financially secure and they spent the whole night talking. They had a connection that he hadn't experienced since he arrived. When leaving the club, they took a cab to his place and when she saw where he lived Vivienne decided that she wanted to go back home. She said that she needed to speak to her mother before they went any further.

Olivier didn't mind being patient so told her that it was fine before the cab turned around and drove to her parents' beautiful home. She was sheepish throughout the drive there and gave him a non-committal hug when they got to her gate. Albeit a disappointing end to the night, he remained optimistic. He thought that with Vivienne he had found someone that he could be committed to.

However, if he thought that the night ended in a disappointing way then the next day was even worse. When he returned to her parents' home the following day, she came out of the gate to see him with an uninspiring expression painted on her face. She explained that her mother wouldn't let her see a man who didn't have any money and no future. He tried to tell her that he had finished his studies and had a grand vision for his business outside of the bank, but she didn't hang around. The mention of being an orphan caused her to shake her head before she disappeared from view. It was obvious that a rising orphan who didn't have family money to rely on was not a suitable candidate, regardless of the heart or the character that he possessed.

With his biggest love prospect not interested in him he reverted to focusing entirely on business. His new job in the bank meant that his working hours were now from 7am until 8pm, however with the increased salary he was now able to expand his business. He opened a small shop in the industrial area where they sold car tyres and other car parts. Jean Claude's younger brother was placed in the shop. Olivier bought a large quantity of rice packets and was forced to form a company. He had "Pure Rice" on each one of his packets and as a result of the professional packets he was finally able to sell to the convenience stores.

He soon learnt that it wasn't easy to do straight business in Congo and to grow his businesses he had to keep putting more and more money in envelopes to pay individuals. If he didn't do this, then nothing would move. Growing up he had high morals but had since adapted to the business environment. He had grown up in a place where there was a clear distinction between right and wrong. However, in the Congolese business arena there were so many grey areas that he was determined to change it if he ever got the chance. Corruption was entrenched in most of the systems, political and otherwise.

After two and a half years he became a branch manager, many of the people that reported to him were much older than he was. He moved out of his place and into a residential home. He was also able to buy a new car. He was delighted to move away from public transport. The minibuses brought him so much stress because the drivers took too many risks and behaved like they were the only ones on the road. It was normal for the bus to drive on the pavement or park between stops to pick up just one more customer. They drove on the wrong side of the road when it suited them and assumed that other cars would stop to give way.

As luck should have it when he was settled and secure, he came across Vivienne once again in the supermarket. She asked him how he was doing and was very impressed with him being a manager. When asked what she was doing he was told that she was still unemployed and living with her parents. She seemed more inclined to be with him, so they started dating after they went for a drink together that evening. He knew within himself that she would leave him if things took a turn for the worse; she was obviously only a girl for the good times. However, she had the most captivating smile he had come across, but it was her eyes which got him. Once they locked, he felt there was no where he'd rather be.

Early into the relationship he felt the pressure; Vivienne was constantly asking him for things. Her whole life revolved around his dealings and this started to annoy him. Every single piece of information he shared about his business she would go around and tell all her friends about it, but not before she asked him for some of the money. He was constantly digging into his pocket to pay for her hair, clothes, and her car and eventually this extended to her demanding a monthly allowance. He encouraged her to finish school, but it never materialized, and it became more and more evident that her parents saw him as the last resort for their daughter to have a promising future. Vivienne obviously felt the same and Olivier regretted the fact that in those early years he didn't do more to bring her out of that mindset.

Chapter 3

Stepping Into Politics

A YEAR AFTER Vivienne returned to his life, he bought a small farm and began to produce wheat and livestock. This was when his business just took off. He cared deeply about his community and after several discussions found himself in the government. His income from his out of office operations was much greater than his salary at the bank. His businesses grew rapidly every month from that point. Once he left the bank his first government position was as a Member of Parliament in the National Assembly. He won it with ease and thus found himself at the helm of political power.

This was how he joined politics and after what seemed like nonstop political battles, he went on to become the governor of Katanga, Congo's richest province with an unprecedented amount of mineral wealth. This did not come easily as it was seen to be the best job in the country aside from becoming president. It was also the final steppingstone before one went on to become president. His businesses continued to grow as he remained a member of the ruling party throughout his political career.

Olivier was now one of the most powerful men in the country which was an indirect threat to the President. With the federal system of governance, it was only natural that the perfect man to take on the presidency would be a governor. In Katanga he sent sixty percent of his tax revenue to the central government and the remaining forty percent was in his control for however he deemed best to allocate it within his province.

He stopped thinking about his history when they arrived where Olivier's family hut used to be or, so he had been told. The truth was that he hadn't a clue. They were given directions by one of the village elders who swore to have been close to his mother, but when they arrived there was empty land. The hut wasn't there anymore. Either the rain had washed away that poorly constructed mud house or someone had deliberately dismantled it. Whatever the case Olivier wasn't going to see the place where he spent his early years.

The fact that he didn't have any photographs of her meant that he could barely remember what she looked like; he had hoped that the house would help. His wife decided to stay in the car since she didn't want to get her shoes dirty; he wondered why someone would wear high heels when she knew that they were going to the village. He was bound to a woman who knew nothing about suffering and sacrifice; she couldn't humble herself even in a village. His wife only knew about swiping credit cards.

He reentered the car and the driver drove a little further to his mother's burial site. It was just a pile of dirt. He couldn't know for sure whether it was hers, so they left. A day that was meant to have been a meaningful walk down memory lane turned out to be highly disappointing. Nothing except that hospital was enough to validate their visit. He thought that sometimes it is better to leave ones past where it is and focus solely on the future.

On the drive out of the district young children ran after the car waving. Olivier waved back while his wife continued to read her glamor magazine. When the children could no longer keep up, he thought about how the first patient known as patient X came from his beloved Yambuku village. This would forever ensure that his community would have to live with being the home of one of the deadliest viruses that the world had ever known, Ebola. Named after the vast Ebola river that flowed through Yambuku Village.

Olivier had to get back to Katanga and meet with his advisors. The President was about to enter the last year of his third term. Olivier had recently told a journalist that he would be extremely interested in contesting for the country's presidency. This had caused controversy within his party because this announcement came a week after the president began intra party discussions on changing the constitution to implement yet another seven-year term. There was a mixed response, and the party was divided on this issue which was when the violence began.

He feared for his family and their wellbeing but believed that he had enough measures in place that he could survive. Olivier did not wake up one day and decide to approach the presidency and he had made powerful allies both locally and abroad who were backing him to obtain it. He was confident in the contingencies that were in place but couldn't know for sure how it would all go.

The year after he became Governor of Katanga Olivier decided to change his name from Clancy to Katanga. He appreciated all that Doctor Daniel Clancy had done for him by adopting him and so forth, but now affiliated himself with the people of the Katanga province and felt the desire to have an indigenous African surname if he was to make even further progress up the political ladder.

Chapter 4

Mohammad of Damascus

IN THE SYRIAN TOWN of Damascus, Mohammad, a simple house servant, remained focused on his task at hand. He was sweeping the leaves off the lawn before he noticed that the front door was opening. His boss, Omar, stepped out of the house into the bright sunlight wearing a sharp, pinstriped navy suit with black sunglasses. The driver immediately rushed up the front steps towards the boss to grab his briefcase. Dashing back to the car, opening the back-passenger door. Mohammad continued to sweep and didn't look up at the car, his heart was racing.

Mohammad felt fortunate to work on a large estate. It had two large iron gates at the property entrance. The house was a tall double story with a wide balcony across the entire front. There were five bedrooms in the main house with two elegant guest cottages in the back. There was a large swimming pool with an island bar built in the middle. There were tall white Greek statues and water fountains all around the majestic white house. Mohammad thought about how blessed those people were, they were more privileged than anyone he knew.

As soon as the boss entered the vehicle it began to reverse and the guard opened the gate before saluting; as if the boss even cared. There were two guards, one who watched the perimeter of the house and one within. They both held rifles and didn't speak to the servants. They were not part of the staff but were merely a signal to any intruders that they would be dealt with viciously. Within the house there was only one housekeeper, Mohammad was expected to help with certain household and maintenance duties and also cleaning the windows.

The housekeeper was a young girl who appeared to be very fond of the lady of the house. In fact, everyone seemed to be appreciating the lady of the house, especially Mohammad. The boss had inherited a family business that Mohammad couldn't understand though he knew it had something to do with oil and the government. All he knew was that he was employed by a powerful man, the type who could kill and still be able to walk the streets freely.

Mohammad was no stranger to death. He was surviving in a country that had been engulfed by civil war for so long that he could not remember a time without chaos. He walked in the streets with one eye looking out for a car bomb or a shootout and lived his life in a manner that allowed for a quick escape. On his meager salary he could not afford luxurious items. This brought him some comfort as he had nothing of great value that he would have to abandon if a situation broke out.

It had only been thirty minutes after the boss had left when his wife, Azmina, came to the front door in her flowing silk night gown. Mohammad tried not to look, but he couldn't resist.

The moment that their eyes locked she used her index finger to tell him to follow her inside the house. He looked at the guard, but he wasn't paying attention. Mohammad strolled towards the house cautiously, it had been like this for the last week, yet time had done nothing to erase his nerves.

Once inside he climbed the long wide stairs. The housekeeper looked at him and smiled as if to say that he had nothing to be worried about. He ignored her as he gravitated towards the master bedroom. When he reached the door, he took a deep breath. The door was ajar. He pushed it gently. Once open he saw Azmina, sprawled on the bed completely naked, wearing nothing but a smile. He smiled back at the lady of the house before gently clicking the door closed behind him.

Without a word he walked to the bathroom to wash his hands and face before spraying some of her husband's cologne over his now naked shoulders. He admired his image in the mirror of the marble clad bathroom; it was built for a king. There was a television on the wall that was showing international news. The bathtub was massive, and the shower could easily fit two people, he knew this from experience. Everything in that house was perfect and expensive. It was hard not to envy the man of the house. Mohammad took the risk of continuing this affair because for a few hours he got to feel what a rich man's life was like.

When he was finished, he strolled towards the lady of the house still naked on the bed. They entered a long silent embrace before they began to make passionate love for a hunger-filled hour.

Their illicit and risky affair began two weeks ago. Mohammad had entered the master bedroom to collect the laundry when he discovered that Azmina was in the shower. He yelled to alert her to the fact that he was in her room. Suddenly the shower stopped, and she told him to wait. When she left the bathroom, she was in her towel, so he immediately looked to the ground. She told him to close and lock the door before she dropped the towel.

The night after their first sexual encounter he went home after work and contemplated fleeing Syria. He was worried that Azmina would have confessed everything to her husband, yet for some reason he returned to work the next day and the affair continued. After sex they would lay in bed and talk. She liked to know what was happening in Syria with the civil war; she was so excluded from it and felt bad for those people in her country who were suffering.

Mohammad always had a horrific story to tell her. By the third day of their affair, she convinced her husband that it would be better if he lived in the cottage on their estate. Now Mohammad was fully dependent on this man, but from the minute that he came he knew that his purpose was just to be her lover. There was a certain adrenaline that came with this secret life, but he was so worried about it that he wasn't sleeping well. He would stay up for hours in his bed each night contemplating all the ways that this thing could backfire; there were many.

The housekeeper didn't say anything, but Mohammad could sense some resentment. Was she becoming jealous because she liked him or was she frustrated that she was being sidelined as the favorite servant? He didn't know what it was but felt that he needed to appease this lady. After all, if she was really against him then she could be the catalyst to his harsh demise.

He shared his concerns with Azmina, but she dismissed them without a second thought. She was too confident in her housekeeper's loyalty that she even went on to claim that the housekeeper was one of her closest friends. Azmina's words did little to ease Mohammad's concerns yet he was in a position where he was forced to accept them.

After they were done talking, he was getting ready to leave the room when he heard a car honking at the gate, the driver was blaring frantically, and it sounded like the boss's car. Mohammad was horrified and pushed away from Azmina. They both couldn't understand why Omar had come back so early. This was completely out of character with his daily routine. Mohammad put on his trousers and shoes before bolting down the long stairs. The housekeeper was standing at the bottom of the stairs with an angry expression on her face. Grabbing at him she announced to him that Inshallah would ensure that he would pay for his adulterous ways. "The master will kill you, he will kill you, he is a good man and you betrayed him." He realized then that he could not stay there for a minute longer. As he had suspected the housekeeper was disgruntled. With one phone call she betrayed their secret.

He pushed her out of the way as she attempted to block his path. His mind raced as he heard the front gates open. The engine roared as the car sped onto the property. He decided to use the kitchen for his escape so made his way towards the backdoor as he heard the boss's car screech to a halt at the front of the house. The sound of the car doors slamming aggressively only served to add greater pace to his escape. Mohammad ran towards the large oak tree that was nearest to the tall brick wall that separated him from death and freedom. There was no point in trying to make it all the way to the second gate. Was it locked, were the guards already there? Mohammad clamored into the tree like his life depended on it, which it surely did. Before he jumped into the next yard, he heard a gunshot and realized that his life did depend on a fast getaway.

The bullet from the shotgun flew over his shoulder and provided more than enough inspiration for him to jump. The distance between the tree and the fence would have been an almost impossible task during normal times, especially with the electric fence in his way, but the fear of being shot provided the inner strength that he needed to make the leap. He didn't bother to see who was shooting at him and heard another shot while he was inflight.

He landed on his face in the neighbor's yard and was immediately pounced on by their dog. The will to live enabled him to beat off the ferocious beast before he dashed to the neighbor's back gate. He knew that he had been bitten on the neck but didn't feel a thing. The neighbor's gardener watched him and stopped the dog from following Mohammad off the property. The landscaper and Mohammad knew each other well so even though the man wasn't going to help Mohammad he would not stand in his way. Mohammad didn't have time to think about where he was going but knew not to stand on ceremony. He had to get out of there and was more than encouraged when he heard his boss yell at the guards to get him. The command was so loud that his voice echoed in the streets.

Mohammad knew that running on the main road wasn't a good idea. He dashed as fast as he could even though his left foot wasn't moving as it should, he suspected that he had sprained his ankle, but there was no time to think about it. He didn't bother to turn around when he heard a car in pursuit of him. He managed to maneuver his way into an alleyway and noticed a United Nations convoy circling the street in an open van with troops in the back.

He was so grateful for this and could barely believe his luck. No one would think of opening fire on the United Nations troops because the ramifications would be extremely severe. He smacked the back of the truck viciously until it eventually came to a halt. The driver scrolled his window down so Mohammad went up to him and explained as quickly as possible that he was a political refugee who was being pursued. He spoke quickly and could sense that they were skeptical to let him in until Omar's guards appeared with guns moments later.

The guards exited their car and Mohammad began to scream and plead. This encouraged the peacekeeping troops to jump out of the van and protect Mohammad. There were four troops between Mohammad and Omar's guards. The guards demanded that he should be handed over to them, but they couldn't tell the troops what they intended to do with him or what crime he had committed. The driver walked out of the van and tried to enhance his understanding, but the guards weren't very good actors. It was obvious that if handed over Mohammad would face severe torture.

The driver had a quick discussion with the troops before he refused this request. The guards were not brave enough to become aggressive with their firearms. They were outnumbered and weren't willing to lose their lives for such a cause, instead they retreated back to the car. One of them told Mohammad that he wouldn't be able to hide for long. The final threat reiterated the peacekeeping troop's stance.

Once in the van Mohammad began telling the troops a false story that he made up as he went along. He explained that he had been kidnapped by members of the government's intelligence wing because he advocated for one of the opposition political parties. He had managed to escape and that was why they were chasing him. He explained that he didn't know where he was being kept because he had been blindfolded on the way there. He lied that he had been running for twenty minutes but was the only prisoner so there was no one left to rescue. The troops seemed to be satisfied with this and didn't press on to ask him anymore questions. They assured him that he would be safe in the refugee camp.

He shuffled uncomfortably as the vehicle maneuvered along the bumpy road. He was also not at ease because the pain in his ankle was becoming more and more unbearable. He said that the government was prosecuting him for being pro-democracy and that he wanted to seek asylum in the United States. He went on to explain that he could clean floors in America just as well as he cleaned them in Syria. He had lost family members during this fighting and had been so privileged to have a job in Syria even if it was such a terrible one. There was nothing left for him there, he was now an orphan and knew that in this cruel country it was survival of the fittest.

He kept asking to be sent to America or Europe, but the troops didn't respond to this. Instead, they ignored him and reminded him that he was safe now and would soon be in a system that was helping to improve the lives of several of his countrymen. He was taken to a refugee camp and was told that he would soon be transferred to one of Syria's neighboring countries once his documentation was processed. Fortunately, he had his national registration card in his wallet, and it wasn't destroyed during his hectic escape. He knew that he wouldn't survive in the refugee camp. Omar would find a way to get him from there, this he was certain of.

Normally he would have waited in a long queue but was fortunate enough to be allowed in the gates since he was in a United Nations vehicle. The group dropped him at the registration office, and he was immediately confronted by individuals who were moving around with photographs, asking if anyone had seen their loved ones. Mohammad sympathized with them. He felt that the worst part of war was not knowing whether a person's family member was dead, free or had been incarcerated by either the state or the rebels.

After a few hours he eventually registered himself and was directed to a tent that had three families packed in there. They seemed to welcome him, but he was still in shock so was less hospitable. His mind went back to his close encounter with death, if the bullet was a few inches to the left than he would have been hit and only God knows what would have become of him. He decided to flee from the camp in the night and make his own way out of Syria. This refugee camp was run by Syrians who would have no issue in handing him over to Omar for the right amount of cash.

That night Mohammad waited until the families were asleep. He walked out with his hands in his pockets as he looked around. There were peacekeeping troops by the gate; they couldn't force him to stay so he walked up to them confidently. The gentlemen at the gate asked him several times if he was sure that he wanted to leave the camp. He thought about all the diseases he could catch in that place; the pit latrines were disgusting. He was determined not to use them again. Not to mention how full that space was. He was also aware that these numbers would only increase. He signed off at the gate and was reminded that they couldn't protect him outside of the compound. He looked ahead at the dark road and decided that he would take his chances.

Chapter 5

The Complications of Politics

OLIVIER RETURNED to his well-guarded home in Katanga. He gained added security from the fact that his driver was a professional assassin trained in Russia, originally by the state before he entered private work. His house was designed and positioned to protect him. It was in a secluded area with several evacuation options should it come under fire. He had a plane in the shed, they had an underground bunker and there was a speed boat that could be used to cruise along the Luvua River. He was prepared for every emergency, or at least that's what he hoped. As soon as he arrived his guard known as Commander One informed him that a letter had been delivered from a government official, it had been placed in his office. As soon as he heard this he rushed into the house.

His wife remained outside in the garden, but her voice could be heard in his office as she was clearly unhappy about something. Olivier decided to lock the door in case she thought to discuss the landscaping problem with him. He found the letter neatly placed and sealed. He ripped open the envelope. It simply stated that he had been summoned to Kinshasa to meet the President. He closed his eyes, leaned back in his chair and began to think.

This was extremely risky especially because both he and the President had been using the media to criticize one another daily. They exchanged political blows every morning and the press got their headlines. As a result of the fact that the two most prominent party members were at loggerheads it had caused division. The President had a group of senior party members who were so used to the way that things were done that they agreed with his proposal to amend the constitution and enact a fourth term in office for himself. He had done this before when his second term expired, but things were different now.

The party was now half filled with a younger generation which vehemently supported Olivier as they believed that he could change the status quo. Olivier had another advantage, and this was his grip on Katanga, the richest province, and he knew how much the people from this region loved him. He had built schools, roads and through his policies several international companies were entering the region which was creating jobs. However, he wasn't as noble as he tried to present himself. He realized that to get anything done in Congo money needed to exchange hands.

Before he entered politics in order for his business ventures to grow, he was forced to send envelopes with cash to the homes of the individuals who awarded government contracts. Before he would even bid, he then would be reasonably assured that his company would win the contracts. When he entered politics with the ruling party, he didn't need to do this anymore as the contracts were guaranteed so he felt less guilty albeit within his heart, he knew that if he fell out of power then the good times would cease to exist.

Companies owned by individuals from opposing parties were not awarded any government contracts no matter how many envelopes they sent. In Congolese politics either you were with us or against us, however he knew that this culture was shared around the African continent. Olivier did believe that he could knuckle down on corruption if given the chance, especially when the wrongdoing was at the expense of the wellbeing of his fellow citizens. His eyes opened when he realized that a call was coming in from the gate. Commander One informed him that he had a visitor.

Olivier's first meeting since his visit to Yambuku was with the Chief Executive Officer of his group of companies, who was none other than Jean Claude, the man who had been there from the start. Olivier unlocked the door when he heard the knock. The two men shook hands and Jean couldn't wait to be seated before he started complaining. He had met with the senior management of an emerald mine in the region. This company were wondering why their mining licenses weren't being permitted even though they had followed all the procedures for foreign investors. They didn't understand how things worked in Katanga. Jean Claude went to inform them that before they would get their licenses, they needed to enter into three-year trucking contracts with "Transcontinental Logistics" which was Olivier's trucking company and they needed to enter into a five-year arrangement for Olivier's other company to supply mining equipment.

The arrangement stated that the mine would purchase from his company first and would only contact other suppliers if Olivier was out of stock or they were looking for specialized equipment that he couldn't supply. Most of the agreements were verbal, but each party knew where they stood. In Katanga business was going very well, but outside of that Province things began to change. Suddenly Olivier was losing bids for government contracts and the tax man was hounding his offices. This was the price he paid for announcing to the country that he was a presidential aspirant. He anticipated these negatives long before he came forward. However, he still had control of the business environment in Katanga.

When Jean was finally seated, they video conferenced some of his partners around the Southern African district to look at how he would withstand the business pressure now that he was distancing himself from the top dog. His partners were confident that he could endure; after all, Olivier knew the system better than most. He ensured that his Zambian, the country which was formerly known as Northern Rhodesia, and South African partners did not belong to any political parties involved with his divorce from the President, they would have been expected to cut him off too.

When the video conference ended Jean moved onto the topic of political news, despite the fact that he officially operated in the private sector he very much had a destiny tied to the political environment so he constantly monitored it. While Olivier was at his mother's grave site a few of his supporters outside Katanga had been brutally assaulted by individuals who wore the President's face on their shirts. The President claimed that this group had acted independently because he didn't condone violence. Thus, another potential topic to be discussed in Kinshasa with the President.

Olivier was now at a crucial point. He never believed in the armed struggle, he was committed to keeping the battles to issue-based debates. For the first time in his political career, he considered the need to arm his supporters because the closer it got to the general election; the more violent things could become. They needed to be able to defend themselves. He explained to Jean that he wanted to visit some of the victims of the attacks but wanted them to go in Jean Claude's car to avoid attention.

They spent that afternoon visiting some of the people who were in hospital many of whom had been cut badly by machetes. He offered encouraging words and promised that their support would not be in vain. He promised to defend them and that he would pursue the culprits until they were brought to book. As expected, the press followed him as the word got out that he was visiting the injured. He spoke strongly about obtaining justice for his supporters, not to mention how he reiterated that Congo was now a democracy and that the people had the right to support whoever they pleased. Olivier asked his other supporters to keep calm and not carry out retaliation which could backfire and lead to their own incarceration.

Chapter 6

Azmina's Punishment

OMAR WAS IN THE BEDROOM with his wife, while the housekeeper remained outside with her ear to the door. The rest of the staff had caught wind of the situation and there was little to no activity around the house; everyone remained in suspense. He had been in the bedroom for only a few minutes and the house was completely silent, yet everyone knew that it would soon erupt. Omar had a temper during normal times, the staff knew that they were about to hear the full extent of his wrath because he finally had something to be angry about. For a man of his status to have been sharing his wife with a cleaner had them all thinking that they were about to witness a murder.

"So, when I am at work you spend your day in my bed with a garden boy." Omar whispered, not like he was asking a question, but was stating a fact. His wife was taken aback by this response. The man in front of her was not the type to speak calmly. He would raise hell if his tea was cold when he came down for breakfast. She swallowed hard before fervidly denying his accusations. Her husband was standing with his hands folded while she sat on the bed. He let her speak without interruption for possibly the first time in their marriage. When she was done, they stared at each other in silence, this was when she noticed that his hand was shaking. Looking away from him would make her appear guilty so she maintained eye contact but couldn't prevent herself from blinking rapidly and in turn her hands too started to shake.

"No Omar, this is not true. He comes to do the housework and to clean. Who would tell you such a horrible thing?" She questioned him. This last desperate attempt changed everything; Omar walked towards his wardrobe in silence and lifted one of his belts. He stretched it out while holding it in the air as if to assess its adequacy for the task at hand. Azmina started breathing heavily as she watched him, she wasn't sure whether to continue talking or if speaking would only make it worse. Either way her fate was inevitable.

"So, you don't respect me, you want to lie to my face. You convince me to put that boy in my house so that you can insult me every day!" He screamed at the top of his voice while he tapped the belt on his open palm in a vicious manner. Now she couldn't look at his eyes, they suggested that she was in for a terrifying couple of days. She looked to the floor and began to cry uncontrollably. There was nothing else she could do. Cry and await the punishment with meager attempts to convince him that it was unwarranted.

"It's not true Omar, I respect you so much!" She stammered, but that simple sentence took a long time to come out of her mouth. She struggled so much with that sentence that she couldn't speak anymore.

"Shut up you whore!" Omar yelled out before spitting in her face. He grabbed her by the throat and threw her on the bed before he began whipping his wife viciously and the screams echoed throughout the home much to the delight of Nihal the housekeeper. Nihal was a young girl who had a boyfriend but didn't want to marry a poor man. She had called Omar and told him what was happening that morning. She wanted him to catch them in the act, but unfortunately, he was a bit far away when she called. The housekeeper now hoped that he would choose her to be his second wife or to replace the current one. She had lost respect for his wife when she allowed Mohammad to move into the estate and that Azmina was living the life that Nihal dreamed of while carrying on this affair with Mohammad that was the final nail in the coffin.

She couldn't take it by the second week but kept smiling when the lady of the house talked to her about it, how foolish of her to think that they were friends. Nihal didn't want anyone to know what her true intentions were and covered them up by acting like all was well. She continued to listen to Azmina's cries which could be heard after each lashing of the belt. Nihal was interrupted by a knock on the kitchen door. With excited anticipation she went downstairs hoping it was Mohammad, captured and returned to receive retribution.

Instead Nihal was greeted by the guards who stood by the door. Their faces suggested that the news wasn't good. They explained that they were too scared to inform the boss but told Nihal that Mohammad had escaped. The housekeeper shouted at them authoritatively before making her way up the stairs. She knocked on the door and told Omar that the guards had returned before telling him about Mohammad's escape. The lashing in the bedroom immediately came to a halt.

When Nihal was finished relaying her message the door opened and Omar walked past her before making his way towards the guards. The housekeeper took a glimpse in the room but couldn't see Azmina. She decided to follow Omar. Nihal found her boss informing the guards that he would find Mohammad in his own time. He sent the guards back to their posts. Anger was chiseled on his face as he opened the fridge to grab a bottle of water. He drank it like an athlete would on their halftime break before making his way back upstairs to continue the punishment of his wife.

He tortured his wife for the way that she insulted his manhood. Next he would torture and kill Mohammad in a manner that made all his staff both in the office and at his home aware of the ramifications of such dissent. He didn't want any of them to bring this up again or to even look at his wife. Nor would Azmina be ever allowed to leave their home again. This was a complete disgrace and she would be forced to live as such for the rest of her life.

Omar knew that he couldn't spend the entire day at home as he was needed in Aleppo for one of the biggest deals of his life, but he couldn't leave things hanging. He decided to lock his wife in one of the dog kennels. He grabbed her by the hair, and she didn't resist, he opened the gate and the dogs barked in excitement. He pulled her towards the last one which was empty and shoved her inside. She crawled into a ball and began to weep as he locked the cage.

He returned into the house and told Nihal that he needed her to remain for the night as he would only return from Aleppo the following day. He explained that his wife was to be fed through the cage and allowed to use the toilet only once, if she refused to return into the kennel afterwards then she should get the guards involved. Nihal gladly took the instructions and thought it was the perfect time to advance her agenda.

"I was thinking, after this disgrace maybe you could consider taking me as a second wife. I could..." Nihal was interrupted by the impatient Omar.

"Shut up woman, you think I'm like her who beds with peasants. My family has a rich history and luckily for her Azmina's family does too. That is why the marriage will not end and even if it did, I would rather remain unmarried then to marry a woman of your low class. Just do as I have instructed." Omar yelled, and his saliva hit Nihal's face as he did. She realized the terrible mistake that she had made, it was all for nothing. The day guards were very alert, but she knew that the night guard was a drinker, he would eventually fall asleep.

Later that night Azmina had finally stopped crying from the pain of the lashes on her back. Her husband had whipped her so much that he left no space untouched on her back. She continued to weep over the other issues; the fact that she was cold, hungry and didn't know what would happen next. The kennel smelt putrid, but that was the least of her problems. She had to figure a way out of there. This man was going to kill her she thought repeatedly. She continued to pick at the lock until she heard footsteps; she immediately pretended to be asleep.

"I know that your awake, no one would be able to sleep in this after the luxurious life that you had." Nihal said in a completely different tone. Her entire demeanor had changed from a sweet girl that Azmina had come to care for. Azmina didn't reply, she knew that the woman was the one who had informed her husband. She wished that she had listened to Mohammad when he quizzed her about Nihal's loyalty. Instead, she dismissed his suspicions and now both of their lives were at stake as they remained in this terrible predicament.

"I asked your husband what he is going to do with you, and he said that he will leave you here for three days. Then you will be allowed back in the house. He is not giving me any more information, but I know what will happen. He will eventually forgive you, he may take another wife now, but you will always be his main woman. But I know how unhappy you are, and your life is only going to be more secluded after this. He will never trust you again and will beat you over the smallest mistakes. So, I will open this gate, the guard is asleep so you can use the second gate. Then you must leave and never ever return here." The housekeeper relayed her proposal which was very attractive and caused Azmina to pay attention while she thought to herself. Nihal was right, Omar would only keep Azmina to make the rest of her life a living hell.

Azmina eventually nodded her head; even though a part of her feared that it was a trap. She didn't know where she would go. Her parents were so afraid of her husband that they would only advise her to go back to him. She had never worked a day in her life and had married in her last year of secondary school. She was afraid of what would come next in the world, alone, but knew that this would be her only chance to find out.

Chapter 7

Mohammad Moving On

MOHAMMAD WALKED along the dirt road. It was daybreak and he was happy about this. When he started his journey, it was pitch black and without the presence of streetlights he had stepped into a few potholes. He had stumbled several times when he started his journey, which did nothing to help his injured ankle. He didn't know where he was going but was following the road. His foot had begun to feel better after a couple of hours, thus reassuring him that it wasn't broken, a fact that he had been concerned about as he could not afford medical treatment.

A vehicle roared along the road and he put out his hand to ask for a lift. He had done this with every car that had passed since he started his journey, but no one seemed interested in a hitchhiker who could potentially turn out to be a thief. Finally, a vehicle stopped and turned around towards him. He couldn't make out who was inside because he was blinded by the full beam. The truck parked in front of him and he ran up to it. He was so relieved to get a ride; several cars had driven past him without any hesitation. When he caught up to it, he found two gentlemen seated who went on to greet him with a smile. They introduced themselves and as soon as he mentioned he was named Mohammad, they said in unison "Like the Prophet". One of them jumped out and Mohammad sat in the middle. He told them that he could sit at the back, but they insisted that he should remain inside because of the cold and so they could chat.

"Where are you going my brother?" The driver asked Mohammad excitedly once they were back onto the main road. "My name is Tariq and my brother there is Hussein. But, out of respect I call him Mr. Hussein. Welcome Mohammad." He thought them to be very friendly and extremely trusting to let him sit in the car with them. He was grateful that he hadn't been told to sit in the back of the pickup because he was already very cold, and it was much more comfortable inside the vehicle. Being inside also made him feel safer, he was living in volatile times and civilians usually got caught in the crossfire during civil wars.

"To be honest, I just want to leave town. Wherever you are going I will drop of there and start afresh." Mohammad said with a grin, he thought that they would be happy to know that there was no need for them to divert from their current path. The two gentlemen seemed elated and looked at one another as if they were having a conversation in their minds.

"What is your religion my brother?" The driver asked as his eyes returned to the road. Mohammad was taken aback by this. It was not uncommon for individuals from different religious affiliations to have violent fights with each other. He knew that roughly ten percent of his fellow countrymen were Christians so felt confident in telling the truth that he was a Muslim. Once again it appeared like he had stumbled across the correct answer however suddenly he felt like he was in an interrogation rather than this being casual chit chat.

"Good, that is what is most important. Inshallah your needs will be provided for. What type of work do you do?" the driver pressed on. It felt like he was probing for something rather than making conversation. What was also strange was that the other guy was staring at Mohammad quietly but reading his expressions. His face suggested that he was in deep thought over anything that came out of Mohammad's mouth. The only time his face changed was when he smiled at the answers, but what if Mohammad gave an answer that he didn't like? He was worried about what would happen then.

"Anything manual, I have been a cleaner, gardener and farm worker," Mohammad expressed positively, he needed to focus on the positives and the biggest one was that he went from walking on the road to moving in a vehicle. He would get much further from Omar now and was safe from bandits that would have pounced on a lone individual.

"Good my brother, we will find you work in Raqqah," the driver informed him whilst striking fear into Mohammad's heart. He couldn't hide the horror from his face. Raqqah was one of the last places that he expected to end up. He had heard the whispers of atrocities that were taking place there. Not to mention the hardships that people were going through.

"Why would we go there, isn't it a stronghold for ISIS?" Mohammad almost shouted. This caused the other passenger to finally speak up, his voice was hoarse. Mohammad had indeed stumbled upon a statement that his hosts didn't want to hear.

"Why should a Muslim be afraid of an Islamic State? Are you really a Muslim?" the man expressed in a tone that was filled with disappointment. Mohammad realized that these were sympathizers of the terrorist group. He wouldn't debate them but was certain to go on his own way when the opportunity would arise. He didn't know what to expect from them and this worried Mohammad. Was he better off on the road after all?

"Yes, I am really a Muslim," Mohammad defended himself before looking out of the window. He wanted to end this question and answer session and derived that the best way for it to come to pass would be if he slept. That was exactly what he intended to do.

"Then there is no problem," the other passenger said as he locked the door and told Mohammad to relax because it was a long journey. Mohammad was not going to argue, although he felt that entering the pickup could have been a mistake.

Chapter 8

Olivier Pushes Forward

OLIVIER TURNED ON THE TELEVISION, clicking until he found some global news. He sat alone in the dark with beer. The headline story was that there had been an assassination attempt on the life of the Syrian Defense Minister, General Jamal Ali Ahmed. His entourage came under fire before they left a hotel where he was having private talks with army commanders and select Syrian businessmen. Jamal had collapsed after taking a bullet to his lower back. He had fainted in the car park as he was trying to escape however during his fall, he hit his head on a large rock which knocked him out. The official report was that his condition was stable, unlike some others who had lost their lives in the shootout.

The reporter went on to explain that doctors had successfully removed the bullet from his back and expected his wound to heal. It was also expected that swelling from his concussion would heal in the next couple of days however were unsure when he would come out of his coma. Initial signs led the medical team to believe that he would suffer some memory loss. The news crews from four different broadcasters waited outside of the hospital doors eagerly awaiting any new information on his recovery. Soldiers guarded the hospital as his family made a direct request for extra protection.

The chief government spokesman said that a plane was on standby should his condition worsen as they would fly him out of Syria to Singapore especially if he required major surgery going forward. His situation would be monitored on an hourly basis. No one had taken credit for this attack which was uncommon for terrorist organizations. The common trend for such groups would be for them to release videos shortly after the attack. The journalist went on to explain that some groups like ISIS owned media companies and were producing threatening videos on a weekly basis. Their mass media messages were extremely efficient at radicalizing members of the public. They were recruiting soldiers from the Middle East and abroad using this medium. Women were not spared on this social media campaign as they were promised faithful jihadist husbands if they came to offer support.

At the time when he was shot Jamal had been attending a meeting with the head of military intelligence and elite businessmen. The reporter explained that the agenda for this meeting remained unknown however information from an undisclosed source suggested that a potential arms deal was underway. The businessman known as Omar had been killed on site; he had been running a family business and was survived by his widow Azmina. The widow had been visiting her parent's when she was informed of her husband's untimely demise. Azmina was the sole recipient of Omar's will as they did not have any children together and he was an only child.

The news's broadcaster went on to discuss the destruction that the Civil War was causing on the Syrian people. Over the years it had become unclear what people were fighting for. There were many factions of rebel groups, some that were working together against the government whilst others were firing at everyone who wasn't with them. It was chaotic and the world was looking on, knowing that intervention was necessary, but the manner of which it should be done was unclear. Some people suggested that the current regime should be removed, but what would replace it? Syria's opposition had a mixture of radicals and intellectuals, it was unclear as to who would rise up to the challenge of unifying the country, rebuilding what had already been destroyed and most importantly the country needed someone who could attract foreign investment again. In the meantime, the only thing that the international community could do was facilitate peace talks and conduct airstrikes on ISIS territory. They were the only obvious enemy, evident by their beheadings of international citizens.

The broadcaster went on to explain that Islamic State were the best funded terrorist organization of all time with current estimates suggesting that the group made over a million dollars per day, through kidnappings, selling organs on the black market and selling oil in the same manner. A huge source of their income was cash from banks in the towns that they overran. What was particularly worrying about this group was their ability to convert recruits with the use of social media, stretching from within the Middle East to Western countries. The biggest problem was that their support base was growing tremendously in the local communities as were their teachings, brainwashing and bullying in their strongholds. The attack on General Jamal was the first time during this civil war that a member of cabinet had been successfully gotten to. With a person of his prestige falling victim to a brutal attack, the world and local attention was not only on his recovery, but also the ramifications that would soon follow. The broadcast ended.

Starting his day with news of a political assassination attempt did little to calm his nerves. He was due to make a speech that morning to his supporters, he turned off the television as he was procrastinating. He knew that what he was about to say would completely rock his world and put his life very much in danger. Congo had a long history of violent transitions of power particularly at the presidential level. Large crowds had gathered with a heavy media presence, he did not hesitate. As soon as the car stopped, he rushed to the platform to make his address.

"Brothers and sisters, we are delighted to be here with you all today. We are happy that we can show off all the infrastructure that we have built in this region and are confident that we will only do more great works in this province. However, we could do even more if we do not insult our democracy. A person must serve their terms and then move on to other things. The leaders must not grip onto power and take away freedom from the people. Therefore, as people have been asking me whether or not I will contest for the Presidency I've withheld my answer but I will answer today. The answer is that I have respect for the party structures. As stated in the party manifesto we must go to a convention and elect a party president. The incumbent leader will no longer be eligible at the end of his tenure. If this is respected, then I and my supporters will also be able to respect the law. But if the law is broken and those with the power to uphold it choose to use a blind eye, then we will raise our voices until they are heard!" Olivier yelled at the top of his voice at the end of his rally. He was standing on a platform in a park that they had reserved for a few hours. At the end of his powerful address there were huge screams from the crowd and his name was chanted with great volume; however, he was used to this. He had made many speeches, most of which were to endorse the current president, but now he was endorsing himself.

As he walked off the podium several prominent party members who were endorsing him stepped forward to speak in great length about why he was the man for the job. They made promises on his behalf on how the nation would benefit if he was elected into office. They spoke about his humble beginnings and manipulated his life history to make him appear nobler than he was, Olivier didn't mind this. They made it seem like he returned from the United Kingdom to lead his people even though he had been very successful abroad.

He didn't care too much for what they said but was more interested in the fact that he had assembled a strong campaign team. Here in the Katanga region where he had become an extremely popular governor he expected to do very well, but if he was going to appeal to the entire nation then he needed a carefully assembled team with each of the individuals selected with great care.

Olivier understood in the rural parts of Congo the peasants, who were very much in the majority, voted following three simple principles. They voted on a tribal basis, they voted for great orator and they voted for people who they had previous experience of dealing with them. The peasants seldom tried new things. The fact that he was in the ruling party ensured that the villagers would be familiar with him. He ensured that his campaign consisted of people from the various tribes and he could give powerful speeches in most of the local languages. He went to great lengths to learn them. For the areas where he didn't know the language French was usually enough.

This rally was very peaceful, but if the president decided to ignore the manifesto and run for yet another term then any opposition, both within and outside of the party would be met with great violence. It was the nature of their politics. With a high unemployment rate, it was very easy to assemble a bunch of supporters and arm them with machetes before instructing them to ascend on your opponents. Then the leaders would stand back and claim that their supporters acted on their own. These cadres just required a warm meal and their favorite alcohol before they would do whatever they were told.

After the rally he invited the party members who spoke on stage to his home for lunch. They had really done a lot by openly siding with him. This took both a lot of courage and great integrity. Before joining him, they would have been faced with a big decision to make, their lives would now change either for the better or for worse.

He opened the meal with a prayer before Vivienne sat by his side. Hosting and socializing were the areas she was good at. She made sure that the chef kept bringing in different delicacies and the bartender continued to pour drinks throughout the night. She loved to dance, and she would always play oldies at the end of each night before she opened the floor to the other ladies.

When some of the men would join on the dance floor, she would conduct herself in a respectful manner until Olivier would also make his way to join in.

Once they were next to each other they would dance intimately for the rest of the night. Guests would leave there having had a great time and they would all concur that Olivier and Vivienne were a perfect couple. He needed to present himself as a devoted husband and father, it showed stability. However, when the guests would leave, and it was just them then things would soon revert to the status quo.

Chapter 9

Discovering Who You Are

GENERAL JAMAL'S EYES OPENED, but his head felt like it was spinning. A woman started to scream excitedly when she noticed that he was awake. She hugged him as he lay on the hospital bed and tried to kiss him on his lips. He could barely move his body but shifted his head to avoid this. It was inappropriate conduct, especially because he hadn't a clue who she was.

"Excuse me, who are you? What happened to me, why am I here?" he whispered as he opened his mouth, his lips felt like they were glued together at first. His tongue was extremely dry. He was craving a fizzy drink of some sort. He asked the woman for a beverage and she immediately informed him that he was diabetic, so his choice of drink was odd. This was news to him. He asked her for a drink of any kind, and she went away before soon returning with a glass of water in a plastic cup. He finished it within seconds of her placing the cup to his lips.

"Jamal, it's me. Shahad, can you not see properly? You were shot remember, but you have suffered some head injuries," she tried to remind him with great energy. He could see so much joy on this stranger's face but was more concerned with why he had been shot. Had criminals tried to rob his family and were his parents and younger brother okay. Rather than rushing into those areas he decided to understand his own situation first.

"I can see just fine Shahad, are you the doctor?" Jamal said much louder as his voice was returning to normal. He shifted around in the bed and felt disgusted when he saw the apparatus for him to urinate in next to his bed. Fortunately, it was empty, yet he wondered about his hygiene. The stench of his body suggested that he hadn't had a proper bath in a long time.

"No, I am your wife. We have been married for over thirty years," she broke into tears; she had been waiting by his bedside for weeks on end waiting for the moment that he would be brought back to her. However, laying there was a man who didn't know her name. The shock on his face when she told him that they were married couldn't have been acting. Had she lost her husband? She was so worried that the brain damage would be permanent but was determined for him not to forget her.

The doctor walked into the room and asked Shahad to step back. She kept saying things to him that he couldn't remember like they had four children and a dog and that he was one of the most important men in the country. As Shahad became more hysterical the doctor called for a nurse to escort her out of the room because she wasn't helping, instead they monitored an acceleration in Jamal's heartbeats the more that she rambled on. Jamal tried his best, but he could not recognize that woman.

His mind was completely blank, and he couldn't just trust that he was married to the first woman that he saw when he opened his eyes. Was he really meant to believe that she was his wife just because he was being told? The doctor conducted some tests on Jamal when he stabilized. After twenty minutes of mental and physical tests the physician was confident that there was no internal bleeding. The doctor sat on the edge of the bed before he began to question him.

"General Jamal Ahmed, what is the last thing that you remember," the doctor asked as he was fixated on his notepad, ready to jot down his notes. Jamal also noticed a camera outside of the hospital window, but the journalists were being ushered away by the security guards. "Am I really one of the most important men in Syria?" He questioned himself before responding to the doctor.

"I remember graduating from University with a degree in political science. I remember being part of the student counsel that ran University affairs and supervised the annual student elections. I remember how proud my parents were when I finished my tertiary education and they told my younger brother to follow in my footsteps. I do not remember that woman who just left my room. Where are my parents? Bring them into the room," he asked needing some familiarity. He was a twenty-four-year-old man, so he couldn't possibly be married for thirty years like this woman suggested. Unless someone was going to convince him that thirty years of his life were erased from his memory. He also wanted to make sure that the rest of his family hadn't been injured when he was; it was the only thing that could have kept his mother away from that hospital room.

"General Jamal Ahmed, your parents have both been dead for many years," the doctor explained cautiously. He was both worried about the fact that he didn't remember this and how his patient would react to rediscovering this fact. The smallest shock would trigger emotions that could send him back into the comatose state.

The remark from the doctor startled Jamal as he racked his brain trying to remember. This made him weak and instantly provoked a severe headache. The doctor could see the pain in his eyes so advised him to rest for a while. Before the doctor left the room, Jamal asked him why he was being referred to as General. For Jamal to be in the military was hard for him to believe, he thought that if he was in the public sector then he would have been a member of parliament.

Jamal had always been against violence and so couldn't comprehend that he was a soldier. The doctor informed him that he was the Minister of Defense and that he was doing very well for the country. This brought him some comfort before he re-entered into a slumber. He hoped that when he woke up once more after his next sleep that most of his memories would return to him. The information that he wanted to recollect most of all was what he did to anger his citizens so much that they would make attempts on his life. A part of him suspected that this was simply a bad dream and after he slept, he would wake up to his real life where he was a twenty-four-year-old bachelor with his two parents and younger brother.

He turned his head to the left; he wasn't bothered about who would walk into the room next. The turn of the neck hurt him during his stretch, but he ignored the pain. He closed his eyes and within a few minutes was fast asleep.

After a few days Jamal's wife insisted that he should be allowed to return home. She made this directive even though the doctors recommended that he should stay in the hospital for another week, his wife wanted the familiar surroundings in the household to help to refresh his memory. Jamal agreed that he needed to be discharged but for completely different reasons.

Being isolated from the world and spending each day trying to remember who he was had become very frustrating not to mention the fact that he had begun to find Shahad very irritating. She was trying too hard to help him remember everything and he really wanted to, but at that moment she was just an annoying woman who refused to give him a moments rest. The more affectionate she became the more he wanted to be left alone. He at least thought that in their house he could get up and walk about when her constant chatter brought him headaches.

That morning he had managed to bathe himself for the first time, which was good. He was self-conscious about the nurses doing it, but it was worse when his wife did it. She made jokes to him and tried to use it as an opportunity for intimacy. She got so upset that he didn't want to cherish the private moment. He enjoyed showers more than baths anyway; he always thought that sitting in the bath was like stewing in your own dirt.

His preference was a shower with cold water, he had gotten used to them when he was younger. They helped to ease his tight breathing whenever he was suffering from an asthmatic attack. However, even when the asthma left him, he carried on with all of the habits that he developed to keep it at bay. He forced himself to grow out of it, illness could be used as an excuse to be weak and he had been born with determination to do great things.

The doctor agreed to his release but insisted that he should have weekly checkups for the next four weeks before he got back to work; whatever the work entailed. Jamal had no idea what he had been doing during his career in the ministry of defense, not to mention his life history since he graduated from University.

He was excited about the prospect of leaving the hospital so walked to the bathroom to get away from everyone, when he got there, he looked in the mirror and saw an old man with streaks of grey in his hair. Jamal had a thick beard but was informed that he came to the hospital fully shaved with a thin moustache. He quite liked the beard, as a student he had struggled to grow one, but now he had a thick bush of facial hair.

He had seen a picture of his children and their families. All of them lived outside of the country and were advised against entering the country due to the security risks, but constantly called to find out about his condition. When they did telephone, he asked them general questions, but went silent when they tried to recap past events with him such as "My boss is saying hello, he still talks about when you and mum hosted him". Jamal would go silent during such comments and his wife would step in and take the telephone from him.

He could see himself in his children's faces, well, his younger face. His strong family features had been passed on. He blinked after speaking to his first-born and could remember holding a baby. But he didn't know which one of his kid's births he was remembering or whether he just wanted to remember something significant so badly that his mind was fabricating memories.

He was fascinated by his weight. He had been lanky as a student, yet everyone was telling him that he had lost a considerable amount of weight since being admitted to the hospital, but in his eyes he gained tremendously. He moved from left to right so that he could fully admire his body, the only thing that disappointed him was his belly; it had been neglected in the gym.

What impressed him the most about his new body were his arms, they were very big and strong. His wife informed him that he visited the gym three times a week, and one of those visits was at the army gym where he would do a big work-out with the soldiers. In his abundant spare time in the hospital bed, he had taken time to read articles about himself and listen to news reports dedicated to him to get a greater picture of his character. If he just listened to the people in the hospital, then he would have thought himself to be some sort of saint. This however was not quite the case. Articles written by Western media seldom mentioned him, but when they did, they said he was a key player in a brutal regime. Others referred to him as "The Executioner" and some said that he was operating a secret police that worked with the intelligence agency to find any individuals who spoke out against the current regime.

Articles that were published by the local media houses were completely different. All newspapers within the country made him out to be a patriotic strongman, reiterated by the fact that he survived the assassination attempt. They said that he was leading the fight against terrorists and would not give up until the terrorists were squashed and stability was restored. He did not read anything about philanthropy, and this disappointed him. If he was indeed such an influential and powerful person with his own children safe and educated, then why couldn't he help the poor?

The police had captured, and were interrogating, two suspects for the attempt on his life. Suspicion was that one of them had died in police custody however this was not confirmed. All this had been accused by the Western media. Jamal was reasonably sure that he was brokering some deal when he was attacked and while he was in hospital, he decided that he would visit the widow of the businessman who was killed. He read that her name was Azmina. He had seen pictures of the lady at her husband's funeral, she was dressed in black from head to toe and her face had been completely covered up.

There was a knock on the bathroom door which broke him out of his daydream. Jamal knew that he couldn't stay hidden away forever and needed to face his current reality. He walked out and realized that he was alone with a nurse. The lady encouraged him to take a seat in a wheelchair which baffled him. He insisted that he could make the short walk to the car but was told that his wife demanded that he should use the wheelchair.

The nurse pushed him in a wheelchair up to the glass sliding doors, but his so-called wife took over before he left the hospital building. Shahad thanked the nurse before she continued to trolley Jamal out. He realized why she had done this when he was hounded by the media who bombarded him with questions and his wife came across very humbly as she answered all the questions on his behalf.

"General Jamal is disorientated and fatigued. He needs to rest before he can address the public, but what is important is that he is alive. The terrorists will never win!" She said all at once into the microphones that had been shoved into her face. Jamal nodded his head to agree with her, he hadn't a clue what to say in that situation but was relieved to be helped into a black SUV.

The car drive was extremely extravagant. There was a police motorcade escorting him to his home. The hospital was only a few minutes from the house, but along the way he stuck his head out and was amazed by the city, it was certainly more modern than he remembered yet after every few minutes there were abandoned buildings that looked like they had fallen victim to heavy firepower.

The car pulled up to a huge mansion and he looked at Shahad in awe. She smiled back and told him that they were home. There was a security checkpoint by the entrance and the guards greeted him with a salute, he couldn't help, but to reciprocate. There was a huge water fountain on the right-hand side, but the rest of the yard was huge with a dog chasing its own tail before it started to follow the car. The driver parked the car close by the steps that lead to the front door. The police motorcade did not follow them into the yard but dispersed once they saw Jamal walking out of the car with a walking stick. The dog began to bark at him viciously. It looked like it was prepared to pounce on an intruder and Jamal began to retreat back into the car. Shahad ran around the car to rescue him from the dog.

"Sit down!" His wife yelled at the canine before the gardener came to restrain the animal. She told Jamal that the dog probably wasn't familiar with his rugged beard. He was hesitant to leave the car again but didn't have a choice. Shahad kept telling him that the dog had been locked up.

Chapter 10

Mohammad's introduction to ISIS

MOHAMMAD WOKE UP IN RAQQAH. Throughout the journey he asked if he could just jump out, but his request was denied time and time again as they assured him that he would be better off with them. The two men would exchange roles as driver allowing for the other to sleep, but Mohammad was always told to sit in the middle. Pressed against them he could feel firearms on both of them, but never saw the guns so he couldn't be sure if that was what the objects were.

The closer they got to Raqqah, the more he saw destroyed infrastructure. Instead of running away from the war, they were moving towards it and this caused him to feel tremendous levels of regret. Surely, he would have been better off in that refugee camp waiting to leave the country. He lost the opportunity to go to America or Europe but promised himself that he would not make that mistake again.

The car slowed as they entered a queue. After rolling the car at a very slow pace they noted that there was a roadblock. Mohammad watched as each car gave the armed gentlemen some money before being allowed to pass; it was some sort of a toll booth. These soldiers were not the government ones, they belonged to Islamic State. This was clearly shown by the flags and their attire. They were dressed in black from head to toe and anyone from a Syrian to an American could recognize their emblem. The road was dilapidated and some patch up job had been done but didn't make much of a difference. The rumors were true. Raqqah was an Islamic State stronghold.

When it was their turn to pay Mr. Hussein dropped the window and showed a badge. The soldier welcomed them back and they drove past without paying. Mohammad thought this rather odd because everyone before and after them had to pay. They were exempt at the next three check points and it was evident that Mohammad had not only allowed himself to be captured by ISIS sympathizers, but these men were so entrenched in it that they moved around with impunity. They continued to drive through Raqqah and turned off the main road. Eventually they entered a farming estate that appeared to be producing cotton. Mohammad was reluctant to ask any questions and Hussein could sense this, so he began to explain.

"My family has been running a cotton farm for many generations. When ISIS emerged and I fully understood the message I began to support them. From the very beginning I gave them money and advice. They have grown and grown to this well set up organization. This is only the beginning; they will continue to expand until the entire country is over run. Western and State media call ISIS terrorists, but throughout history whenever there is an evil regime that kills its own people freedom fighters emerge. Usually in the beginning they are referred to as terrorists until they gain some level of power and free the people. ISIS will liberate us from the current regime and from the Western devils who want to brainwash our youth with their immoral thinking. Most of them do not even believe in God, they only believe in America because they think that America is greater than God. But we will show them that God is with us! I give the leaders some money from cotton sales, which is no different from when I used to pay tax to this regime. They socialize on my property very often and me and my family are protected. I made the mistake of sending my eldest daughter to the United Kingdom for her University and she has refused to return home. However, my sons are studying within the state in the curriculum that will be spread throughout the country as they claim more territory. So, my sons will be among the first graduates with qualifications that will be recognized in the New Syria." Hussein preached proudly while his comrade nodded enthusiastically. Mohammad didn't know what to say in response to this however he was hoping for the best; he could have been shot in a tree not long ago, so anything was better than that.

The rest of the car ride was in silence, however when Mohammad entered the estate, he couldn't hide his amazement. It was a huge property with armed guards outside the entrance to Hussein's home. Mohammad gasped; the man who was driving the car did not appear to be that wealthy. Once out of the car Mohammad was guided to the servant's quarters by the other gentleman whose name he had heard during the trip but it eluded his memory.

This gentleman told Mohammad to clean himself because there was an important meeting that evening and he would need to serve the guests. He asked the man once more for his name and the gentleman smiled before saying that he was Tariq. Mohammad asked him what his job was and was told that he had many roles. He was the driver, bodyguard and personal assistant for Hussein, but he didn't live on the farm. Tariq disappeared and left Mohammad sitting on his single bed.

The workers facilities were very good, and there was no other worker although there was enough room for others. Mohammad felt that he had been too hasty when he judged his situation to be dire. He thought that maybe this wouldn't be so bad. He was living better than he was before and the property was well protected. Not to mention the fact that his boss was not directly involved with Islamic State. He was just a financier, who would not be a target if pro-government troops entered Ar-Raqqah.

He didn't want to be late for his first assignment so hurried into the shower. As soon as he was done and changed back into his clothes there was a knock on the door. A maid came to bring him some fresh clothes; she explained that the men on the property had to wear the brown uniform whenever they left the servant quarters. The maid waited outside while he changed his clothes and they walked together to the main house. Mohammad did not look at the maid for too long, nor did he speak to her too much. He had to be focused on surviving and the last woman that caught his eye almost got him killed. He thought about Azmina for the first time, he wondered if she was still alive, but doubted it.

The two of them entered through the kitchen door and Mohammad was told to remain completely silent during the meeting. He would not react to anything that was said, nor would he repeat to anyone what was mentioned. He was told that there would be stern consequences for disobeying these instructions. He didn't bother to ask what the consequences were but knew to obey the instructions as his imagination ran wild.

He removed his shoes in the kitchen before walking along the carpeted floor that led to the lounge area. The meeting was just about to start so he stood in silence and waited. A part of him wanted to apologize to Hussein for being late, but Hussein did not seem to be bothered nor was Mohammad prepared to break the most important rule; keeping his mouth shut.

"This gentleman has come from Nigeria to tell us about the progress that Boko Haram are having in the region. We know that if we can succeed in spreading in the Middle East and in Africa then we will own the world. Those Western Devils will not exploit our resources anymore and will be begging us for assistance." the gentleman said with a huge grin on his face. Mohammad was surprised that the men were drinking pure juice; his past employers would drink alcohol in the house but pretended that they didn't when in public. Mohammad, himself, enjoyed a glass of whiskey. However, he sensed that this was probably banned on this property.

"Very well, what is it that you would want from me?" Hussein said in a non-aggressive manner. These men had a tremendous amount of mutual respect. Mohammad didn't look at them, instead he stood like a robot staring at the painting that was directly in front of him. It was an interesting image. A little boy was kneeling near a river; his hands were locked as he was drinking. Mohammad could understand the resentment towards the West. Most of the people he knew drank water from streams and lived in immense poverty. Then they were told about a country where its average citizens lived comfortably, he heard figures like the average American earned fifty thousand dollars a year. That was money that he probably wouldn't earn in his lifetime.

"We would like to host our Nigerian friend from Boko Haram here at your beautiful house. Then we can show them how we are working with local businesspeople. Without commerce we won't be able to run successful economies," the gentleman announced as he walked around the room congratulating Hussein on his family's success and wishing him more decades of it. Hussein remained seated and clearly reveled in the compliments.

"Very well my brother, we shall prepare for you," Hussein said with a grand beam. They made several jokes that Mohammad found hilarious however forced himself not to respond. It was so important that he kept this job because he had nothing else to fall back to. There was not a single note in his pocket and the only food in his stomach and been given to him by Hussein and Tariq.

After the meeting was complete and the guests dispersed the boss asked Mohammad if he was comfortable. Hussein told him that if he kept his head down then good things could come his way. Mohammad thanked him profusely for the opportunity and promised that he wouldn't disappoint him. Hussein told him that the staff ate dinner outside of the kitchen at eight so he should join them before the food finished.

Chapter 11

A Potential Second Wave

OLIVIER WAS WOKEN by his son who had decided to jump into their bed. His son gave his mother a kiss and a hug before he hugged his father. He had just returned from a school trip to Kenya which coincided quite nicely with their trip to Yambuku. Olivier had a drumming hangover but smiled before they started to wrestle. Then as usual Olivier would lay still as Pierre would pin him down and win the match. Vivienne laughed as she chased them both out of the bedroom, and Olivier knew that that boy was the key to the happiness in their marriage. That was what made his decision so difficult.

He lifted his son and walked towards the living room as Pierre told disjointed stories about the school trip. However, at the end of each story Pierre was the hero and to this his father would reply "fantastique!". When they got to the living room Olivier placed his hand on his son's shoulders.

"Pierre, I have decided that you will join your sister in Paris. You will be going to boarding school over there…" Olivier was interrupted by his son's protests. He changed the narrative to state that he didn't enjoy Kenya and wanted to be home. But

Olivier raised his hand to silence the boy and explained that his decision was final. The school wasn't starting for another three weeks but Olivier had arranged for his son to leave in the next couple of days. Tears rolled down his son's eyes before he stormed out of the living room. Olivier guessed that he would have gone straight back to his mother who would probably need to comfort him for an hour or two.

Olivier didn't want to send his son away but wouldn't have been able to forgive himself if anything happened, not that he thought it would, but he had to be cautious. He would be a target, but his family would not be, going by the unspoken rules of the game. But he trusted no one and if his fortunes would take a turn for the worse at least his children would be away from it all.

Since his presence in the bedroom wouldn't be appreciated, he turned on the television and put the news on. The international news broadcaster announced that the current Ebola outbreak originated in the Meliandou village in Sierra Leone. An infant child, now known as patient X, was the first to die before his immediate family shared the same fate. The first family of the current crisis infected people who subsequently travelled to other villages and caused the virus to spread. This was the first time that Ebola cases had been reported in Sierra Leone which led to a considerable time before it was recognized as what it was.

In March 2014 the World Health Organization announced, that the virus had spread rapidly into Liberia, Guinea and Sierra Leone. The first time that Ebola had reached a capital city was when cases were reported in Conakry, Guinea's capital. By April the virus had found its way to Liberia's capital city, Monrovia. Finally, by July, the virus had reached Freetown, Sierra Leone's capital city. The fact that Ebola had gone from being a virus that only affected peasants in villages to now being one that was in capital cities of countries that possessed international airports was of extreme concern. The broadcast ended.

Olivier turned off the television. He was a child of the first Ebola outbreak, but now the virus had the potential to spread to any country in the world and international media made sure that everyone knew this. This was sure to cause even further panic. He had been following the surge in causes and analyzing the responses to it by countries. Within African countries they appeared to be responding by isolating themselves from each other in a desperate attempt to protect their countries. In the process they were closing their doors to trade opportunities in the region. This was not to mention the reaction from several international companies that were ceasing their operations and calling back their expatriates. Then there was the effect to foreign direct investment as several investors held onto their money as they waited to see what would transpire in the region.

Production in Sierra Leone, Guinea and Liberia was coming to a halt in key industries such as mining and agriculture. From what Olivier had read, farm workers were abandoning the properties where they worked due to fear that they would contract the virus from their colleagues or the general public when they took their produce to the market to sell. Orphans had become outcasts as there was fear that they had caught the virus from their parents who had died, leading to an increased number of street kids and rises in criminal activity that appeared to be correlated.

Olivier also felt that the weak health care centers in these countries did not help. Even prior to the outbreak they couldn't withstand the current health care needs of the citizens with issues such as malaria and HIV ensuring that their hospitals were always full. Medical treatment in public hospitals was always delayed, not to mention the fact that there were never enough doctors. Statistics showed that for every medical doctor there were eleven thousand patients. Surprisingly the governments in these countries couldn't understand why their graduates opted to work in private hospitals or overseas instead of their public ones where they were not always paid on time and were understaffed and had long working hours.

Many African governments had been criticized for not investing their own money in research and development of the cure and relying too heavily on foreign countries to uncover the antidote including his own. Olivier didn't forget about the Ebola virus and constantly probed the Health Minister on what would be the government's response if it ever returned. These questions were never addressed as over the years his view on a second wave was never shared.

The Ebola virus is a hemorrhagic fever that spreads between human beings through the exchange of bodily fluids. To date there has been no cure so how could cabinet not have a plan for its return? Was this not inevitable? Patients were only to be treated through isolation and staying hydrated, was this the only plan in the result of an epidemic?

The virus spread through eating fruit bats which is a common source of food in the villages, Olivier's calls for removing bats from around the villages in Congo were also ignored due to cost. The common mistake that was being made in the villages was the disposal of the dead. They were not taking the proper precautions and funerals would often result in many of the mourners falling ill, thus propelling the multiplier effect. Not to mention the spread in the hospitals and mortuaries. The situation was becoming direr and global concern was increasing. Many governments had to answer the cries of their people who were asking the same question, being, what their government would do to ensure that Ebola did not enter their borders. It wasn't yet in Congo, but the question was for how long.

Chapter 12

The Negotiation

THE DAY AFTER HIS SON ARRIVED in Paris, Olivier arrived in the capital city for his meeting with the President. Some party officials who couldn't decide which camp to follow opted to broker this sit down in an attempt to establish some form of a power-sharing agreement within the party's structures to avoid further dissonance. Either the President would proceed with his plans to change the constitution and implement his fourth term or Olivier would be the party's presidential candidate for the general election. They did not expect to reach a conclusion early nor one at all; they just hoped that they could. They felt that fighting in the media would only provide political mileage for the opposition, whichever that might be.

They met at the Grand Plaza hotel and their vehicles drove up to the entrance at the same time. The president's limousine was in front of Olivier's. Olivier waited for the president to exit his first before he followed suit. The two men walked up to one another and embraced each other with hugs and laughs as the media snapped away with their cameras. They stood side by side and posed for photographs before continuing to greet other party members. Olivier knew within his heart that the boxing gloves were not on until after this meeting. For now, they had to continue as if it was business as usual.

The other officials all greeted each other before proceeding into the hotel. They were taken to the conference room where they found lots of drinks and snacks on the table. As a courtesy Olivier waited for the president's entourage to serve themselves before, he stepped forward with his own entourage to do the same. The doors were closed by one of the senior party members, Moses Nelele, the man who had pleaded with Olivier to attend. A few members of the press were camped outside of the room, eagerly anticipating the conclusion of that meeting. Moses explained that the security guards would inform the state press to leave the hotel.

Once all the men were done eating their snacks, they took their seats around the long table with the President seated at the top and Olivier on the opposite end. The laughs and jokes came to an end as the President began to clear his voice. He would be the first one to speak, as expected.

"As you all are aware, we are looking into amending the constitution and implementing a fourth term, like we successfully managed to do at the end of my second term. I am still the most popular candidate in the party. However, once I win the presidential election then I will shuffle my cabinet a bit. I won't go into great deal on that right now, but the position of Vice President will go to Olivier Katanga," the president explained with a large grin on his face. However, his beam didn't last long as he could tell that Olivier did not share the same enthusiasm. Another one of the senior officials who had clearly been brought in to tip this discussion in the president's favor leaned forward in his seat and took the floor, as if the discussion was scripted. Fabrice Mpuka looked at Olivier to try and win him over; they had been long time friends. In fact, prior to that day, Olivier attributed most of his success to Fabrice's mentorship.

"We are very happy that you would decide to open this discussion with such a generous offer for the governor, who will be placed well to take the presidency once your fourth term is over." Fabrice responded on Olivier's behalf. His contribution reminded Olivier of a mother who was promising a crying child that even though he couldn't go to his friend's house that day, he would be allowed to go next time. Olivier mustered all the frustration within him and placed it on his face. Fabrice knew that his lack of neutrality meant that he had picked his team and all that he had done for Olivier would be forgotten.

"That is exactly what I was thinking. I just need one more term to ensure that Olivier becomes a nationwide figure so that when I step aside the party can continue to rule. If we are too hasty, then we can lose the general election instead of making victory a priority. I know that some of the party members feel like they must choose between myself and Olivier. However, if we walk out of here, embracing one another as brothers, then we can focus on the national election so that all of us keep our jobs," the president concluded with murmuring approvals from his supporters who were now in the majority. The unbiased officials had shown their allegiance within moments of the meetings commencement. So much for their stances of simply being the custodians for this coming together, Olivier thought to himself.

"Governor Olivier Katanga, do you have nothing to say about his Excellency's generous offer?" Moses Nelele, the grey-haired traitor pressed on. He was concerned that Olivier showed no sign of emotion towards the president's proposal. Olivier decided that he wouldn't waste any more time here. He had other meetings in Kinshasa so wasn't going to spend any more time at this scripted debate. It was obvious that the president was not willing to compromise, and neither was he. Not only should they respect the party's manifesto which only allowed for two terms, but so did the national constitution before he amended it. Now he wanted to change it again.

He was spitting on both documents and he had been allowed to do it before, but not again. Olivier opposed President Mbuyi's third term but didn't have enough support to do anything about it previously. That was not the case this time. His eyes in the intelligence agency told him that he was now more popular than Mbuyi. Olivier was done with the niceties; the gloves were now on. It was time for the bell to ring and the fight to begin.

"Number one, he was talking about a fourth term even before I stepped forward to challenge him. This shows that it is just greed that motivates him and not the party. Number two, before his last election he promised six people the Vice presidency, including myself. This man will not keep his word. Number three is that I am popular enough on the nationwide level, which is why you are even bothering to sit down with me. The intelligence department must have informed you that I am more popular than you and the most capable candidate to replace you," Olivier replied as arrogantly as he could be. It was now official; these men were at war and could no longer walk around like the party was united. It was time for party members to pick sides and he was ready for any and all consequences that would follow.

"Olivier, I only offer friendship once. Now if you are not my friend then you are my enemy, and everyone knows how I deal with my enemies. You would know very well, however, my colleagues are protected so even though you know what I can do, you have never experienced it." The president responded with venom in his eyes. Olivier knew who he was dealing with. His country had secret police that would harass any individuals who supported the opposition. The areas of the country that were opposition strongholds would not receive medicine for their hospitals or general development. The people knew that the fact that their towns were so terrible was simply because they had different political viewpoints. Olivier was saddened by all of this. He strongly believed in democracy but knew that he couldn't cause any impact from the outside. He knew that he could only create a democracy if he aspired to the top position. He knew all about corruption and prayed that his own morality wouldn't be comprised; he couldn't become like that man who was seated across the table from him.

"I guess then I will soon experience it. If you try to run for a fourth term, then you and I are no longer friends." Olivier announced. The senior officials tried to intervene and discuss party unity and how they must achieve a mutual goal of staying in power. The meeting lost its order when Olivier's entourage also yelled back in his defense; it was becoming a big mess. He decided to remove himself from the anarchy.

Olivier stood up and walked away towards the main door while Fabrice pleaded with him to stay because they were all brothers. Olivier just continued and opened the door as Fabrice said that it was rude to depart in that nature. When in the lobby Olivier was startled by the fact that there was no state press, he had hoped to find them and be filmed with his furious face. He envisioned tomorrows headline reading "Governor Katanga of Katanga walks out of talks with President Mbuyi". However, there was no one in sight, even the hotel's staff members were missing in action. One of them could have been used to leak his exit to the press, but this wouldn't be the case.

His car was brought round by the hotel's valet. He was informed that his driver would return shortly as he was in the bathroom. As he waited in the car alone, he noticed a newspaper man walking around and the headline caught his attention. Olivier stepped out of the car and walked across the street. The headline wrote that the Ebola virus was spreading rapidly in Liberia, Sierra Leone and Guinea. He couldn't believe it. This virus divided his family and changed his life, he wondered if it would stay in West Africa or whether it would come knocking on his country's doorstep yet again. He paid for the paper and stopped on the pavement as he continued to read the article in further depth for five minutes until there was a huge explosion across the street. He looked up in disarray. The car that he had been sitting in a few minutes ago had just blown up. Olivier froze. His mind raced back to the moment when he was an orphaned child in Yambuku village standing hungry outside of the hospital. Alone, defenseless and afraid. This sensation took hold of his gut and for a moment he felt paralyzed.

Chapter 13

The Recollections

GENERAL JAMAL WAS FINALLY OFF DUTY. He spent his first day back in his mansion. He never thought that he would ever live in such a spacious house. For him it was truly incredible, yet its majesty didn't help to restore his lost memory. He was still not even believing that his wife was his wife. They had a fight the night before. She wanted to make love and pamper him, but he was tired after being away for such a long period of time. All he wanted was solitude to remember and sleep in the guest room. After an hour it was decided that he would sleep in the master bedroom to aid his familiarity and she would sleep in the guest room. Despite her disappointment this didn't prevent her from bringing him breakfast in bed.

After enjoying what was described as his favorite breakfast, he made his way down the stairs. He used a walking stick although his left leg was feeling stronger as each day went by. Once on the ground floor Jamal decided to summon one of the butlers to sit with him in the lounge.

"I need to meet a lady known as Azmina; she is the widow to the gentleman who was killed at the meeting where I was shot. His name is Omar," he explained as he sat back in his chair to get comfortable. His back had been sore, so a masseuse had been working on it the day before. She was an incredibly beautiful woman and he had been chatting away with her when his wife walked into the room. She gave him a stare and commented about how he barely said two words to her before leaving in anger. The massage didn't actually help, and he didn't expect his wife to call the same company again.

"Yes Sir, is that all. This morning you received many sympathetic phone calls from well-wishers not, to mention your colleagues," the butler replied almost robotically. This gentleman showed no emotion and Jamal could sense fear in him. He thought to himself for a moment. He wanted to change the atmosphere here, because whoever he had been was not going to influence who he would be going forward. The first thing he wanted to introduce was controlled philanthropy; he knew that people needed to learn how to fish rather than being given a fish. His programs would teach people how to stand on their own two feet.

"Okay, I will return some of the phone calls. Now tell me, what I am like to work for. As you know I am suffering from memory loss," he instigated before the man had the opportunity to excuse himself. Suddenly the butler shifted his jaw rather uncomfortably. Clearly this was a difficult question to answer. The gentleman blinked twice and cleared his throat.

"You are a great employer Sir, and I am lucky to have this job. My family is extremely grateful because we wouldn't have been able to survive if not for it." The butler went on and on about how there was tremendous suffering in the country and that working at such a safe home and receiving such a generous salary was something that he would not take for granted. He complimented all that the party was doing to keep the terrorists at bay and then he suddenly shut up. It was as if he didn't trust himself not to say the wrong thing.

Jamal thought for a moment, he asked the gentleman to take a seat. He pulled his chair closer to the butler before he whispered.

"Be honest with me, I can see fear in your eyes. Tell me, what is the worst thing that I ever did to you. Your job is safe, I promise." He told the butler that he was trying to change, but he couldn't do that with everyone telling him that he is a great man. He needed to know more about himself, not only so he could change but also to help him to remember. He needed to find out why there was an attempt on his life as quickly as possible. Finding out could save the lives of other people.

The worker took a deep breath and swallowed his saliva so slowly that you could visibly see it going down his throat. He whispered back at Jamal.

"I left your clothes on your bed once, but forgot to put a belt. You screamed asking for it, when I brought it to you. You grabbed the belt and whipped me with the buckle near my eye. That is why I have this scar," the gentleman stood up and moved towards the wall as if he expected some negative consequences. His arm was shaking rapidly; he immediately regretted what he just said.

Jamal closed his eyes in pity for this man but was suddenly filled with a vision. He remembered whipping that man across the face. Afterwards he recollected going to the gym and lifting weights for a few minutes before calling all of his children. He remembered everything about his kids and how relieved he was that they no longer lived in Syria. Information about them entered his brain such as their birthday parties and school-teachers. The many times when his youngest son was naughty, and they needed to punish him. Also, the fact that he shouldn't let the youngest boy drive his car was cemented in his mind because of all of the car accidents his son had over the years. When he opened his eyes, he thanked the worker and apologized for the scar.

His wife walked into the room and told him that his brother Abdul-Aziz wanted to see him, she seemed to be upset about this, but Jamal was delighted. Abdul walked in and looked quite frail, Jamal embraced him with a huge hug and a kiss on the cheek. During the greeting he could smell the stench of alcohol, yet it was still early morning. Abdul smiled politely, but remained silent as if he was scared to speak. His brother scratched his elbows and arms, it was obvious to Jamal that there was something wrong with Abdul. This was evident by his blood-red eyes.

"Abdul, I am so happy to see you. Every day in the hospital I was hoping to see you." Jamal decided to ignore his conjecture; he was standing with one of the familiar faces. Abdul didn't answer, he simply scratched his head before mentioning to Jamal that he had come for his pocket money. Jamal was taken aback by this. He stood up and walked to the kitchen where Shahad had retreated to after announcing Abdul's arrival. He found his wife drinking a glass of water and asked her about the allowance. Jamal had no idea where to get the money from, not to mention how much it was supposed to be. Shahad passed a comment saying that she had hoped that hitting his head would help him to realize that giving his brother money would only contribute to his drug addiction.

Jamal stormed out and asked Abdul if he took drugs. His brother couldn't speak because he was high and drunk first thing in the morning. Jamal ordered the butler to escort Abdul off of the premises. As his brother stumbled towards his car that had two female passengers in it, Jamal finally came to the realization that things would never be the same. He could not spend his time yearning for the good old days, re-linking with high school friends or wishing to awake from this dream. He needed to solve the problems that were created prior to the assassination attempt; whether he remembered them or not.

Chapter 14

The Near Escape

AS SOON AS THE CAR EXPLODED Olivier dropped the paper and ran into the nearby park. A crowd of civilians started to gather by the newspaper stand as the seller emphatically explained the events that just took place. The gentleman who sold him the paper would have known that Olivier had just escaped death by the skin of his teeth because he saw him leave the car. Olivier wasn't sure whether it was a bomb or there was a gun man out there. It was highly possible that there was a sniper, it was the Central Business District and the area would be ideal for shooting him from one of the tall buildings.

Olivier cowered underneath an oak tree as his mind raced through what he should do next. If he went back into that conference room to throw punches at the President, then that would be treason and he would be locked away. As of this moment he hadn't given President Mbuyi any reason to throw him in jail and it needed to stay that way. He wondered who in that room knew about the bomb and how quickly the order was given after his refusal of the Vice Presidency. Finally, he considered how open and obvious the attempt was, it smelt of desperation. In their politics opponents would be given what they called "slow kill" or be involved in "car accidents". Car bombs hadn't been used since Mobutu's era.

After five minutes of hiding and staying completely still he could hear the fire brigade racing towards the scene. Olivier finally rose hesitantly before dusting himself off. He mustered up all of his strength to climb the tree just enough for him to see the site where the explosion had occurred. A larger crowd had assembled across the street. Olivier climbed down from the tree and made the decision to flee the scene.

He knew that he could obtain political mileage by telling the press that it was an attempt on his life by the President shortly after he refused a proposal for him to enact a fourth term. However, something within him urged Olivier towards leaving the country and only increasing his status when he was thinking clearly. Right now, he was only thinking in the short term and that required a plan for him to escape DRC unharmed until he organized himself. He was breathing rapidly, and his blood felt like it was boiling.

Fortunately, he remembered that his luggage had remained at his hotel which was on the other side of town. He would have stayed at the Grand Plaza, but because of his other meeting his secretary booked him at the Karome-Bensadaa Hotel, albeit Karome-Bensadaa was somewhat decrepit. He knew it was risky for him to return there without a bodyguard, but maybe now was the best time. His attackers probably thought that he was dead. It would take some time before it was discovered that his body wasn't in the wreckage. The fact that the President was so near to the blast meant that the priority for the police would be to ensure his safety and that he was evacuated as quickly as possible.

As Olivier walked back out of the park and kept his face down, he could hear the police sirens that were right on cue. If seen he would have to go to the station and give a statement. He didn't want anyone to recognize him, civilian or otherwise. He walked for a few minutes with his eyes fixed on the pavement until he was confident that he was out of sight. With his eyes firmly focused on the ground he stuck his hand out in the air. From his earlier days this was the way that a person was meant to wave down a taxi.

Before he could hail a cab, several minibus drivers hooted at him as if he was a prospective customer. After what felt like a couple of minutes, he realized that it would be easier to catch a cab at a taxi stand so he enquired from a passerby where he may find one. After ten minutes of walking blindly, his faith in his understanding of the directions guided him there. It wasn't much of a rank, just a bench with a shelter that protected the drivers from the heat. Before he even approached the rank the fact that he was moving in their direction caused the group to stop what they were doing.

The drivers hounded him by them shoving their car keys in his face and waiting for him to pick one. Olivier simply pointed at the one who was nearest to him. When they weren't selected the other drivers immediately lost interest in him and swarmed onto the next potential client who was an old lady with a number of grocery bags.

As soon as he was seated in the cab Olivier noticed that there was a newspaper on the backseat so he used it to cover his face, he knew that he was being somewhat paranoid, but would only calm down when he made it out of the country. He was even suspecting that this cab driver could turn him over to the secret police, as if the whole nation already knew what he just said to the President.

The driver kept trying to discuss the bomb that he had heard that went off near the Grand Plaza, but Olivier simply replied by telling him to hurry up because he was late for an appointment. The cab driver needed little motivation to drive like a lunatic and this request from Olivier sparked him off. He drove on the pavement and hooted at civilians as if he was meant to be driving on their walkway and the pedestrians were in the wrong. Whenever there was a traffic build up the driver would switch to the opposite side of the road and push his way back into the correct line whenever a car was coming. Olivier contemplated telling the man to calm down, but then remembered that it wasn't his car. If this guy was stopped by the traffic police, then he would simply exit the vehicle and catch another one.

Olivier was no stranger to radical driving from his own personal driver's behavior. However, in his daily movements the public knew to move out of the way when a government official was moving around town with the national flag waving on the front. The community never openly showed any dissent towards the crazy driving that the official's drivers would do. However, with the cab driver he was receiving and sending out several insults throughout the journey. Olivier wondered why his lanky cab driver had such an aggressive mouth. Some of the individuals who he was insulting on the road were twice his size and Olivier was not prepared to step in to solve any physical altercations if someone got out of the car to sort him out.

It suddenly dawned on him that his driver and bodyguard were not at the vehicle. If they had been then they would've seen the bomb being placed. This was standard protocol and he felt it was far from a coincidence for both of them to be away from the car when the bomb went off. If they had been compromised, then who else? He suddenly realized just how alone he was. He could sense incipient betrayal building up from those closest to him.

By the grace of God, they arrived unharmed. Once they reached the hotel Olivier continued to cover his face with the paper as he paid not only the cab fare, but also for the paper. He moved through the reception inconspicuously ignoring all of the staff member's greetings as he made his way to the elevator. He wasn't sure if there were cameras in the lift, so he only ditched the newspaper when he got to the top floor.

His rooms were always on the top floor, he was deserving of the presidential suite, he often joked, because he was determined to be president one day. The top floor only had one room and he had to use his keycard in the elevator before he could even proceed to his room's door. He felt very safe there with this safeguard even though he did not intend to stay for very long. The first section of the suite had a living room, the second section was a dining room, the third had a kitchen, and the fourth section was his bedroom that had a balcony and bathing facilities. From the terrace he could overlook the poolside and could even see into the city.

He poured himself some whiskey and drank it like it was water. He hurried around the room re-packing things that he had taken out of his suitcase only a few short hours earlier. He checked his briefcase several times to make sure that there was nothing that could stop him from entering Nigeria, even something as trivial as a yellow fever certificate could have been a deciding factor. Once satisfied he went onto his laptop to look for commercial tickets. Flying anything other than a private jet was something that he hadn't done for a long while. He was grateful that he hadn't always been rich because he knew how to survive in the world with very little.

During this period of uncertainty, he would only fly commercial; it would be safer than him using a private plane. The forces that just tried to kill him wouldn't be able to tamper with an international aircraft. His safety was worth the inconvenience and it wasn't like he hadn't flown commercial before. Flying commercial would also aid his political career if he reinvented himself to come across as a humble civil servant whose only wish was to serve his fellow countrymen. Olivier sent his secretary an email to explain that he would soon be leaving the country because of an unforeseen emergency. He Bcc'd his deputy governor who had already assumed his powers in his absence from Katanga.

Olivier took his passport and luggage before making his way back down to the lobby. He checked out of the hotel much to the surprise of the receptionist who reminded him that the state had booked him in the room for two days. He mentioned the urgent need for him to travel because of Ebola, this was good. If asked, then the woman could reiterate his reason for travelling to anyone who came looking. He neglected to mention which country he was travelling to.

Olivier sat in the lobby and drank coffee as he waited for the bus shuttle. The receptionist kept asking if he wanted a private vehicle to take him to the airport, but Olivier refused her each time she made the proposal. The lady must have been fearful that he would leave and complain about the hospitality.

Olivier had to reassure her that he was going to the airport in the bus so that he could mingle with all of the other exiting guests because he wanted to feel closer to the people. The staff members whispered amongst themselves, audibly, that they considered him to be very humble. It was not long before the other guests surrounded him, and he obliged by turning on the charm and entertaining them with some jokes until the driver politely interrupted him to explain that the shuttle was ready.

He made his way to the middle of the bus, if there was a head on collision then he would be safe and if the vehicle was hit from the back, then he would also be fine. He wore a smile throughout the trip but within himself there was turmoil and his stomach was uneasy. During the long drive to the airport, he used his smart phone to check the news, nothing yet had been written about the explosion, but the citizens knew about it from word of mouth. He couldn't wait to get to Nigeria, the African equivalent to Switzerland when it came to banking laws. Nigeria had always been his safe haven for a rainy day. At least it was his African place of safety though he preferred the greater luxury of Cyprus, tucked in the eastern end of the Mediterranean Sea.

He had some friends in West Africa but didn't want to appear scared for his life. If supporters thought that he was running for his life, then he would lose them and their respect. The decision to go to Nigeria needed to have purpose behind it.

So, he logged onto his social media and released statements about how he would travel to Nigeria because of the Ebola epidemic that was sweeping West Africa. He told his followers online that containment of this outbreak was of the outmost importance to him as an individual and to the nation at large. He wrote that he wanted to offer solidarity and advise on containment of the virus.

As he lay back and browsed the web on his smartphone, he eventually found himself strolling through the Nigerian e-newspapers and uncovered that there were several conferences and discussion forums that were coming up with regards to this very issue. He spent his time registering for the various events and made sure to commit himself to at least a week of work.

He bought a one-way ticket to Nigeria and then logged onto his email. He informed his Nigerian counterparts and urged them to invite the press to meet him at the airport upon his arrival. In the airport he made his way to the VIP Lounge after saying his goodbyes to the others who were taking a domestic flight.

After four hours of struggling to pass the time and feeling fearful that police would storm in to prevent his travel his flight was finally boarding. The first-class passengers were allowed to go in first, as usual. The flight, itself was very relaxing. The skies were calm, and he found lots of movies to watch, he would usually use the time to read, but he was too nervous. Every time someone walked past him, he felt jumpy and ordered alcohol each time the flight attendants went by him. He didn't think that food would sit well with him yet. The truth was that that bombing wasn't a warning. It was an actual attempt on his life, and he had to take it seriously.

When they finally arrived in Lagos after a three-hour flight, he found some media presence outside of arrivals. He put on his usual charm and smiles as he walked towards them. Olivier had learnt a long time ago how to hide his emotions. Everything that he felt was addressed in solidarity, when he was alone. He didn't even allow his wife to enter his innermost thoughts. He cleared his throat before he tended to the journalist.

"It has come to my attention that the Ebola virus has returned to our beloved continent and is spreading rapidly in West Africa. I lost my own mother to Ebola and was raised as an orphan until I returned to Congo. The people of Congo have since become my family, yet I sympathize with those affected by this deadly virus. It is with this in mind that I have decided to travel to Nigeria. I am here to provide ground support to the West African politicians so that this virus can be contained. It is spreading rapidly, and we are hoping to contain it before it becomes a worldwide pandemic. I have left my duties to the deputy governor and will only return once the situation stabilizes. After all, if it spreads then it won't be long until the dreaded virus returns to my beloved country."

After which the press hounded him with questions about his presidential ambitions, his relationship with the President and other sensitive questions. All of which his answer was "no comment".

Chapter 15

The Investigation Begins

GENERAL JAMAL WAS INVITED into Azmina's home. It was a beautiful house with a guard outside who didn't bother him for too long. As his driver parked and Jamal exited the car, he could hear Azmina, but couldn't see her at first. She continued to call to him until he noticed that she was by the pool area. She welcomed him by there and smiled as he approached her with his walking stick, which provided him with the necessary support.

She greeted him with kisses on each cheek which surprised him because they didn't know each other. She shocked him further by holding his hand as she walked him towards where they would sit. Sensing his awe Azmina kept saying that she needed to hold him so that no one would say that General Jamal collapsed at her home. He laughed with her, which probably encouraged the casual behavior, but it was nice for someone not to be scared of him for a change.

She raised her voice and instructed the house boy to bring them some refreshments. Azmina was going to take herbal tea so he asked for the same. It was a habit from when he was a young boy to take whatever his hosts were taking rather than being too picky. Once she was done giving the boy numerous instructions she sat back down, somewhat satisfied. Azmina was dressed in all black, but her face wasn't covered which would have been the norm for a widow who was mourning the loss of her husband.

She was much younger than Jamal and was extremely beautiful, even in her long black robe he knew that there was a sexy body underneath. He tried not to stare for too long, but his heart began to beat rapidly. His instincts told him that she was also interested in him from the way she stroked his arm and so forth. Since he had come out of hospital, he hadn't even thought about satisfying his lusts until then and didn't feel any loyalty towards the woman who called herself his wife.

After the houseboy returned with their snacks, he immediately left them alone before Azmina sat closely to Jamal. She had such a unique fragrance. General Jamal felt that her scent would consume anyone that came across her, and it wasn't just the attraction that was causing him to be aroused by her smell. The conversation had been light, but eventually he remembered why he was there and regained focus.

Jamal kick started the conversation. "Did you have any knowledge of your late husband's dealings?" His hope was that Omar ran his business like a family business. If so, then the wife could be extremely useful however if she was kept in the dark like most housewives with rich husbands then this would more than likely be a dead end. Yet he had faith that he was there for a significant reason.

"No, not really I'm afraid. I heard that you are suffering from memory loss," she jested; Azmina must have assumed that this was a social visit. People had been passing through her home to convey their condolences, especially those who hadn't made it to the funeral. For the next three months she would try her best not to go far from her home so that people who were travelling to pay their respects would find her.

"Yes, bad news travels quickly. That is very true, I am trying to figure out what we were discussing that afternoon and how we were ambushed. If it was a secret meeting then it didn't make sense that we would have been in a gun fight, unless we were betrayed. I can't go back to work with a blank mind because I will be setting myself up for someone to finish the job," Jamal confessed the debacle that he was facing. He could see in her face, Azmina was determined to assist his plight.

"I understand, would you like to come inside and look around in his office. Maybe you will find something that will be useful?" She suggested frankly. She continued to sip on her tea and eat the biscuits but did so at a quicker pace after she made this suggestion.

"That will be great, tell me about your husband. What type of man was he?" Jamal asked before he downed his drink and stood up, it was time for him to go and snoop in Omar's office. Jamal also suspected that his driver was reporting his movements to his wife and the party officials who were interested in monitoring him. The driver agreed to take him wherever he wanted, but Jamal noticed that he would immediately make a call before pursuing on his duties.

"My late husband was the type of man who would do whatever he liked and expected others to be content. He was a terror to be with and for many years I thought about being free from him. I must admit that I am relieved to be alone." Azmina said for the first time much to Jamal's surprise. He couldn't believe that she would be so honest with him, yet he had already opened up to her. Maybe she felt that him snooping around was not completely warranted yet she would protect his secret so expected that he would keep hers.

"I know that you must be grieving, I'm sure that you will feel differently in time," Jamal responded before they stood up. He was guided into the house and she walked slowly at his pace. Before he entered the front door, he noticed that his driver was on the phone staring at him. Jamal suddenly felt a sense of urgency.

Chapter 16

Mohammad's Growing Awareness

MOHAMMAD NOTICED that more and more Nigerians from Boko Haram were being hosted at his boss's estate. He never met the Caliph in person, but his title was constantly referred to during all of the discussions. The Caliph was the title given to the ruler of the community; this individual was the modern-day successor to the prophet Mohammad. Very few people in Raqqah had actually seen the Caliph; he wasn't like a politician who could move freely making speeches since there was a bounty on his head. Instead, the Caliph, who was a great orator, was heard via radio broadcasts that played on speakers that had been set up around Raqqah. He would also send messages online however not many people had access to internet in the region. All that Mohammad knew about him was his name, Faraz Khalid Abdallah, and that he was the supreme leader in this territory.

From Mohammad's viewpoint it seemed like some form of an alliance was being sought after. The Nigerians pledged allegiance to Islamic State, and this had been accepted by the Caliph however in the interim efforts were being made to ensure that their teachings were not only similar, but fused together.

The hope was that they would have one universal message so that it would not matter if their supporters were in West Africa or the Middle East. There was also an insistence that the message would be given in Arabic so as to overcome any language barriers that their followers would have to face. The leaders of the two groups didn't want to create confusion by relaying different messages to the Muslim community.

The western style of teaching was out however they wanted these Nigerians to walk away with the textbooks that the students in Raqqah were using. This way they could refer potential students who were unable to travel to Syria or Iran to West Africa. They promised to encourage some of their jihadists to spend some time camped in West Africa where they would fight hand in hand with Boko Haram fighters. The meeting seemed to have been an agreeable one, but it suggested that there was some hierarchy. It was more of vertical integration rather than a merger. ISIS was the parent company and Boko Haram was going to be a subsidiary.

Mohammad continued to listen to the discussions. He didn't flinch until he was sent to get water or food for them all. All the workers on the estate were encouraged to undertake some classes that Islamic state was providing. Even though it was only suggested none of the other workers had refused to attend the lessons so neither did he.

Mohammad had always been a devoted Muslim, but with the Western influence he had lost some of his core beliefs which were now being reinforced. He was beginning to realize that Islamic State or a Caliphate was necessary for the people to become pure in God's eyes. Apart from walking to the tutorials he hadn't left the estate since his arrival, but on this day, Hussein asked him to drive the visitors to the border because Tariq wasn't feeling well.

Mohammad was also instructed to show the guards the letter that Hussein gave him. Mohammad was extremely nervous about leaving the property but was pleased that he was trusted enough to be given this duty. He had created a bond with Hussein that he had never had with any of his previous employers. His other bosses treated him like dirt, yet Hussein made Mohammad feel like he was a younger brother.

Mohammad opened the doors for the Boko Haram visitors before rushing to the driver's seat. Hussein waved them off with a big smile on his face. Mohammad drove rather slowly, and the Nigerians kept saying that he was a good driver.

It was a short journey and as the car reached the border checkpoint, he noticed that there was a buildup of expensive cars in a closed area. One of the Nigerians sat forward to explain why those cars were there since he could tell that Mohammad didn't know the reason.

"Your system here is very good. Those who want to leave the Caliphate state must leave their vehicles that are valued over twenty thousand dollars as collateral in case they stay away for longer than the permitted time," the man explained jovially, Mohammad tried not to be too surprised by this revelation but he was shocked. Up until then he thought that everyone who was in Raqqah was here because they wanted to be, not because of restrictions.

"Their houses as well, if they leave and don't come back then the house is given to a prominent Jihadist as a reward for their loyalty. It is a good system; we don't want people to leave here because they are afraid of the fighting. We know that the people support Islamic State, but the fear of government fighters might encourage them to flee. Either you succeed together, or you die together. We will ensure that it is the same in Nigeria in the Borno state, but we need your help to control the people."

After this statement they noticed some commotion on the road. It appeared that a man was trying to run away from the ISIS soldiers and make his way towards the main gate. The gentleman was shot at and it seemed that he was hit on his legs. Another soldier came forward to stop the traffic, all of the cars were immediately halted. No one was allowed to move, but they could all see the jihadists drag the man's body and lean him against the wall.

One of the jihadists was given a megaphone. He informed everyone that the man who had been shot had tried to leave Raqqah by presenting a fake title deed. The man was hoping to flee without paying the exit tax like everyone else. At this point the other two jihadists held the man against the wall while the ISIS fighter with the megaphone put it on the ground and rolled up his sleeves. The spokesman pulled out a long combat army knife. Grabbing his hair, he held the man's head up for all to see.

Mohammad knew what was coming, he wanted to look away, but his eyes were glued to what was happening in front of him. The Nigerians shifted excitedly in their chairs with huge beams on their faces. The Boko Haram representatives were clearly enjoying the show and delighted to have some entertainment before departing.

The jihadist cut the man's neck slowly causing him to let out loud cries. This is what they wanted, for him to suffer in front of anyone who would dare to attempt what he just did. Eventually the crying and screaming turned out to be his own un-doing as he choked on his own blood and suffocated to death. His body was left by the wall that the locals referred to as "Deserter's Corner".

This was done so that anyone who didn't have the opportunity to watch the spectacle would still be allowed to view the result. As the cars began to move forward again, they crawled even though the spaces between cars were increasing. The administration process was moving faster since the personnel were confident that no one else would attempt to escape.

Mohammad was shaking frantically as he presented his documentation. He thought that if there was a simple mistake then he could be due for a gruesome demise. The paperwork was acceptable, and the Nigerian gentlemen stepped out of the car. Mohammad wished them well on the rest of their journey before they walked out of the gates. There was a vehicle that was waiting for them on the other side of the fence. Mohammad's heart couldn't stop racing as he turned the car around and drove back into Raqqah. He realized then that he could never leave this place. He was barely paid by his employer whose justification was that he didn't need money because everything was provided for him. Up to that point he hadn't even thought about leaving, but now he felt differently.

Chapter 17

Self-Imposed Exile

OLIVIER ARRANGED with his Nigerian counterparts to not only meet him at the airport, but to ensure that the state press was present. He knew that the Congolese media would eventually air his travel itinerary. He wanted everything to appear normal. He read and frequently clicked the refresh button on the media outlets that he was viewing on the internet as well as constantly checking the local news. To his surprise no information had surfaced about the assassination attempt on his life. The only item the media had carried was that a vehicle near the building where important government officials were meeting, including the president, exploded. All the media said was that the police would be carrying out an investigation to uncover why such an event took place however the unofficial report was that a surrogate group of the terrorist organization Boko Haram orchestrated it as an attempt to intimidate the President.

Olivier couldn't believe that the journalists neglected to mention that he was in the car. He realized in that moment that should he have been killed Boko Haram would've been blamed and he would've become the martyr whose death could assist the President to not only eliminate his biggest rival but also provide an excuse for increased militarization of the state. The fact that it wasn't one of his personal vehicles and he fled the scene meant that it couldn't be traced back to him. Fortunately for Olivier, Nigeria was due to host an international conference within the next few days. Dignitaries were flying in to pledge their contributions towards the growing epidemic. This event would help to remove all suspicion with regards to his trip while he figured things out.

As luck should so have it, he arrived at the same time as the Zambian delegation. Olivier actually knew more about Zambia then any of Congo's other trade partners. He felt that Zambia had been faced with a tremendous number of challenges post-independence. By the time the country gained its independence there were less than a thousand graduates with school certificates. There was a serious lack of native education pre-independence with the colonial office opting to delegate this responsibility to the missionaries.

The first indigenous Zambian administration was faced with immediate migration of their educated, non-indigenous staff moving to Southern Rhodesia after independence, which was yet to have gained its independence at the time, and apartheid South Africa where they could continue to enjoy the perks of racial discrimination towards black Africans. The first administration was also crippled by the fact that their trade routes were Rhodesia and South Africa whose governments were hostile towards them and didn't want to support an indigenous regime.

Unfortunately, the first Zambian government considered themselves to be the sole custodians for the people's interests and Zambia became a one-party state. All other political parties were banned, and elections were between two individuals from the same party. Even this small right was eventually abolished, and individuals were appointed by recommendations from the general committee. With the increasing economic pressures and nationalization of not only resources, but also businesses eventually shortages ensured. The Zambian people became frustrated and after two failed political coups the people fought against the one-party state that was introduced by the first administration, thus leading the national commitment to democracy.

Once a multi-party democracy was re-introduced Zambians were celebrating simple things like gas being available at the gas pumps and that their shops now had a full range of goods and the shelves were stocked. On a less mundane level they celebrated that they could now choose between political parties. However, the second administration tested the peoples' resolve yet again as suggestions for the enactment of the introduction for a third term to the post of president was rejected. The rumor was that they had hoped to amend the constitution however the whispers of such a move caused the people to march in the streets towards the state house and the president immediately brushed aside any suggestion that he intended on standing for longer than what was stated in the constitution. They had had several presidents and several parties in power such that Africans around the continent had no option, but to admire them and leaders around the region would do well to learn from them. Yet in Congo, the rumors were circulating with regards to Mbuyi's fourth term, yet the people hadn't used the initiative to challenge him.

Olivier greeted members of the Zambian delegation and exchanged business cards. He was hoping to do some socializing with them when he was settled in. There were several female delegates and with Zambian women recently being voted as the biggest drinkers in the world he knew that he would probably have more fun with this group than any other because he loved a drink himself. Olivier eventually saw a sign with his name on it, he greeted the driver who took his luggage from him. Olivier realized that he needed to buy more clothes since he had only packed for two days. The Lagos airport was always crowded. In fact, everywhere in Lagos was crowded, that was why it was the perfect place for someone who felt that their life was in danger. It was easy for him to get lost in the crowd in this city.

Chapter 18

Putting the Pieces of the Puzzle Together

AS JAMAL LOOKED AROUND the office, Azmina was extremely helpful. She gave him the keys to every compartment and then left so that he could read through the information freely. He sat in Omar's chair with an open folder on the desk. The first couple of documents were title deeds for Omar's various condominiums but as he searched through the documents, he was getting further into the business contracts.

There was a picture of Omar and Azmina on the desk. Jamal lifted it up and stared at the man's face. He really couldn't recall meeting this man. His eyes eventually ventured off to the dead man's wife. She was the most beautiful woman that he had ever seen. Even though in the picture she was swathed, her shapely body and curves could be seen. He had to force himself to return his attention to the files otherwise he could have stayed there looking at her forever.

Jamal hadn't been like this when he was young. He was so focused on his books that he seldom caught himself staring at girls when he was in University. So many sacrifices had been made by his family to send him there that nothing could distract him from reaching his goals.

The heading on each file had a stamp on the top of the page that wrote "classified". The first document that he came across was a government tender that had been awarded to Omar's company for a huge arms deal with the military. It was for tanks, missiles and machine guns. There were images of each of the weapons and every time Jamal blinked, he could remember when he did a physical verification of each of the items on sale.

With his eyes closed he could see this image of himself in army uniform stroking a new tank before he climbed into it. He remembered himself driving the tank for a short while before stepping out of it to take a photograph. With the machine guns he tested them in the army's shooting range where the soldiers stood on opposite sides of him to watch. They cheered as Jamal hit the target right on the bull's-eye. He opened his eyes as he was beginning to develop a headache. If he could remember all of these small details then why couldn't he remember who tried to kill him, he quizzed himself.

Jamal blinked once more and remembered himself marching in a suit while a group of soldiers took time to salute him. He boarded a private jet and sat in it with three other gentlemen. He opened his eyes and continued with this exercise. The fact that his driver was out there watching and possibly reporting on him encouraged his pace to quicken yet again.

He turned the page and found a document written to Omar expressing that the tender had been awarded for a three-year period of arm's supplies. Jamal skimmed through the files because for some reason he felt that time was of the essence. The Syrian leadership were eagerly monitoring his condition and it was almost time for him to return to the workforce. He wouldn't have been surprised if he had been followed to this woman's home. He had been living with the very realistic belief that the attempt on his life was an inside job, not to mention how uneasy his associates felt when they came to visit him, and he couldn't recall who they were. He knew about the inconsistency in politics, friends turned to foes and vice versa quite rapidly. Not to mention that it was an extremely sensitive time with the civil war, no one could truly trust anyone. The fact that the Minister of Defense couldn't remember some of them was extremely worrying because he was meant to be protecting them. How could he protect people who he didn't remember?

At the bottom of the document, he saw his signature and his mind went back to another memory. This time round he remembered the document being brought to his office by his secretary. As soon as she left Jamal, he removed some cigars from his desk and smoked one as he read through the proposal. He remembered getting on the phone and calling Omar as they chatted on the telephone. Later that day he had met Omar in a nightclub where they shared drinks and cigars. He remembered belly dancers were dancing around their table and Omar slipped money into the girl's skimpy satin costumes as he applauded them.

Suddenly Omar's office door opened, and Jamal came back to reality. The flashbacks always left him with a stinging headache on the right side of his head. As much as he loved to remember, he hated the side effect. The fact that he was socializing with someone who was bidding for a government contract made him realize that he was not the most principled individual. His mind swirled with the fact that this wasn't a gray area but it was completely unethical.

Azmina was standing at the door. He looked up at her and she appeared to be somewhat concerned. She asked him if everything was okay. She also informed him that there were people from the government who just called her to ask what he was doing in her house. Azmina had told them that he had come to express his condolences. Jamal realized that he couldn't stay for that long in the house. He asked Azmina if she knew somewhere private where they could meet again later, she told him that he should dress like a civilian and take a taxi to the city center. She would meet him and take him to a secluded spot. He rose up and thanked her for the access, as he made his way to the front door. His driver was sleeping with his seat totally reclined. Jamal tapped gently on the window with his index finger. The driver, startled to see Jamal back to the car so quickly apologized profusely. As the vehicle reversed out of the driveway Jamal waved at Azmina standing in the doorway. She reciprocated with a wave and gentle nod of her head.

Chapter 19

Murder and Abduction

IT WAS A REGULAR MUNDANE MONDAY morning in the quiet town of Anka. Zaki was a government school which was situated on the outskirts of the town, surrounded by uninhabited land. The atmosphere was hot and dry and dusty. The children's ages ranged from twelve to eighteen years old and classes had already began that morning however, one by one, members of the teaching staff were being called to the principal's office. Whenever the headmaster would call his staff members he would do so shaking frantically. He would tell them to follow him to his office before hurrying off. Then after a few minutes he would go out and get another until all twelve of them were in his office.

Eventually the basic school became very noisy with each class filled with students that could sense that their teachers were being held up at some unplanned important staff meeting that was prolonged. The school prefects huddled up and decided to each takeover a class and control things until the teachers returned or at least gave them further instructions.

As soon as the prefects managed to re-install order the school bell rang and it was break time. The students didn't stand on ceremony and hurried out to the playground to enjoy their break. The prefects decided to investigate what was happening. They chose one of them to go and see the principal. The prefects' spokesperson was the strongest academic in year twelve and adored by all of the staff. If the teachers were busy, then they probably wouldn't shout at him for disturbing the meeting.

As the prefect approached the door to knock, he was spotted, and the door was opened for him. When the prefect walked in hesitantly, he was immediately confronted by the atrocity that was taking place. His eyes popped out when he saw all of the male schoolteachers and staff against the wall while the female teachers were being raped. He turned around to try and flee before two of the intruders grabbed him and slammed him against the wall before pointing a gun at his head.

"If you make a sound then you will die. Now wait against the wall with your teachers." He was grabbed around the neck by his shirt before being shoved in his back by a rifle. The prefect stood cowering against the wall. He could hear the trickling sound of his mathematics teacher urinating in his pants. In the background the desperate moans of the female teachers being raped frightened him so much. A pool of his own urine formed around his own feet.

The truth was that all of the men were equally terrified, they expected to suffer too. For now, the suspense of what would happen to them was nerve racking. Woman's suffering was restricted to sexual abuse if they were candid and did not try to fight back, but with men the type of abuse was unclear. It depended on if these militias wanted to keep them or not. If they did keep them, it could be with the purpose of turning them into soldiers or slaves who did their manual labor.

However, if they didn't think that they had a need for them then they could be let go so that they would convey what happened to the authorities. Boko Haram loved to make sure that they took credit for all of their terrorist attacks. The other side of what could happen was the very real possibility that if they didn't need them then they would simply kill the male teachers. Anyone who came after would be able to decipher what took place there if children went missing, female teachers were abducted, and male teacher's corpses were left rotting with bullets infused in their skulls.

It was another ten minutes before the militants were all done with the women and fortunately no other female walked into the principal's office. The female teachers responded to their abuse by weeping together on the floor. The middle-aged ones tried to comfort the younger ladies, but they were all in pain. The women huddled together and mourned loudly in solidarity. The militants didn't care for the noise that they were making. It was time for them to carry out what their supervisors had actually sent them to do.

The male teachers and the unsuspecting prefect were told to walk out of the room in a straight line. Before the door was opened, they were reminded that if anyone attempted to flee then he would be shot and tortured. After what they had witnessed happening to the women no one showed signs of disobeying these instructions. The men were shaking rapidly, they all looked terribly sick. The grade eight teacher vomited on himself; they were all uneasy. It was obvious that their minds couldn't take much more of it.

The women teachers remained in the room with two guards who had AK-47's hanging from their necks, they wouldn't be running away either. The rest of the militants marched out with the male staff towards the playground where the unsuspecting children were nosily playing their games. The children had enjoyed their day. They hadn't had any lessons and now they were experiencing a prolonged break time.

When the teachers came into view the students stopped running around, but continued to talk. When all of the gunmen came into view there was complete silence on the playground. One of the militants stepped onto the platform that the principal would usually use whenever he wanted to address the students. This militant speechmaker smiled sinisterly with a pistol in his hand, he was happy that the children already respected his authority. They would make good soldier's he thought to himself.

"Good afternoon children. My name is Abaeze. Today is the day when your eyes will finally be opened, and you will learn the truth. No more Western rubbish that is not even fit to teach dogs. For those of you who do not know, we are Boko Haram, which means Western education is forbidden. We have come to rescue you from what these people have been teaching you. Now say goodbye to these devils and prepare yourselves to make a decision because those who are not with us are against us! Those who run will be killed also!" He yelled with intensity. His voice echoed in the playground before it went completely silent again.

There was no panic from the students however some may not have known what was coming next.

Abaeze clicked his fingers authoritatively, thus prompting the militants to open fire on the teachers. They must have forgotten that the boy was only a prefect because he was shot down as well. With the AK-47's there was no chance of there being any survivors. When the gunshots erupted the previous tranquility had finally been broken and the playground blew up into chaos. The children broke into screams as they watched their teachers being gunned down.

The shouting only increased when they saw the men gasping on the floor with blood gushing out of them. This execution triggered a few of the students to run, but as promised the Boko Haram militants turned their weapons on all those who dared to attempt to escape. These shooters were prolific and none of the potential escapees survived. It didn't matter whether they ran in a straight line or tried to sway from side to side. All of the targets were hit.

The vast majority of the other students opted not to test their assailants and went to the ground to protect themselves from stray bullets. When it was evident that no one else would try to escape, some of the militants went to retrieve the bodies of the students who had previously tried to flee. They brought them to the front to showcase what would happen to anyone who attempted to disobey them. Those students who were brave enough to raise their heads from the ground broke into tears when they saw the fate of their teachers and colleagues.

The militants walked around the playground guiding the students into lines. Not by grade or age, but the students were arranged by sex and height. The militants taunted the students and told them that either they were with them or against them as they smacked them on their heads. They hit the boys who were in tears and told them to be strong, weeping was for women and children. They were told that they were now men, they were now Boko Haram.

The Boko Haram spokesman, Abaeze, pulled out a cell phone and called in for transportation. It was now time to leave the scene of the crime. He would have usually avoided using a traceable phone because of the obvious risk, but he just threw the phone in the bush after making the call. He had done well. They had assembled over forty new students. The girls would be their brides and the boys would be turned into soldiers. He hadn't lost any of his men and they had even been rewarded with some time with the female teachers. This was an extremely successful day and he expected to be congratulated by his superiors when he returned to where they were camped in the bush.

Abaeze had been recently promoted and was also a teacher. He had studied the textbooks that had come directly from the Islamic State stronghold in Raqqah, Syria. He was also completely fluent in Arabic which gave him an advantage over his other comrades who were now his subordinates.

After about ten minutes the open-back trucks arrived, and the students were loaded. The tall, stronger boys would be sent for direct militant training. The young boys would work on the land and with livestock, the young girls would go where the young boys were going. The girls would go to the camp to be distributed amongst those who were camped there. They would be married and start families with committed soldiers. Abaeze himself planned on taking another two to add to his current two wives. He was earning good money so could afford to feed them. The more wives that a man could take the more prestige that he deserved.

Abaeze had recently received a large payment from the reward money that his unit got after kidnapping a prominent Nigerian businessman. The businessman's family rendered the ransom within a day after they were sent a video of Abaeze torturing the man. Like their brother's in Raqqah, they were gaining or extracting support from several businessmen in Borno. Abaeze made sure that the dead teachers and students' bodies were also loaded. They would sell their organs on the black market, as they were reminded to do by Islamic State. One of the last things left for them to do was to infiltrate some oil refineries.

Chapter 20

Putting Affairs in Order

WHEN OLIVIER AWOKE, he ordered room service. He wasn't in the mood to go to the dining area for his breakfast and was eager to watch news and browse through his emails in his room before the conference commenced. Even though politics forced him to constantly interact with people it was isolation that he appreciated the most. He had trained himself to work with noise around him, but only truly relaxed when there were no eyes on him.

He did some pushups and sit ups on the floor before taking a shower. When he came out, he turned on the television while he changed into a grey suit. The breaking news was that Boko Haram had conducted yet another deadly attack. Before Olivier could listen to the story, he heard a hard knock on the door and quickly went to open it. A young lady had brought his room service and blushed when he smiled at her. Olivier engaged her is some polite chit chat as she set up his meal in the room. He asked her if she had seen the news about the Boko Haram attack. She filled him in about the murders, rapes and kidnapping of the school children. She was enjoying their discussion so much she appeared to be reluctant to leave.

Olivier had received two things with his breakfast. The first was a notice that the conference had been cancelled in Nigeria and was being relocated to Sierra Leone due to the current attack from Boko Haram. The notice went on to explain that there had also been a threat by Boko Haram that they would attack the conference center. This notice disappointed Olivier who had been looking forward to spending time in Lagos so that he could also attend to his personal business interests.

The second thing that came with his breakfast was the local newspaper; it showed the story on how Boko Haram militants had abducted school children. His heart bled as he imaged what the parents were going through. This type of narrative was full of anachronisms and he felt that the conciliatory attitude by the government towards these criminals was why they operated with impunity. This was only weeks after the United Nations building in Nigeria had been bombed by these same militants. The police explained that they already had several Boko Haram militants incarcerated, but the militants responded to arrests by kidnapping children and foreigners.

The girls were often sold as slaves, many of whom would soon become prostitutes. In fact, the younger they were the more they were valued. The girls who would not be sold would become wives for these terrorists and would be brainwashed into their teachings. The young boys would be used to conduct terror exercises around the country. The child soldiers who were killed were of no consequence to the terrorists because the Boko Haram leaders would simply raid another village and take more children. That was the end of the police officer's statement. Olivier put the newspaper down and increased the volume on the television as there was a gentleman in military uniform on the screen.

As he listened through the interview the situation sickened Olivier, he wondered why the Nigerian army general would say things like "Often Boko Haram militias are better armed and better motivated then we are". This was insane when he thought about the fact that Nigeria was Africa's leading economy. If they couldn't stop the insurgence, then what chance did Congo have if these extremists came knocking on her borders. He wondered how an army general could wear his insignia proudly on his chest yet utter such rhetoric.

His morning was ruined, but he thought that international news would help; it didn't. The news broadcaster began by talking about the detrimental effect of the Ebola virus on West Africa, and then they discussed the same Boko Haram raid before proceeding to talk about the refugees from the Syrian civil war and they finished the broadcast with the conflict between Ukraine and Russia. Olivier felt like humanity had little hope with a combination of severe external and internal problems that were rocking the globe all at once. He turned off his television and ate his meal in silence as he contemplated how he would spend the rest of his day.

After his breakfast he made his way out of the hotel. The hotel tried to organize transport for him, but after his previous encounter in Congo he preferred to catch a random taxi. He decided to meet with a Nigerian colleague who was a local businessman. They had done several deals over the years, most of which involved oil and Olivier decided that since he wouldn't be staying, he would meet this man much earlier than they had originally planned.

However, this working relationship was more personal than just two men who made deals with one another. Olivier had some of his money saved in a Nigerian bank in his wife's name and another account that was in his colleague, Aliko's name. Aliko also had money in South Africa in Olivier's name at the same amount as what was being held in Olivier's name; however, there were slight differences due to the varying interest rates.

The idea behind this move was that if either of them were forced to leave Africa and had their bank accounts frozen then the other one would send the money to the one who left, wherever they may decide to reside. They trusted each other and kept their friendship as low key as possible. It was agreed that if one of them feel into trouble then apart from the bank transfer they shouldn't expect anything from the other. It was a friendship of convenience that would only continue as long as there was prosperity.

Once at the gate Olivier paid the taxi driver who kept insisting on entering the yard. Olivier was against this because sometimes cab drivers would enter into a rich person's house and take a mental picture before passing on the information to thieves. This was a trend in his country and he often treated all African countries with the same glove even though he was sometimes proved incorrect.

Aliko was dressed in a traditional Nigerian outfit. His ensemble could only be compared to a dress and he wore a round hat. He was wearing sandals and walked to Olivier with open arms. Aliko was over expressive whenever he met Olivier and hugged him before rendering two kisses to each of Olivier's cheeks. As they walked into the house Aliko held Olivier's arm and guided him into the lounge where, they usually had their chats.

"Why is it that your government cannot end the madness that Boko Haram are causing?" Olivier asked as soon as they sat down in the den. His colleague lived on a farm outside of Lagos. The house was well guarded but couldn't be seen from the roadside. However, you could see the wealth as soon as you stepped into the house. Everything was extravagant and fragile. Olivier thought that it was no place for a child because nothing was straightforward, each item had a story behind it. The first time that Olivier visited the home he was told the background details of the ornaments. Most items were imported from Italy, Japan and Morocco.

Aliko's family was actually home. Olivier was greeted by his wife with deference. The last born was now a twenty-five-year-old son who just would not leave the house. Aliko constantly complained to Olivier about how he couldn't motivate the boy and was more than prepared to kick him out of the house, but his wife would never allow it. Aliko reminded Olivier once more how much he struggled at that age and this was what taught him how to become successful.

When Aliko's wife disappeared, he finally answered Olivier's question about Boko Haram.

"Well, the situation has become more complex the longer that it goes on for. If you notice something, Boko Haram are attacking and killing people in areas where the opposition have strongholds. I have been following these trends. Even Boko Haram know, if they kill people who support the opposition the army's response is much slower and less enthusiastic then if they attack the current government's strongholds. What I believe is the politicians want the people to realize that either they support the current regime, or they will not be safe from Boko Haram. There have also been rumors that Boko Haram members have infiltrated the army as well as the political system. Then there is the issue of the businesspeople who sympathize with them and provide funding to these lunatics. However, let's not forget history, bullies who are appeased become greedy and continue to take more and more until that greed becomes their undoing." At the end of this brief explanation Aliko's son stepped into the den with headphones and walked straight past them in his usual profane persona.

His father yelled and told him to greet their guest. Aliko and the son had a stare down that made it obvious that there was tension in that household. The young man gave Olivier a brief greeting before returning towards his original destination being the fridge. This upset his father once more who yelled and told him to offer their guest a drink. The son grudgingly reciprocated and Olivier could also feel his friend's anger. This boy had all of the opportunities in the world.

With a wealthy father he could have gone to the best Universities and had enough contacts to get a good job when he returned to Nigeria. Instead, he was in the wilderness. Olivier told him that he wanted a soft drink before telling the boy to go to the kitchen and prepare him a sandwich. He wasn't even hungry but wanted to inconvenience this lazy boy.

Once the disgruntled boy went to the kitchen Olivier nodded to agree with his friend with regards to Boko Haram. They went on to speak about a possible oil deal to Katanga, but his friend was reluctant to agree to the terms due to the political turmoil. The fact was that he only came to Olivier because he was the governor. They had already agreed early on that if Olivier was to lose this position, then they would end the relationship.

Olivier understood the dynamics of the affiliation and held no hard feelings. He knew all of those who came to him shortly after his inauguration as Governor. Aliko and Olivier went on to lighter topics. They joked that the reason that Africa is so far behind from the rest of the world is that there is constant manipulation of constitutions and political interference in business. Investors cannot make ten-year plans in Africa because that was too long for the continent. Everyone was taking business one year at a time.

When the son returned with the sandwiches, they kept the conversation going until it was time for Olivier to leave. They shook hands and promised to keep in touch with regards to the Ebola virus and the situation in Sierra Leone.

Olivier read through the conference itinerary. At 3pm there was a scheduled open discussion when any of the delegates could contribute. Olivier decided he would speak and argue why fighting the epidemic with the utmost seriousness was so important before it manifested into a worldwide pandemic.

Chapter 21

Another Step Towards Normalcy

GENERAL JAMAL FINALLY RETURNED to his office. He reported for work and received a warm welcome from everyone. At this point he could remember most of the people there. His receptionist had just graduated from University and was a single mother. She had once asked him for a salary advance which he declined with his door open so that all his other employees could hear his reasons why. The staff was mixed. He had brought in some guys from the army who were degree holders. He felt that until a person had the army discipline that he had benefited from then they couldn't make decisions with regards to the defense of the country. His department needed patriots and even though he didn't say it he felt it needed soldiers, who had the required academic background. The individuals with these two backgrounds were expected to make a lot of progress in his department. He only socialized with the former soldiers and he would put money in their pockets after each drinking session.

There were also the mathematicians, he knew why he needed them but found them annoying. They were always the ones to bring statistics to his desk that often strongly suggested that he was doing a terrible job at containing the rebels. He knew all their names, backgrounds and his past interactions with each of them.

His memory was coming back more rapidly. At the present he could just not familiarize with his wife and he didn't know what was so secretive about the arms deal that he made with Omar.

He searched through his office for any clue, but his secretary kept interrupting to remind him that there was a cabinet meeting and he was running late. There was nothing in writing in his office with regards to the secret deal with Omar thus leading him to believe that everything had been agreed through word of mouth. He looked around his office and there were pictures of his wife and kids. How could he remember these children, but not the person who had given birth to them? He tried so hard to remember and had resorted to pretending that he did. They still hadn't been intimate with one another and his excuse had been that he had back pains. The truth was that he had never been the type to be intimate with someone that he didn't have feelings for. He wondered if he had stayed this way throughout his adulthood.

He was frustrated but couldn't do anything to aid his flashbacks. They came when he least expected them so all he could do was wait patiently.

He had no idea what would be discussed at the cabinet meeting, but when his secretary informed him that the driver was waiting for him in the carpark, he knew that procrastinating was not an option, especially for the Minister of Defense during a civil war. He lifted his briefcase that only possessed a pen, notepad and a few magazines.

He couldn't remember what one should take to meetings of this nature and when he spoke to the party's permanent secretary, he was told that his presence was more than enough. Before he left, he noticed a large iron safe between two cabinets. He placed his hand on it. Like magic his fingers went to the number three, then zero, then the number six and finally the number two. Without consciously thinking about it he remembered that thirty was the day that his wife was born and sixty-two was the year. With a twist of the handle the heavy safe door glided open.

Inside the safe there was money, gold bars, a firearm, a fully loaded magazine and two passports. He was intrigued by the passports because he had seen their passports at their home. He opened them and saw that they were indeed passports for each of them but with false identities. These passports suggested that they were citizens of Zambia.

He placed them back in the safe and locked it before proceeding out of his office. Most of his members of staff were huddled together in their cubicles and immediately resorted to silence when he walked past their desks towards the exit. None of them bothered to look up to him and he felt like a ghost. As he ventured down the stairs, he started to recall some recent history in oil rich countries. In the millennium he had heard a rumor that the United States had enough oil reserves to provide for their entire country, this had worried leaders in the Middle East because oil was their greatest asset and at the time the United States of America was the biggest consumer of this commodity.

With America so vested in their oil it was no surprise that they were prepared to send in ground troops to remove Arab dictators, especially those whose policies prevented their large corporations from taking control of the oil industry in their respective nations. Once trouble started and the people protested, NATO soldiers would enter the country to overthrow the dictator regime whether the dictator was dead or alive. With dictators out of the way large American oil corporations would move in. Troops would remain on the pretense of protecting the transition to democracy. Everyone knew that they were protecting their selfish financial interests in the region. This was Jamal's belief and it seemed justified that countries with dictators who didn't have oil reserves only received sanctions with no direct aggression.

Now the rumors from the millennium seemed to have come true. The Americans had developed a new technology called fracking which was being used to tap into their reserves so much so that the country seemed self-efficient. Ground troops began to return to their home and their interest in the Middle East was diminishing. This meant that it was up to the Syrian people to solve their own problem and those expecting American soldiers to swoop in and save the day were beginning to realize that this was wishful thinking. They were willing to conduct airstrikes on ISIS strongholds and provide technical support, some arms deals could be conducted on credit terms, but Jamal's hope was that Islamic State would continue to provoke them so that they would intervene. He knew that his country was crumbling into ruins, their nation was burning and there was a very real possibility that there would be nothing more than ashes left to govern at the end of this fighting.

Jamal had also remembered all that he had read up on renewable energy, the world was changing. Solar and other alternative energy sources were receiving major funding from investors in research and development and this was enabling them to make great strides year by year.

Once downstairs the driver opened the door to the limousine for him. He greeted him before entering it. He thought that it was a waste of resources for each minister to travel in a limousine when they could simply use one to pick each other up. He was grateful that the air-conditioning was on full blast because stepping outside was like walking into an oven.

After a few minutes into the drive his phone rang and the caller I.D alerted him to the fact that it was Azmina, he had been expecting her call all day.

"I think I have found something very important General Jamal," she explained without any introduction.

"Where are you, let us meet right away." He responded as he made the decision to absent the cabinet meeting. He knew that this was bad but was still receiving sympathy at a level where he could do no wrong. He also was more interested in uncovering the truth more than any other exercise. She gave him the address of the hotel where she was, and it sounded very familiar. He told her that he was only a few minutes away.

"Room number 207, see you soon." She said before hanging up the phone.

At that Jamal opened the car door as his driver slammed on the brakes. Without saying a word, he bolted out of the car and crossed the street. For some reason he knew exactly how to get to the hotel. It wasn't far away at all. He knew that the driver would simply return to the office with his belongings so wasn't bothered.

He walked straight into the hotel lobby. The receptionist recognized him immediately. With a smile she said, "Sir, are you taking your usual room?"

He said no and proceeded quickly up the wide stairs to the second floor. He thought it strange that he would have a usual room in a hotel that was so near to his house. Turning down the long-carpeted hallway he walked straight to 207 where he found the door was open. Without knocking he entered the room. Azmina walked up to him and presented him with a thick file folder of papers. Dropping it into his hands she stroked his shoulder and said she was going to take a shower.

Jamal read through rapidly. Omar kept a diary that Azmina had retrieved from his security deposit box at the bank. He had been paying government officials for many years and kept an exact record of dates and amounts. Jamal's name appeared on that list time and time again. He was always paid, then the next diary entry would be him being awarded a large tender to provide military weapons. The final entry was the night before his assassination attempt. Omar had already met with Jamal to discuss him providing chemical weapons. They had decided to wipe out the entire city of Raqqah because such a large number of ISIS jihadists were camped there. Omar had locked in a date for this attack being the 28th. Jamal was stunned. This genocide was going to take place within two days. So many innocent families would be wiped out by the chemical weapons and he authorized this. He knew that information about this must have been leaked which led to the attempted assassination.

He needed to stop it. The shower had stopped a few minutes ago but he was so engulfed in the diary to have noticed. The door opened and the woman was naked. She walked up to him slowly before pushing him onto the bed. She climbed on top of him and leaned forward to kiss him. Without hesitation he obliged.

While his eyes were closed his mind raced through all the women he had brought to that hotel over the years. His usual room was 309. Jamal's memories jumped to a fight that he had with his wife. She left the house and said that she couldn't take it anymore. He had been miserable without her but by the end of the week he went for the secret meeting. Hussein Raham was the person who shot him. The man was in the military and proclaimed his allegiance to ISIS before pulling the trigger. Hussein was probably planning to kill Jamal. Jamal opened his eyes and pushed Azmina off him.

"I'm sorry, but I love my wife." He said regrettably, his marriage could have ended if not for Shahad coming to care for him at the hospital. The assassination attempt saved his marriage and could now save civilian lives in Raqqah.

"You mean to tell me, General Jamal, that you the biggest womanizer in Syria is going to turn me down?" She laughed; Azmina thought that he was joking with her. All the signs suggested that this was what he wanted; at least that's what she believed.

"I guess so. I am sorry. You have been a great help. I remember everything now. It all came flooding back to me while I read over the file you just gave me. I'm sorry but it's time to right some wrongs and deliver retribution," With a great sense of commitment Jamal stood at the side of the bed, straightened his hair and headed to the door. He did not even hear Azmina pleading for him to stay.

Chapter 22

A Miracle or Disaster

WHEN HE FINISHED HIS SUPPER in the hotel's restaurant Olivier returned to his room. Shortly after getting there, he realized how lonely he was, unlike in Nigeria he knew no one in Sierra Leone. The conference was not for another two days to allow all of the delegates to change their travel arrangements. The isolation was a gift in itself; he hadn't given any time to think about his ordeal. He looked out of the hotel window and couldn't shake the sensation that the President knew exactly what he was doing and even which room he was sleeping in. He trusted no one, emails from colleagues checking in on him heightened his suspicions.

He couldn't call his wife for several reasons. The first and underlining reason was because Vivienne simply could not keep anything to herself. Anything mentioned to her might as well have been published on the front page of the newspaper. The second reason was that he had a growing suspicion that the phones had been bugged. Fortunately for him, being an orphan, he had no other loved ones in Congo and his children were far away from the mess.

The Nigerian government had issued an apology to all of them for the inconvenience caused by the cancellation. The government spokesperson announced that a state of emergency was introduced until the terrorists were contained.

Olivier thought it was good that the venue was forced to change, and the pacification of Boko Haram was finally being taken with seriousness. The other reason for his joy was that Nigeria hadn't been directly affected by the Ebola crisis, therefore a conference in that country would've been prosaic. He had only heard of the country having a few isolated cases in the rural areas. People seldom panicked unless it was spreading in highly populated places.

Sierra Leone on the other hand had been suffering not only from the actual virus, but the economic implications that had followed. Their neighbors had closed their borders in fear of the virus spreading. This was now preventing trade and business-people from importing the goods that they needed to supply to the local economy. Trucks couldn't cross borders into Sierra Leone which had led to shortages in essential items. Most importantly the President was known for being amenable, combined with an inscrutable demeanor, which made him a fascinating man.

Even access to fuel had been prevented; gas stations were filled with angry motorists who were parking for hours on end each day waiting. Some would sleep in their cars so that they could refuel in the early hours of the morning before the stock would finish. People also had, and took, the black-market option that was causing vehicle issues as the fuel was being mixed with water by those who were looking to exploit the crisis.

Foreign direct investment had also been halted; the general understanding was that international investors wanted to see how the situation would pan out in the end. The global companies were recalling their expatriates for fear that they would catch the virus, especially those who were operating in rural areas. These companies were suddenly short staffed and unable to make executive decisions as many of the decision makers were evacuated.

Local farm workers were abandoning their plantations in fear of catching Ebola, either on the farm or the marketplace. The Sierra Leone leadership had to divert funds from other organizations towards the health sector, which was being felt by the economy, stalling most major public works. Olivier thought that with all this difficulty around them then it was more likely that greater ideas would be developed at this particular conference, more so than in Nigeria because now the delegates could feel the struggle.

Olivier strongly believed that when the delegates' movements were restricted because of lack of fuel or when they couldn't buy essentials from the supermarkets or even when they were screened for Ebola both at the Sierra Leone international airports and their home nations when they eventually returned, it would increase their understanding of the crisis and abhorrence towards the virus. The delegates would now live in fear of catching the virus, like the citizens of this land. The fear and struggle would drive innovation.

When Olivier had initially arrived, two hours before, he was shown to his room. The doorman had whispered that he should tell him if he wanted some company for the night and this played on Olivier's mind while he idly sat. Olivier had done everything to stop himself from thinking about the doorman's offer, but like the popular saying went an idle mind is the devil's workshop. At the time he purported himself to be uninterested but as the minutes dragged along sluggishly this played on his mind.

The first thing that he tried to do was some exercise on the floor but stopped after one set of ten pushups. He turned on the television and found himself on the adult movie section. He rented a movie and after ten minutes, he gave in to his lusts. He had called his wife when he had just reached the hotel and she bombarded him with the usual rubbish. She needed him to buy a host of electronics and perfumes for the family, he hadn't told her about the assassination attempt. His inner circle had bombarded his emails and had left numerous missed calls on his phone, none of which he intended to respond to. He didn't want to think about it thus leaving his mind to be filled with ideas of satisfying his lust.

Whilst on the phone his wife ranted on and on that she should have been informed that he intended to travel, the main reasons seemed to be because she would have written him a shopping list and needed things for home. He constantly reminded her that the countries that he was visiting were going through economic crises, and then she had the nerve to tell him to buy her a ticket to South Africa or London so that she could do the shopping herself. She always knew what to say to annoy him and he dreaded having to pick up the phone to call her.

As usual he contemplated divorcing her before he opted for the easier option; some alternative female companionship. If she only knew that after each one of her fights over money, he would indulge in adultery then maybe she would stop. He only got her the same things because he was somewhat guilty, if not, then the money would have stayed in his wallet.

Olivier re-dressed in casual wear before leaving the room. He ventured off to the fitness room with no real objective, but to just look around. He watched the television for a few minutes until another guest walked in and smiled at him politely. After a few minutes that same guest looked back at Olivier as if he was trying to figure out why he was standing there. Olivier pretended to be there to work out, but without the will to exercise the idea lacked merit and became awkward quite quickly.

In that moment he decided to stop procrastinating and make his way to the hotel's lobby to organize what he had been battling with for the last hour. He walked past the reception and found the door man watching the television in the coffee area. It was clear that the staff were chilling out because they weren't expecting anyone else for the day. The gentleman immediately rose and attended to Olivier when he said that he had come for him. Olivier did find it interesting that this man was trying, unsuccessfully, to pull off a British accent. He often came across people who applied different accents depending on who they were talking to.

He asked the doorman to organize him some female company. He tipped the man and reminded him what the room number was as if there was more than one penthouse suit. Before returning to his room, he reminded the doorman that he wanted a high-rise girl and not a mediocre one off the street. This seemed to be understood; the doorman informed him that there was an executive range for men of his status. Olivier passed by the vending machine to buy an energy drink before returning to his room where he waited patiently. He sat on the sofa and scrolled through the channels, spending only a few minutes on each.

For some reason he felt nervous, yet he had done this so many times. He concluded that he was still rattled from his narrow escape back home. He couldn't shake the feeling that something significant would result from this encounter with the girl. Olivier helped himself to a drink to help pass the time and twenty minutes later there was a knock on his door. He opened it cautiously since there was still a lingering feeling that someone was trying to kill him.

Once the door was open the girl came into full view and he was immediately pleased with what was before him. The doorman did not disappoint him at all. The girl was stunning. She was tall with caramel colored skin and brunette hair which was probably a weave. She was wearing a coat and high heels. He smiled and stepped aside to allow her to walk in. When the door was closed and locked, she dropped her coat and revealed her body. She had big breasts and a big bum, yet her waist was thin. She wore leopard print lingerie and asked him if he liked what he saw before smiling with her red lipstick.

Olivier approached her and without wasting anytime they were headed for the bedroom.

Less than an hour passed before they were finished, but it only took a moment for the satisfaction to leave him and the regret to kick in, as it always did. Olivier decided to be a good host and asked what she wanted to drink from the mini bar.

They both shared a glass of wine in the bed while he turned on the television and lowered the volume until its last bar. The woman didn't seem to be in any particular hurry to leave and he didn't mind the company. He didn't specify to the doorman how long he wanted her there for so decided to go with the flow.

Olivier had put most of his money and valuables in the safe anyway, so wasn't even worried about falling asleep. He also wasn't tired because of the energy drink so thought that he would probably be awake for another couple of hours. The girl, whose name was Kandy, went on to ask him what he was in town for, she didn't have a great variety of vocabulary which led him to believe that she had limited education, no surprise there.

Olivier explained that he had travelled to attend the International Ebola conference. As soon as those words came out of his mouth, he immediately regretted them. What if this woman wasn't really a hooker and went to the conference looking for him? He realized that it was too late to take his statement back so quickly explained that fighting Ebola meant a lot to him because he had lost his mother to Ebola. He thought that this aspect was good enough reason for him to attend because he didn't want Kandy to know that he was a politician.

Even though he didn't really remember his mother, he had become so accustomed to adding her death to his explanation for being there that it came naturally. It stopped people from asking him more questions with regards to why he was there instead of the foreign affairs minister. Kandy had become chattier with the wine and went on to tell him her own story with regards to Ebola.

Kandy explained, "I have a girlfriend a bit older than me that is also in the same hospitality work as me. She is also sexy even if she is about the same age as you. She told me that she also lost her mother during the first Ebola outbreak in Congo. At least she thinks she lost her mother. I forget all of her story, but she said she had been waiting outside the hospital with her younger brother all day and they fell asleep and when she woke up, she had been dragged away by some men. She told me how much she kicked and screamed, but there was nothing she could do. She was kidnapped and forced to sleep with men through all the countries that these men travelled to until they got to their home in Sierra Leone. When she was eighteen one of them died and during the funeral confusion she managed to run away. After years of struggling, she finally made her way to the capital. It is such a long sad story. For me I like my job taking care of men and the money is good but for her she is not educated so she continued with this work throughout her life. She has such a nice name that her mother gave her, she is called Sunshine. All the men like that name too."

Olivier quickly sat up in bed. He instantly remembered his sister's name for the first time since his childhood. Even after all those years it rang as clear as a bell. He dropped his glass to the floor as the memory shuttered to the surface. Startled by his reaction Kandy asked if she had said something wrong. She got out of the bed and tried to clean the spilled wine with tissues as Olivier sat their mesmerized by his past. His mind and heart raced as if he had seen a ghost. His mind still swimming he questioned the odds of Kandy's friend Sunshine actually being his long-lost sister. With a jaw dropped pale complexion he mustered the energy to respond to Kandy.

"I need you to take me to this woman you call Sunshine. There will be more money for you if you do. We need to go there right now. Let me jump in the shower for two minutes then we can go. I want to go right away. Is that okay?" Olivier asked in almost a whisper while Kandy finished cleaning the floor. Kandy abruptly stopped cleaning while she thought with worry about his request. She simply smiled and told Olivier that it wouldn't be a problem for her to take him. She continued jabbering whilst on the floor, but Olivier wasn't paying any attention. Her voice had just become sound in the background while his mind continued to swirl about the possibility of seeing Sunshine.

He stepped out of the bed and thanked Kandy for cleaning up the mess before he headed to the shower. He stood in the shower and turned on the cold tap hoping that the cold would shock him back to reality. He didn't want to stay in for very long. His sister Sunshine was back in his thoughts. He was not going to lose another second.

Initially when he entered government, he tried to find his sister with the use of state resources, he knew that this was wrong, but couldn't help himself. During the course of his search, he met one hundred and sixteen girls who were not her. Over the course of his search, he wondered if he had seen her, but just didn't recognize her, it wasn't like he had a picture to go by. He was relying on the memory of a young boy but didn't tell the girls why he asked to see them.

He simply got their life history and eighty percent of them still lived with their biological parent which was the first threshold. Only about thirty of them were orphans, but out of the thirty, twenty were younger than him and those who were older did not come from his village nor were they two years older than him like his sister was. He eventually gave up and sold himself a dream that she lived in Europe somewhere with a new family. He never once allowed himself to contemplate the very real possibility that she was abducted. Knowing this made him feel like he didn't do enough to save her. He could have hired private detectives around Africa and should have conducted a massive manhunt; he certainly had the capacity to do something like that.

He showered for almost exactly two minutes and when Olivier returned to the bedroom he was greeted by the silence of the empty room. He walked over to his trousers that were draped across the chair. He leaned down and patted the pockets and discovered that his wallet was gone. What was he thinking leaving a prostitute alone with his stuff let alone something as valuable as his wallet? His mind began to swirl again. He didn't even care about the money. All he could think was that he may have just lost the only opportunity he had to see his sister again. He sat on his bed completely deflated. He could barely breathe. He held onto his chest tightly before he collapsed on his bed in agony.

Chapter 23

The Planned Atrocity

JAMAL LEFT THE HOTEL and booked a taxi, he had to inform cabinet that the wheels were in motion for mass genocide. The cab driver was stopped by the state house security. Jamal reached forward and gave him the fare with a generous tip before he opened the door and walked out. The guards recognized Jamal and apologized profusely for the inconvenience as they undertook their security checks. He was vetted from head to toe for several minutes before he was allowed to enter. He was escorted by one of the guards who told him that he had missed the meeting and that the president along with most of the ministers had already left, however the secretary general was still there. Jamal walked in and knew where all the offices were. His instinct guided him towards a door where he found the secretary general.

"General Jamal, we missed you at the meeting. Everyone was extremely disappointed, how are you feeling?" The secretary general asked with a mixed expression, first he looked disappointed then switched his reaction to one of concern. Jamal knew that people were reaching the turning point where they would begin to lose sympathy for him and instead would expect him to be the person he was before the incident. However, Jamal felt that even if he had a complete recollection of every experience that he had had, he would never be the same again.

"I apologize; I was trying to conduct personal investigations so that I would know why there was an assassination attempt on my life, who betrayed me and who actually pulled the trigger. Now that I know all three, I feel that I can now return to my duties. But first, you must know that the meeting was being conducted with the purpose of purchasing chemical weapons. These were intended to be deployed on ISIS strongholds, but would cause devastating effects with large numbers of civilian casualties. Such collateral damage cannot be allowed to happen." Jamal expressed passionately as he pulled a chair for himself, even though he was never offered one.

"I think that you are aware that you were given one mandate. To use all means possible to evade use of the various terrorist groups so that this country can start to rebuild. With that in mind, we expect you to do whatever is deemed necessary for the greater good." The secretary general replied to him still with a smile. He was strongly suggesting that Jamal would leave this alone.

"I simply cannot authorize mass genocide on innocent people." Jamal countered him as he placed his big arms on the desk to intimidate his counterpart, this move usually worked for him. His exterior and the guns that were backing him would make him an extremely difficult man to negotiate with.

"Are you really calling them innocent people? Those people are living in ISIS strongholds because they support the terrorists, if not then why wouldn't they simply leave. Soldiers cannot prevent all of them from moving away, let them come here to Damascus then we can protect them! Jamal this thing is happening, you already approved it." The secretary general went on to explain to him that everything had already been agreed on. He was simply informing him as a courtesy since defense matters lay in his portfolio.

General Jamal spoke with a firm tone, "I understand that the wheels are already in motion and there is little that I can do but allow me this one courtesy. I wish to send in troops to conduct a rescue mission?" His tone was resolute, "Any and all of those who are living there against their will can flee then you can do as you wish." Jamal changed his approach and sat back submissively. Sometimes you needed to bully people whereas at other times one must try to appease the person who was in a stronger position than he. Jamal needed to think of a way to buy time as he figured out what he was really going to do.

"The first target is Raqqah, you have one week to come up and execute whatever rescue mission that you think can save them but knowledge of the chemical attacks that will follow must remain a state secret, revealing knowledge of them to any individuals of the public with be received as treason. If you even hint to these people that they must leave because something bad may happen soon then you will become an enemy to the state." The secretary general warned him. There was clearly no trust between these two men. Jamal was thinking of doing something to help the people in Ar-Raqqah and the secretary general read his mind.

He thought about how simple life was as a boy. The biggest kid bullied the smaller ones, but now he was sitting across from a short, bald, man who wore thick eyeglasses and fit the description of a nerd perfectly. However, tables turn and the boys who were nerds become bosses and the bullies who neglected books to chase girls and terrorize others must work for these same nerds when they are older.

Jamal accepted this and wondered why the secretary general felt that he could give him orders. He needed to play it cool though, as if he was against the use of chemical warfare, but not so much so that he was willing to disobey his comrades. His memory was back and even his knowledge of how to play politics, however one thing had changed in the interim. His moral compass had changed. The next thing that he needed to rectify was his relationship with his wife who deserved some tender loving for sticking by him. After all, if things took a turn for the worse then their lives would change tremendously.

Chapter 24

Chasing Hope

OLIVIER WAS DUE TO SPEAK on the second day of the conference in Sierra Leone. He had signed up to present a statistical review of the socio-economic and macroeconomic issues. He had prepared several PowerPoint presentations to show the correlation between the outbreak and areas such as agricultural productivity, foreign direct investment, government spending outside of public health and youth crime. The criminal activities were meant to indicate to the delegation that several of the orphans who lost their parents were stigmatized by their communities and resorted to crime as a means of survival. Yet through his testimony these orphans were a linchpin to Sierra Leone's future.

Olivier attended the first day of the conference with his laptop and notepad, but his mind was elsewhere. He was so concerned that he wouldn't rescue his sister that he started daydreaming through most of the opening address. This was egregious for him because his brain had always been sharp, nothing ever distracted him. He could go from a heated disagreement with his wife to a board meeting without another thought of the fight until he saw her at the end of the day.

The opening speaker would have given Olivier an opportunity to jot down key phrases and statements which he could refer to when he stood up to present the next day. He knew that commenting on his colleague's addresses was always appreciated and made him popular amongst all the delegates. The story of his dead mother could only take him so far; he needed to couple it with some strong points. Half of the people there had lost their parents, he wasn't in high school.

The other aspect was that he was dealing with a group of intellectuals who would probably ask him tough questions because he was a government official. Smart people in the international community seldom let an opportunity pass to quiz African public officials on issues such as misappropriation of funds; delayed responses to economic problems and the accusation of the day would probably be that "they weren't doing enough." Olivier didn't mind engaging in debate with intellectuals because he considered himself to be one, not to mention the fact that he could hold his own. Other party members often misinterpreted criticism as disrespect and reacted harshly towards their critics. He had seen several journalists being deported and local ones losing their jobs, or worse, being sentenced to jail. All these harsh measures to simply thwart freedom of speech disgusted him, but there was little that he could say to convince his colleagues otherwise.

What he did take from the two opening speakers was a need to collect money from the international community. In typical African fashion they had started the discussion by putting their hands together and begging for crumbs from the tables of their international counterparts. The developed world must have considered Africa to be a hopeless case. Our leaders' contributions to these conferences ostensibly portrayed us as such.

We blamed colonialism for our stagnation then after we received our emancipation then we went on to blame our inadequacies on the effects of colonialism and the fact that the skilled foreign settlers returned to their motherlands after independence. We wanted money from the international community but didn't want their citizens to prosper in our countries nor did we want them to control our policy or interfere with human rights abuses. Then after the international community left us to our own vices, we reverted to sitting with them not to explore or discuss innovative ideas but simply to beg for support. Very seldom did African leaders come to seek guidance or contribute.

Olivier realized that he was not equipped or in the right frame of mind to make a speech so opted to remain silent during it all. He usually liked to make his presence known by asking compelling questions to the speaker, but for the first time in a long time his mind was completely blank. The cameramen did zoom in on him several times and that was enough to validate his purpose for leaving the country. Mission accomplished. His final mission was to locate his sister before he returned home. There was no reason why he shouldn't return to Congo. His supporters would see him at the conference, and everything would appear like business as usual or so he hoped.

At the end of the first stage of the morning gathering he was spotted by members of the Zambian delegation who marched up to him for a chat. He really needed the interlude, because he had struggled to stay awake during most of it. When he woke up that morning it was as if he hadn't slept, his asthma had returned and caused his collapse the night before. The twenty-minute breakfast was exactly what he needed, but he didn't think that he would return to his seat afterwards. He had to save his sister earlier then he planned lest his time in the conference would have been in vain.

Olivier was happy to finally be fully engaged in the conference. Setting his sister, Sunshine, aside for the moment he leaned forward with a question, "From your country's history what do you think is the best way forward for African states? Do we nationalize our resource industries? That way the mineral wealth will be directly felt, or do we simply allow as much foreign investment as possible so that we focus on politics instead of biting off more than we can chew?" Olivier asked sincerely. From his studies of African history, he knew that over the years the Zambian economy had been governed with both methods for long periods of time. He felt that in their region he had a lot to learn from the Zambians.

He found Patrick Mweene, the great Zambian diplomat orator, was always surrounded by people and displayed absolute delight at the prospect of being able to show off his intelligence to the audience by answering the questions of such a prominent political figure. He placed his hand on Olivier's shoulder to prevent him from moving as he spoke to him loudly so as to keep an audience engaged.

"Olivier, in my opinion we need a mixed policy. I think that every African government should own one mine so that, as you've mentioned, the citizens can benefit directly from them. However, from our post-colonial experience nationalization quickly becomes a political tool and you will find that the government of the day will be filling up top positions with their supporters rather than the most capable individuals. The other negative effect of nationalization is that profits are directed to political interests, such as campaigns and can fund projects that will increase political mileage instead of economic growth. Then there are the problems with nepotism, cronyism, and tribalism. With nepotism if a person places their relatives in top positions in parastatals, then they will find it difficult to motivate them in the manner that others would do with their employees. The individual won't have that fear of losing their job that serves to motivate staff in the workforce, nor will the other employees be able to tell them off when they make mistakes or are doing things inefficiently.

With cronyism, if a person places their long-term friends at the helm of power and subsequently uncover that those persons are embezzling then they will feel inclined to protect the individuals, especially if their friends are sharing the loot with them. Finally, with tribalism it is discriminatory and allows people's capabilities to be judged based on their place of birth, this in itself explains all of the problems that will result. Now with all of these unavoidable problems that come with nationalization, in an industry like mining where one needs to be prepared to spend large amounts of money on exploration as well as keeping a high level of reserves to combat price fluctuations, often it needs private investment to maximize productivity.

What I recommend for Congo is that you just install fair tax and royalty terms. Put in place measures to monitor and punish tax evasion and corruption. This corruption is mainly between the tax man and the mining companies. Also be mindful of the foreign owned mines that will allocate large sums of money on their statements of comprehensive income to management fees. This tool can sometimes be used to ensure that they reduce their tax liabilities. If you put in strong transfer pricing policies and push out corruption, then foreign investment is fine. These people aren't going to leave Congo where they make so much income. Threats that they will leave if taxation policies are changed are empty. There's too much wealth for them to walk away from our continent. While you do all this, run the state mine without tribalism, cronyism and nepotism." Patrick Mweene advised him passionately. Patrick and Olivier were actually meeting for the second time. Their original encounter was at the airport, but Olivier already found him to be an articulate and intelligent individual.

"That is very true my friend." Olivier responded as he placed his hand on Patrick's shoulder. He didn't want to enter a long discussion so opted to just agree even though he could have continued the chat. His eyes were firmly on the exit, but before he said goodbye Patrick pulled him close and whispered in his ear.

"I tell you these things and hope that you will continue to consult people from within and outside of Africa when you are President." Patrick replied before locking eyes with Olivier. They shook hands before Olivier expressed his apologies to the rest, as if the Zambians were the conference organizers, as he made his way out.

Patrick's comments surprised Olivier, even though he believed that he could do it this gentleman was so confident in him. The fellow said "when" he became president instead of "if" almost as if it was Olivier's destiny. This comment was very peculiar in politics, people often stood back and watched quietly. African counterparts often only came to show their allegiance once they achieved victory. It was usually only the West who liked to speculate aloud.

While Olivier checked out of the event, which was the requirement, he thought about his actions in the morning when he woke up to an empty room. He immediately ran downstairs to the reception. When he was sure that she wasn't there, he asked the doorman where he could find her. Olivier's demeanor made the doorman very nervous; he could see how the gentleman's hands were shaking. The doorman insisted that he should just be telling him when he wants to see her, but Olivier instructed him to bring the girl's address immediately.

He knew that telling the man that Kandy robbed him would only cause panic, so he bordered on the truth. He explained that the lady knew one of his relatives who was her neighbor, so he wanted to visit his relative and not the girl. The doorman gave him her address which wasn't far from where the conference was being held. So, when he left the conference hall Olivier caught a taxi and went in search of his long-lost sibling. The driver explained that the charge would be high because he had spent one whole night waiting for the fuel. Olivier didn't care.

During the car ride his heart was racing. He hoped that she was someone who could be reasoned with. He also hoped that she would believe him. He would be going to a woman to try and convince her that she should abandon her life and follow him to Congo. She could slam the door in his face, or she could pack her bags and follow him. Either way there was only one way to find out.

Chapter 25

The Truth of the Law in Raqqah

MOHAMMAD HAD BEGUN to enjoy his stable life in Raqqah. His former immoral life of sleeping with his boss Omar's wife had finally faded into the past. He was finally seeing the value in the moral lessons taught in the volunteer classes that he was attending. He was growing morally and spiritually though he attended what seemed to be a peculiar lesson that day. Both males and females were in one classroom. He took the opportunity to sit next to one of the maids for the first time. Until then they had always been taught separately. Mohammad had been courting Yasmina, a young maid for a while. He had made little progress because of the social restrictions but he could tell that she liked him. He was even considering making a proposal; he felt that his employers would welcome this as they would have a couple who worked for them.

The two walked home together after religious studies. Normally she would walk with the other ladies, but Mohammad insisted on being the one to take her home. He told her that he liked her, and she smiled. She was very shy. As they strolled along the road, they heard gunshots. Mohammad held her hand

and guided her into an alleyway. He continued to hold her tightly while the shooting continued; they heard footsteps which came closer and closer. The girl moved into his chest for protection, but they both knew that there was nothing that could be done.

In front of Mohammad were three ISIS militants who had surrounded them.

"What you are doing is against our law, unless this is your wife. Are you two married?" one of them asked in a manner that suggested that he already knew the answer to that question. They were extremely intimidating, and Mohammad knew better than to argue with them.

"No, we are not, but we heard gunshots and she was scared so I only held her in case there was danger." He explained as he let her go. It was against the law for an unmarried man and women to be holding hands; especially in public.

"Holding her would protect her from gunshots? You are also a liar I see, there have been no gunshots here. You and your girlfriend were doing immoral things in the public domain and now you think you can get out of this mess by lying to us. That is ten lashings for both of you." The verdict was given, and their punishment had been announced. Mohammad was terrified for her, he knew that he could take a beating, but she was a young girl.

They grabbed the girl and guided her into a nearby abandoned building while one of them stayed behind giving Mohammad a look that suggested that if he moved then there would be severe repercussions. He could hear screams from her but no sound from the armed men. He was so close to the building that he thought it strange that he couldn't hear the belt. They kept her in there for ten minutes before one of them returned; as he walked, he zipped up his trousers. His colleague smiled and they whispered to each other for a few moments before Mohammad's initial guard walked towards the same building. While he was there Mohammad sat with fear and anger. The woman that he had hoped to marry had stopped screaming, and he knew exactly what was happening to her.

Eventually the two other gentlemen returned. They removed their belts simultaneously and whipped him with the buckle end. As promised, they did it ten times each. Mohammad did not want to give them the satisfaction of letting them know how painful it was. However, the fact that he was not screaming encouraged them to hit him harder and harder. When they were done, they warned him about what would happen if he and his girlfriend complained, they promised to do much worse. Once they walked away, he lifted himself and ran limping into the building. He found her on the ground in tears. When he placed his hand on her shoulder, she lashed out at him and told him not to touch her. There was blood on the floor and her dress. She had been a virgin.

Chapter 26

Undoing past mistakes

GENERAL JAMAL ONCE AGAIN MET with senior army officials. This time they were heavily protected not only by armed guards, but also by tanks and special unit officers. He was comforted by this but knew that if someone infiltrated the army then these precautions would be futile. Albeit the citadel made the interlocutors feel secure and with most possessing elan attitudes. He had become greater in their eyes; it was evident that the fact that he was shot and survived exalted him in these circles. It showed that he was a real tough guy. The officials all pledged fealty to him and with the return of his memory he felt omniscient as he sat with them.

Jamal opened the discussion.

"We need to go to Raqqah to conduct a very severe rescue mission. We will be retrieving civilians who have been unable to leave because they are being held for ransom by the terrorists. Some will refuse to leave their homes, business and family members. There is nothing that can be done to help these people. If they stay out of your way, then they are of no concern to us. ISIS soldiers will resist us and with it being a stronghold they will do so with the outmost enthusiasm and hubris. As we have established from past peace talks, we cannot reason with them. We can't request a cease-fire and expect them to respect it. It will be a stealth mission conducted in the middle of the night. We will kill the guards who are blocking the city with snipers. Our ground troops will move from house to house in compounds. Do not bother about the rich. Anyone with a house or a job or business could afford to leave if they really wanted to, it is with insularity that they choose to stay. As you know ISIS receive title deeds from those people who want to leave the region as security. Or they take twenty thousand dollars. Anyone who can afford to be in the residential area could probably have found a way out. We are going to rescue the peasants." He announced before sitting back. From his first look he could see unconvinced faces. He needed to adopt a different approach, one that encouraged these men more.

"In theory that is a nice idea, but the truth is that if we go into their stronghold without all guns blazing then we don't stand a chance. If just one soldier sees our operatives, then he will alert the others and there will be an onslaught. I think either we go in hard or we don't go in. If those soldiers are captured, then they will receive some of the worst torture that a human being can do to one another." One of the generals responded while the others nodded their heads to agree. Serendipitously an idea entered his head on how to change the narrative.

"The peasants are most of the population. If we want to finally see an end to all of this, then we will need their support. There is great strength in numbers. If we have the masses with us, then the handful of businesses that support these terrorists won't be able to achieve anything." Jamal responded to show that there was party gain and it was not only a humanitarian effort. He would make up more incentives for the army as they progressed.

"Jamal, let us speak openly for a moment. Everyone here understands the penalties of treason so information will not leak. You want us to bring out peasants before the chemical bombings begin so that we will have people to vote for us when the general election comes?" The same general asked with a smile on his face, Jamal returned a guilty smile and nodded his head.

"Well, I'm glad that you have an ulterior motive. There were rumors that you had become a saint. I can see what you are proposing now. After we clear out these terrorists then the people who have been rescued will be so grateful that they will side with us when things stabilize, and the electoral process recommences."

All the men laughed and congratulated Jamal on his foresight. They were now more willing to discuss the operation because they could understand the benefit to the party and most importantly the benefit to themselves. Jamal knew that valiant acts had to be compensated; he couldn't act like he was simply a humanitarian who was thinking of just doing well for his fellow man.

Jamal knew that the rescue mission proposal would buy him some time. Immediately after his meeting with the army he drove out of Damascus in a private car. He had arranged to meet a Western journalist who was in Syria. The gentlemen's name was Graham Adams and he promised that there would be complete anonymity with regards to what they discussed.

Graham told him that he wanted to have an interview that would be broadcasted worldwide however the camera would focus on Graham and Jamal's voice would be manipulated.

Once the cameras were set up and Jamal was comfortable enough that there were no witnesses near their spot in the mountains the interview commenced.

"I am here with a credible source in the Syrian capital. The individual's identity will not be revealed however he has an important message to relay. Sir, what are the Syrian government's plans in their fight against terrorists, rebels or opposition as some would say?" Graham began the interview. Jamal's heart was racing rapidly; he was terrified but could see no other way to stop the attack. He informed the viewers that the government was planning to exterminate its enemies using chemical weapons. He went on to explain that the attacks would be aimed in areas where opposition groups have strongholds.

"Now, how will the government be able to target only the terrorists? Won't civilians be caught up in the crossfire?" Graham pressed on just like they had rehearsed. The questions were poised to set up an opportunity for Jamal to alarm the international community.

He explained that the chemical weapons would kill innocent people in those regions. There would be a mass exodus if these plans were achieved. Men, women and children who are not fighting the current regime would fall victim to those chemicals and would suffer painful deaths. Jamal compared what was to come to the extermination of Jews by the Nazis.

"These are crimes against humanity, and we have seen world leaders sent to and receiving long prison sentences for making and executing decisions of this nature. What do you expect to happen next, being someone who is on the ground?" Graham continued as they were nearing the end of their discussions.

Jamal said that he expected the international community to prevent these attacks otherwise there will be genocide here in Syria. Graham asked whether there could be an end to this horrible civil war that was displacing and taking the lives of many Syrians.

"Well, there are so many groups fighting for so many different causes. I hope that the people respect the existing regime. Give the government of the day a deadline for when they must re-introduce democracy and hold free and fair elections. Let us fight each other using our words in parliamentary sessions and not through bloodshed." Jamal concluded before Graham thanked him for taking the time to meet with him.

The next morning General Jamal was called to the state house. The President informed his cabinet that the United Nations was sending an emergency commission of enquiry due to reports that the Syrian government would use chemical weapons which was a direct violation of human rights. The President had been informed that sanctioning genocide on his own people would lead to severe consequences from the international community.

The commission wanted to see all the government's arms stocks and if chemical weapons were found then they would leave the government with two options. Either they were going to face worse international sanctions which would devastate the economy that was already suffering so badly, or they would have to destroy them on site. A decision on which option to use would need to be made within an hour of any evidence being uncovered.

The secretary general, Fadi Hasim, looked at Jamal throughout the President's address and tilted his head in a manner that suggested that he was thinking of him. Jamal sat there looking shocked and outraged just like the others. The President wasn't pointing any fingers yet. In cases like these investigations were usually already underway and he would wait for the results. Workers at the warehouses would be interviewed as well as customs workers who were responsible for inspecting the equipment that had been imported. None of the cabinet ministers would have been pointing a finger at each other.

Once their leader was done explaining the extent of the situation that they were facing he put his notes down and looked around the table. At this moment the television was turned on by the minister of information. He walked towards the screen and inserted a memory stick. He scrolled through files until he clicked on one labeled "The Rat".

As soon as he pressed enter Jamal's interview with Graham Adams began to play on the screen. The video started and Jamal continued to maintain an angry expression on his face, in accordance with the other ministers. However, within himself his heart was racing at a rapid pace, like someone was going to turn around and point him out whilst proclaiming him to be the traitor. Fortunately, Graham Adams had done a fantastic job of protecting his identity. Jamal's voice had been manipulated and he sounded high pitched, like a young man or a woman. The camera remained focused on Graham Adams as he explained that the identity of his colleague was being protected as a matter of life and death.

Jamal watched as he gave away intricate details of the current regime's military strategy and how their plans would have a more detrimental impact on civilians then other strategies that could be employed. As he listened, he realized that he was short of breath, but was determined to hide this until he was far away from these men. Fadi Hasim and he locked eyes, before Jamal squinted angrily. He was beginning to get extremely frustrated with this man's constant lurking, even though he knew that the secretary general's suspicions were completely justified.

Once the interview finished the television was turned off, the secretary general decided to take the floor. This was extremely brave because normal etiquette would call for the President to give an address first before others could contribute. There were murmurs amongst the ministers as Fadi stood up and placed his hands firmly on the table to attract everyone's attention.

"We need to find the mole; the person in that interview must be in the government because only a handful of people knew about our plans. Therefore, there is no point in starting our investigation at the bottom. We were shipping in the pieces separately and the chemical weapons had been assembled here in Syria so let us not even bother with customs officers." Fadi announced before once again looking at Jamal, if someone followed his eyes then they would be able to sense that there was a problem between the two. However, Jamal didn't sit idly, he responded by also getting up and giving a passionate contribution. After all he was the minister of defense; he was actually the person whose contribution would be more appropriate than his counterpart.

"It must be the same person who infiltrated the meeting where I was shot. We must find him otherwise information will continue to leak and more of us will be put in harm's way. I will dedicate my personal time and resources to finding this rat as the minister of information correctly labeled him. However right now we must prepare for our guests from the U.N." Jamal announced while Fadi sank back into his seat. The other ministers agreed with Jamal and so did the President.

Fadi knew how popular Jamal was, if he accused him of betraying the party without proof then the ministers would prefer that Fadi was ousted from the party to maintain unity. After he was shot, they all exalted his name in party meetings, but the fact that he was sitting here with them as dedicated as before meant that he was a party hero, second only to the President in popularity.

The other ministers followed this new procedure by also standing up to give passionate declarations and contributions with regards to pulling in their ministries to fight the leakage of intricate information. Finally, the President closed the meeting by saying that he agreed with Jamal wholeheartedly and would let him take leadership in managing the UN visitors.

Before they all left the boardroom, the secretary general asked Jamal if they could walk together to discuss his strategy for the UN commission. The President heard this and smiled to encourage their dialogue before he and the other ministers raced off in different directions. Jamal slowed his stride to allow Fadi to keep up with him, yet he knew that the conversation was bound to be an aggressive one.

"If I find out that it, was you who passed on information to the Western journalist then I will personally make sure that you get what you deserve. The great General Jamal's legacy will be crushed within moments of me finding evidence against you." Fadi whispered in his ear as he held Jamal's hand firmly with his own. Jamal found it almost humorous that this frail individual was trying to exert physical strength over someone his size.

"If I find out that it, was you then you will fall victim to the same fate. Now if we are done, I've got to leave and attend to my duties. Unlike you I am actually going to find the real culprit rather than wasting time with empty threats against my fellow minister. Everyone knows that I command the loyalty of the army and the respect of the cabinet. You are treading on thin ice." At that Jamal shoved Fadi off and the secretary general crashed against the wall. The noise caused both men's bodyguards to stand still. The guards didn't know what to do. Jamal simply walked towards his vehicle and didn't look back; more provocation would be considered real intimidation to Fadi. Jamal felt justified that he had done the right things. Thousands of innocent people would continue to live because of his courage; however, he was not prepared to suffer for his choice. He wanted to continue with his work so that he could control government defense and ensure that it did not enter the unwanted territory of genocide and public suffering.

As he drove away from the state house, he was informed that the UN delegation had arrived. He went to the airport and met them with hospitality and not hostility. He knew that in dealing with people in this nature that the first approach should always be appeasement. If that didn't work, then leaders often resorted to aggression however this would not turn your enemies into your friends. It would just transform them into greater enemies. When he reached the airport, he quickly ensured that the belly dancers and party supporters were there to welcome them in the same way that they would a minister.

Jamal met with the United Nations delegation and gave them the grand tour of the countries defense mechanisms. Two journalists followed him closely behind recording each and every word that came out of his mouth. He conveyed welcoming arms and said that he was disappointed that their visit had not been a social one, but in the nature that it was in. When asked if there were chemical weapons in the country, he did not give them a straight answer. He told them that during a civil war, weapons of all types were finding their way into their country. To know whether or not chemical weapons were in the country they would have to sit down with each of the terrorist groups and find out what arsenal they had at their disposal.

Jamal also joked that if the journalists interviewed Islamic State militants, and they were not beheaded, then they should ask them not to destroy any more historical sites lest their descendants never see Syria's rich history. The joke on the beheadings was only laughed at by the state press; Jamal threw that remark in to remind them that there was a much greater threat in their country.

Jamal was meant to take the leaders of the delegation around while the other delegates did a more thorough search. He had sent a secret letter to Graham Adam informing him where the chemical weapons were being hidden and this was passed along. Within an hour of their arrival the chemical weapons were found. The delegates became very hostile towards them once their mission was achieved. Photographic evidence of the warehousing facilities where the bombs were stocked was sent back to the UN headquarters; there was not enough time for the administration to hide them elsewhere.

Despite Jamal's futile attempt none of the delegates decided to stay except those who would stay to observe the destruction of the weapons. The plane left and within hours the President was contacted by the United Nations Security Council. The cabinet agreed that their leader would pass the blame down his hierarchy and proclaim profusely that he would never permit weapons of that nature.

After the weapons were destroyed the President travelled to Geneva. A monitoring team was sent to Syria to ensure that Omar's chemical weapons were indeed destroyed. Jamal acted the part but was so relieved that he had saved those lives. He just hoped that he hadn't jeopardized his own cover because the secretary general continued to pass comments about crushing him if he found any evidence. The man was convinced yet had not taken his suspicions to anyone else.

Chapter 27

The Reunion

OLIVIER'S TAXI DRIVER HALTED the car and pointed to the house across the street. He was in the shanty town. The car drove along some of the worst roads that he had ever seen, if they could even be called roads. The houses were close together, without any fences to separate them. Most of them had been built using brick and mud.

He told the driver to wait for him as he opened the door and stepped straight into a puddle of mud. He didn't bother to brush off his shoes. Instead, he marched towards the front door where a skinny dog began to bark at him. He was not concerned about the emaciated animal. It seemed so fragile that biting him would probably hurt the dog. He knocked on the wooden door and within moments an elderly man came out.

"I am looking for Kandy; she is a friend of mine," he lied with a pleasant smile on his face. The skinny dog continued to bark almost as if it was attempting to show off for its owner. Olivier's reason for being at the front door did not seem to please the gentleman. He stammered a little bit but went on to say.

"There is no Kandy who lives here, I'm sorry." He replied before attempting to close the door, but Olivier put his foot in the way to stop him. He smiled while doing this to appear as friendly as possible. Olivier went on to open his new wallet and remove some notes which he handed to the man.

"I am a friend of hers, there is no problem." He repeated himself reassuringly, the man decided to open the door wider before walking forward and cautiously taking the money. Olivier knew that this meant that he would be more helpful. The second that his fingers touched those notes the elderly man had been compromised.

"She rents the guest room behind my house; she is just my tenant." The man responded before retreating back into his house, even though he took the money he didn't want to see whether or not Olivier was telling the truth.

As he approached the guest house two chickens scurried out of his way as they squawked loudly. Suddenly Kandy's image appeared at the window before she quickly ducked and tried to hide. He could hear things shuffling in a panic inside; there was obviously only one entry and exit point however he didn't want her to find an alternative way to flee. He really needed to reassure her and hope that she believed him, in her line of work she would have heard a tremendous amount of lying from men.

"Kandy, I am not upset with you. Please let me in. The lady you were telling me about called Sunshine. I think that she is my sister; I was the brother who she left in Congo. I lost my mother. I couldn't care less about the money otherwise I would've come here with the police." He raised his voice all the while knowing that she was paying attention because the noise inside had stopped. He heard some cautious footsteps that stopped right inside of the door. She was breathing audibly on the other side, he was careful not to startle her. He simply kept saying "Please. Please come out and talk to me. I need your help.".

After a few moments the door was opened. Olivier pushed it open cautiously and had to duck his head as he stepped in. Once inside Kandy stood in front of him with a knife in her hand as she was shaking frantically. He didn't expect her to hurt him, so he walked past her and sat down. It was a tiny place. The television and sofa were in the far left, the kitchen appliances were right by the entrance and a black curtain covered the area where he assumed her bed was. There were shoes everywhere. Olivier made his way and sat down on the couch.

"I'm sorry that I ran away with your money. Your wallet is still here, but I have already spent the money." She announced as she put the knife down. She remained standing as she tapped her long nails on the table. Now that he was in the house Olivier didn't feel the need to be so nice. This woman had robbed him not to mention the anxiety that she caused him by disappearing.

"Where is Sunshine?" He said strongly as his eyes remained fixed on the television's blank screen. She moved towards him in a seductive manner. She obviously wasn't sure about why he was really there. He didn't seem interested in the money that she took yet insisted on meeting Sunshine. She couldn't figure him out; could it really be possible that Sunshine was his sister?

"I thought you were a police officer or something. I have been to jail already so I am very scared. You were just asking weird questions and I didn't know what was going to happen…" He interrupted her. Clearly, he needed to be sterner otherwise he would've spent the entire day going back and forth on this topic and he simply did not have the time.

"Kandy, please focus, I don't care about why you ran away. Just take me to Sunshine!" He almost yelled at her; he didn't want the old man to think that there was a problem after he promised to be her friend several times. Kandy was taken aback, by this.

"Okay, let's go. She is my neighbor," she finally blurted out. She changed her footwear into flat shoes before explaining that she needed to find out where Sunshine was. Olivier was being extremely hostile, which was a complete contradiction to what he had been like. This bothered Kandy and she was trying hard to chat and rekindle the nice man from the day before.

Kandy texted Sunshine, in front of Olivier, asking if she was home. While they waited, she offered him something to eat and drink, but he said that he was fine. There was complete silence for one minute until her phone alerted that a text message had been received. This was extremely comforting for Kandy who walked to Olivier and showed him the response from Sunshine saying that she was home.

Kandy went behind the curtain to the bedroom and returned to him with an empty wallet, but at least he got all of his cards and I.D. back. Although the bank cards would have been of no use because he had already cancelled them, but things like his driver's license were back, however he never drove himself. As they walked Kandy told him how much she enjoyed the other night and asked how long he would be around for. He didn't bother to answer her and she could tell that that part of his holiday was now over.

They used the side gate which led directly to Sunshine's front door. Kandy didn't bother to knock, but just walked in. Olivier followed her in and saw that the accommodation situation was the same as Kandy's.

"Who is this handsome man?" Sunshine asked. She had a large beer belly and a cigarette squeezed between her fingers in her left hand. She was wearing a pink gown, small shorts and a t-shirt that exposed her belly ring. She smiled at Olivier and he looked back at her red eyes, they looked alike. She swayed from side to side as she walked towards Kandy. Her demeanor suggested that she was drunk or high on some drug.

Kandy opened her mouth but failed to explain so Olivier stepped in.

"I am your brother," Olivier said expecting this opening sentence to kick start some kind of emotional awakening. It didn't, she gave him a kiss on the cheek before she replied.

"So, my brother, what have you come here for? You want group sex?" She said with a smile, but it was a real offer. Kandy opened her mouth yet again but decided to stay out of it. She would only be the custodian for this reunion, but not a participant.

"Sunshine, when you were a little girl, you had a brother in Yambuku village in the Democratic Republic of Congo. Your mother was sick, so she went into the hospital while you and your brother waited for her outside. I am the brother who waited with you on the field outside of the hospital. I was adopted by a missionary when I woke up and you had left. He named me Olivier, but I never forgot my sister's name. So, I searched through Congo for you many years ago and eventually gave up. Kandy told me about her friend called Sunshine last night and I've come to get you." He explained with more energy, she looked at him completely confused. She put her hand on her head, before placing her other hand on his face to look at him carefully. She reeked of alcohol, and tried her best to concentrate. It would have been better if they found her sober but Olivier was happy that she was beginning to understand.

"Wait, I follow Congolese politics. You mean to tell me that the governor of Katanga is my brother?" Sunshine asked as if she had just won the lottery and was thinking about how her life was going to change in no time.

"We will have to take some DNA tests to make sure, however I can see from your face that you are my sister. When we are certain than I can take you back to Congo to live with me, you will come back home and I will make sure that you have a good life. I can't change the horrible things that took place in your past, but trust me. Your future in Congo will be much brighter." Olivier explained while holding back the tears. He didn't cry, but this was really as close as it was going to get for him.

Sunshine was very excited and hugged him. Kandy also tried to involve herself in the celebration. She mentioned to Sunshine that she was so happy for her before asking Olivier if he also wanted her to come. He explained that he was married, but she said that she didn't mind. He could just see her whenever he was free and that way Sunshine would at least have her best friend.

Sunshine didn't say anything to promote him taking this girl. Olivier declined; he wanted his older sister to forget this horrible life that she had lived in for so many years. That meant forgetting about all of the old friends, acquaintances and enemies. It was a new start.

Chapter 28

Tying Up Loose Ends

GENERAL JAMAL ARRIVED at the state interrogation center. The need for such an institution came shortly after the UN declared that Syria was in a civil war. Barbed wire around the perimeter prevented any of the captives from escaping and those of them who would succeed would be pounced on by the trained dogs. Jamal hated coming here because it was worse than prison but he had received a call explaining that Raham, the man who shot him, was in their custody. It had taken the state several weeks to locate him and Jamal wanted to have a chance to speak to him before he was tortured to death.

He was certain that Raham was not only the one who shot him, but also part of ISIS. His conclusion was derived from the manner in which the assassination took place, but those who had apprehended Raham explained that he had an ISIS tattoo on his shoulder. Raham had been in the army for several years but somewhere along the way he had been infiltrated. Jamal was hoping to find this out.

Jamal remembered how the attack began. Raham was one of the guards on duty during the meeting. After about twenty minutes Raham moved briskly towards the main entrance, unlocked the door and turned around to shoot at Jamal before running into the corridor. Immediately after that ISIS militants rushed in and the gun fight began.

Jamal fell under the table holding his shoulder, the bullet had actually ripped through his flesh. He lay on the ground in pain however managed to pick his pistol from his holster. When the shooting ended only one of his guards was alive, the rest of the people in the room were dead. This man helped Jamal up, even though he was also injured, and they went towards the car park where another gun battle was taking place.

The guard tried to cover Jamal as he made his way towards his vehicle but before he could enter his car everything went dark. He assumed that that was when he was shot again and fell hard onto a rock. Jamal was very fortunate to have been knocked out because that would have made him appear dead, and none of the assailants bothered to check.

The guard who had tried to save him hadn't been so lucky and was found dead next to Jamal. If his memory hadn't returned then no one would have known about Raham's betrayal and the man would have continued to do his work unnoticed.

Jamal walked along the dark corridor and heard screams from the other cells. There was so much suffering in that place yet Jamal was happy that Raham was in there and knew that that man would never see the light of day regardless of if the information came out the easy way or the hard way. The guard opened the door to Raham's cell and Jamal immediately saw the man hanging from the wall, chained by the wrists. The man's body had been whipped all over and his face was so swollen that he couldn't open his eyes lids widely.

There was a strong stench because Raham had gone to the toilet on himself and no one bothered to clean up after him. Jamal had been around worse so wasn't fazed by the smell; he was more focused on achieving his goal. He walked around the puddle of urine before he asked Raham why he wanted to kill him. The man was conscious but decided to ignore the General and continued to stare at the ground. This infuriated the guard more than it did Jamal, the guard marched up to Raham and struck him several times while Raham yelled in agony. When the guard was satisfied that he had done enough to motivate the prisoner. Jamal stepped closer and asked Raham once more why he tried to kill him.

This time Raham lifted his head and looked Jamal in the eyes before spitting in his face. The guards shouted in anger for assistance and others came in. They beat Raham with batons while Jamal wiped the spit off his face with a handkerchief. Jamal told Raham that if he cooperated then the torture would stop, but the prisoner's only response was that the Caliph was the true leader of the Islamic world.

Raham continued to yell a variety of patriotic sentences while he was beaten severely. Raham spoke about how he was prepared to die for the Caliph and nothing done to him would cause him to talk. Jamal realized that this man was not going to be of any use. The insults from Rahma were so severe that Jamal was thinking about getting involved in the beat down. Being spat on was one of the biggest insults and he didn't care what happened to Raham in the end. He came there with the spirit of reconciliation and was prepared to transfer Raham to the general prison if he cooperated, but now Jamal didn't care.

He left the room and walked back to his vehicle. He was somewhat at peace, the gentleman who tried to kill him was in police custody and even though he knew that this would not stop ISIS from regrouping and planning future attacks at least he had closed that particular chapter. The chemical weapons had been destroyed and this would make the regime play by the rules at least for a while. Something triggered in his memories. Everything flooded back to him as if he had never forgotten. He was delighted that he remembered everything, especially his wife. He was instantly convinced that he would be a dedicated husband and an honest politician. He was optimistic that the future would be very bright for him but it was going to be dim for his country.

He had been informed by the minister of intelligence that over two hundred thousand people had been killed since the fighting began in 2011. This fact was the main reason why over two million women and children were refugees; such staggering figures could not be ignored by anyone who heard them. There were over five million people who had been displaced from their homes because of the fighting. He wondered how many years of rebuilding would be required once the fighting eventually ended. Even though Jamal had prevented the major attack he heard the rumors that over two hundred civilians had been killed using sarin gas across the country.

The other item that the regime had to deal with was the growing momentum for the National Coalition which was a group of several opposition camps that had grouped together.

They had even been recognized as the legitimate representative of the Syrian people by most of the international community. They were seen as the biggest political threat. However, the Free Syrian army was seen as the greatest military threat as that group comprised of army defectors. Jamal and the other generals were poised with the challenge of preventing soldiers from joining them as they too were building momentum and would be well positioned to undertake a coup d'état.

The state also had to combat the jihadist groups who were fighting them, but fortunately the jihadists had lost direction and were also fighting the Free Syrian army. They welcomed the fighting between opposition parties and ensured that information leaked on the whereabouts of the opposition to one another. The only saving grace was that Hezbollah fighters who pledged allegiance to the current regime were entering into Syria to fight ISIS. These militias needed very little motivation, all they wanted were guns.

Jamal also knew that the Organization for the Prohibition of Chemical Weapons would be constantly sending in monitoring teams to ensure that the entire chemical weapon stockpile was destroyed. The president had to agree to this because the last thing the regime needed was for sanctions to be placed on arms and military equipment. Jamal fully expected OPCW to be on his case for a while.

Jamal wasn't too concerned about direct military intervention from the superpowers because the UN Security council was split. The fact that Russia and China were vetoing efforts to further sanctions and introduce military intervention worked well for the regime. Then there was the fact that within the U.S. congress they weren't allowing direct intervention and the House of Commons was doing the same in the U.K, but Jamal knew that in times like these positions could change the longer the war lasted.

Finally, Jamal thought about how relations with Turkey were at an all-time low after the Turkish jet was shot down in their airspace, however, once car bombs were set off in the Turkish border town the government declared that it would use physical force to protect its interests if such attacks continued.

So even though Jamal felt a sense of relief he knew that there were more headaches and complications to follow in the near future. As the driver left the interrogation center Jamal asked him to go straight home.

Chapter 29

Returning Home

OLIVIER HAD ASKED SUNSHINE to take a full medical once the DNA test confirmed that she was his sister. Olivier knew that she would be in contact with his family and because of her career he needed to be sure that she didn't have Ebola before taking her home. As they sat in the waiting room for the results from her medical examination Sunshine shifted around the chair nervously. The fact that she was so concerned forced Olivier to ask her what the matter was. She took a large gulp before she explained that she had HIV and Aids. She closed her eyes while telling him as if she expected this to change everything. She thought that he would no longer be interested in taking her. Olivier put his arm around her shoulder to reassure his sister, he didn't want her to live her life on egg shells, and he wanted her to be more comfortable around him.

"Let's see what the doctor says, don't worry about that. We have good hospitals in Congo; my physician will be able to guide you on the best diet not to mention the best ARV's in the market," she immediately stopped shaking; she was calming down and realized that she wouldn't miss her chance. Olivier just wanted to be sure what her condition was like before exposing her to his family. If there were severe risks then he would accommodate her outside of his house. Either way he was going to save her.

When they were eventually called in the doctor told them what they already knew, but also went on to tell them what they didn't. The illicit drugs that she had taken would stay in her system for a few months. She needed to introduce a fitness regime into her life to stabilize her high blood pressure. After this revelation Olivier asked her to leave him alone with the doctor. Once it was just the two of them, he was told that there was nothing contagious that she was harboring that could infect his family. She was also okay to travel.

Olivier was relieved and had a sense of mission accomplished. It was only in that moment when he felt that he could no longer run away from his life. His wife would find out about Sunshine when he walked in with her or via a text message, he was yet to decide. Calling to inform Vivienne now would only allow her time to frustrate him by bringing up all the reasons why it was a bad idea.

His mind was set, he wanted to protect his sister by keeping her as close as possible. He also hoped that he had given it enough time for tensions to relax in the political arena. He would play politics and get a message to president Mbuyi that they were on the same side. This should have been enough to buy him sometime until he figured out how best to approach his pursuit of the presidency.

Olivier and Sunshine left the hospital and went straight to the airport. Olivier bought their tickets for the late afternoon flight, but even though they had several hours he didn't want to risk it. The Ebola screening procedure also meant that the boarding process had become a little longer. After another costly cab drive, they went straight to the business lounge where they had lunch and drinks while they waited for the flight and caught up on a lifetime of being without each other.

Sunshine asked him what happened after Doctor Clancy took him overseas. Olivier was reluctant to talk about it because he didn't want to show off his good fortune; however, she squeezed it out of him by pestering him for an answer whenever he tried to change topic.

"Well, Doctor Clancy took me back with him as that was his last mission. I went to a Catholic school and he was just like a normal father to me. He was strict though and I had to work for my allowance by washing his and his friends' cars on the weekend as well as delivering newspapers in the neighborhood during the week. So, I often had more money than other students and as I entered upper school, I sold snacks out of my locker, candy bars and chips, during break time which I would buy from a local wholesaler. Doctor Clancy was seeing a widow on a regular basis and I often accused them of being boyfriend and girlfriend..." Sunshine interrupted to ask him about his relationships in Ireland before he met his beautiful wife. Olivier didn't comment on Sunshine's remarks about Vivienne's beauty. Instead, he went on to explain that when he was growing up, he focused on his Christianity and academics. He admitted that he had gone astray somewhat with regards to his faith.

He seldom allocated time to anything else and so Vivienne was his only serious relationship. Sunshine went on to ask about his children, a topic that he was happy to talk about. He realized only while he was going on about them that he didn't ask whether or not she had had any children of her own. He assumed that she hadn't because it was a general rule of thumb that most mothers wouldn't abandon their children.

Olivier didn't ask her any questions in return, and she seemed happy with this. Their cocktails arrived with a Margherita Pizza that they decided to share. After their first round of drinks, he was surprised at how quickly she drank, as if she noticed his shock, she explained that she was nervous because it was the first time that she was flying in a plane. He encouraged more cocktails so that she would just sleep on the flight, it wouldn't be so bad for her, especially since it was business class.

They boarded the plane and once inside he gave her a reassuring smile before stretching back in his seat. He placed the headphones on and listened to classical music while he sipped on his wine. He needed to relax himself because he was about to enter a battle at home and a war in the political arena. These were going to be his last few moments before all of the chaos broke loose.

Chapter 30

Panic

MOHAMMAD'S HEART WAS RACING. He had reported the incident with the soldiers to his boss as soon as they returned to the property. Mr. Hussein immediately got onto the phone and called some of his friends in ISIS to his house. Now Mohammad was waiting outside the main dining room while his boss discussed the episode with the ISIS superiors. Mohammad didn't have a second thought to the threat that he would be killed if he reported them because he knew how important his boss was.

After an hour Tariq came to retrieve him. He was summoned to the table and asked to explain exactly what happened word for word. Mohammad was glad to hear that the culprits had been identified and were scolded on the phone by the superiors but to his surprise Mr. Hussein told him to apologize for not only being on the streets after curfew, but also holding the girl in public.

Mohammad couldn't believe what he was hearing and immediately refused to apologize. He spoke about his scars from the abuse and insisted that the men should be arrested for sexually abusing the girl. His remarks caused a lot of tension;

from the faces it was clear that he was offending the ISIS senior officers. Mr. Hussein decided to prevent the situation from escalating so he rose up and slapped Mohammad across the face before repeating that he should apologize.

That was the first time that his boss had struck him and it was obviously done to impress their visitors who couldn't help but smile at Mohammad. It shocked him, but he remembered what he had seen the militia do at the border so he grunted an apology. This apology seemed to be acceptable and Mohammad was informed that the incident would be forgotten.

Shortly after that the guests stood up to leave and Mr. Hussein and Tariq hugged all of them. Mohammad gave them handshakes as they walked out of the front door. When the guests had driven out of the property Mr. Hussein told Mohammad to take a seat with him and Tariq.

"Sir, the soldiers can rape and beat her then I am expected to apologize? That does not make any sense to me whatsoever," Mohammad protested as he was huffing and puffing furiously. Tariq looked at him angrily but Mr. Hussein tried his best to calm him down.

"Just leave it alone Mohammad, complaining is not going to take it back. They didn't know that you are associated with me, I did my part and now you will be fine going forward. In the future Tariq will pick up my workers in the car when they are attending late classes. Do not stress, okay." Mr. Hussein got up as he thought that that was the end of the discussion however Mohammad wasn't done with what he intended to say.

He was so disappointed with this conclusion that he was ready to leave Raqqah. He would return to a refugee camp and make his way out of Syria; there was nothing left for him there anymore. The woman that he thought he would marry had been defiled right in front of him and she didn't even want to see him anymore. Things had been good for a while, but it was time to pack up and move on.

"I cannot stay in such a place. I thank you for what you have done so far, but I am leaving today." Mohammad blurted out before Mr. Hussein could leave the room. His boss stopped walking, but didn't even turn back to look at him. Instead, he simply told Mohammad that he wasn't going anywhere before Tariq was told to escort Mohammad to the servant's quarters. Tariq was elated because the manner in which Mohammad had been speaking to his boss had been infuriating him. Tariq grabbed Mohammad and dragged him to the servant's quarters while repeating that he was there to stay and the only way to leave Mr. Hussein would be in a coffin.

All the workers watched Mohammad being dragged across the lawn and none of them were prepared to intervene. Once inside Mohammad was pushed onto the floor and both of his elbows were cut. He decided to stay on the ground because it would hurt less when Tariq beat him up.

Instead, Tariq stressed that he didn't want to hurt him but would be forced to if Mohammad tried to escape. He told him to forget what happened and that things would be better going forward. After that final statement Tariq told Mohammad to spend the rest of the day in his room and to only return to his duties the following evening.

Once alone Mohammad looked around the room and realized that he had been a prisoner from the moment that he entered that car with Mr. Hussein and Tariq. He wished that he had stayed in that refugee camp because there was no way for him to escape. Even if he somehow left the property, he didn't have any money to pay the militia at the border so it was pointless. Mohammad sat on the bed and wondered if he was ever going to get a chance to escape, even though he didn't know where he would go the thought of staying was much more frightening.

Chapter 31

A New Chapter

OLIVIER ASKED THE DRIVER to escort his sister to the cottage that was behind the main house. He told her to make herself feel comfortable and that he would come to get her when it was dinner time. Sunshine was taken aback by the house. She repeatedly mentioned that she hadn't been in such a house before. She thought to herself about how terrified she was to say the wrong thing, and all this would be taken away from her. She hugged her brother in silence before following the driver and he was delighted to have her there.

He already had ideas as to how he would go about changing her life. He knew that she needed to become independent so he would let her work in one of his businesses during the day and then pay for her to do afternoon classes in whichever industry that she wanted. He knew that it would be difficult for a mature person to start from scratch academically but would insist on this.

Olivier had taken his sister shopping at the airport because her clothes were not appropriate. Even in the stores with him he noticed that she gravitated towards the items that exposed her body and Olivier was not going to sugar coat his distaste. He wanted her to know exactly the type of woman that she needed to become. Sunshine was to be a classy, mature student who he could be proud of.

As Olivier watched his sister walk to the cottage, he took a deep breath before nervously proceeding to the front door. It was time for him to face the music with Vivienne. He had sent his wife a text message that she neglected to respond to, but the amount of time that she spent on her phone made him reasonably assured that the message had been received. He dragged his suitcase inside and found her in the lounge room. He left the suitcase just below the stairs before facing the music.

"Hello Vivienne, did you receive my text message?" Olivier asked as he removed his suit jacket. He also gave her the gift bag with all her requests. Jewelry, perfume and Brazilian hair; it was always the same stuff. She took the bag and placed it on the chair behind her, she wasn't going to let her gift sway her from what she intended to say. Knowing Vivienne, she would have been practicing for their dialogue throughout the day.

"I read something about you finding your sister who is going to live with us," she responded in a tone that suggested that she wasn't impressed with the manner in which she had been informed. He had deliberately sent a text message so that he wouldn't have to enter into an argument until his sister was already unpacking in the guest room. He knew that it was too late for Vivienne to tell him that Sunshine couldn't stay there.

"Yes, it is quite incredible that she and I would finally cross paths. However, we did not share the same fortunes. Her life has been extremely difficult, so she will need to stay with us until I can rebuild her into someone who can be independent," Olivier expressed decisively, hoping that that would end the discussion whilst knowing that it wouldn't. He was dealing with a woman who spent the whole day thinking about his every move. The fact that their kids were abroad had turned his wife into a rabble-rouser.

Vivienne went on to ask how he even knew that the woman was really his sister, she strongly suspected that she was a scam artist who was probably just trying to steal from them. She went on to tell him that it was extremely irresponsible for him to expose his family home to a complete stranger and further expressed concerns that witchcraft had been used on him. She alleged that spells had been cast on him numerous times throughout their marriage, it was ridiculous.

"I did a DNA test and she is the one, Vivienne, I'm not stupid," he responded harshly as she was already beginning to irritate him. He could barely remember a time when this woman didn't annoy him. After all his success she actually believed that he would bring someone home if he wasn't completely sure. Of course, there were millions of women who would have loved to live in his home in whatever capacity.

"Why does she have to live in my house? Can't you find her an apartment, I'm sure she would rather be doing her own thing than here under our roof," Vivienne yelled back at him. Their talk had gone from a discussion to an argument in the blink of an eye. This was why Olivier ensured that his son went to boarding school, which child would be happy with their parents' fighting every other night? Even though he didn't want his kids to know what they fought about Vivienne would always run to their rooms and tell them just how bad their father was. She constantly exposed them to mature discussions and he kept them out of the house so that they could focus on academics because he noted how the arguments directly impacted their performances.

"Unfortunately, she had been forced into prostitution. If she lives out of the house right now, then I am sure that she will fall back into those old ways. She is staying here where I can keep an eye on her progress. I'll keep her busy, working and studying until she is a qualified person. I don't intend on taking on another dependent for life if that's what you're worried about," Olivier snapped as he turned on the television. He realized that the argument would go on for some time so to make it more productive he would have the news on in the background. He would hate to waste thirty minutes of his life listening to Vivienne when he could watch news instead. Just as he scrolled to the correct channel, Vivienne asked him how he met his sister.

"I was at the Ebola conference and explained to a colleague that I lost my sister many years ago in Yambuku. He happened to know her and after the introduction I did what was required to ensure that she was indeed the one," Olivier responded with his eyes fully focused on the television. He knew that the story of how he met a prostitute who happened to know his sister would really be the tipping point. If he could emerge from this side of the discussion victorious then he was home and dry.

"I think that you went looking for prostitutes, you found one that you like and now you want to keep her in my house so that you can have two wives! My children will not be exposed to that rubbish here at home!" Vivienne announced as she threw the gift bag at his head. Olivier stood up and kept checking the side of his head to ensure that he wasn't bleeding. Vivienne looked at him as if she expected a fist fight of some sort.

She knew that he wouldn't lay his hands on her, but he was still angry at how far she was prepared to go to test his resolve. He had been hit with a frying pan before, not to mention the scar on his arm from when she threw hot cooking oil on him. She had scratched him with her nails on numerous occasions and throwing perfume at him was simply adding to the list of physical offences. If it was the other way around, he would be called a monster but because it was a woman abusing her husband then it would be embarrassing for him to report her to the authorities.

"I think you are so worried that I will have to spend some money on this woman, and it will divert funds from your extravagant shopping. Don't worry dear, unlike you she understands that she can't depend on me forever. She will leave when I have empowered her, but she is staying for now." Throwing papers onto the table he said, "Feel free to read the doctor's report. You will see that we are brother and sister not to mention the virus that she is dealing with. If you lord, her illness over her then there will be severe consequences. Now, I am going to take my bag upstairs, shower and then bring her in for dinner. I hope that you will put yourself in my shoes and be more considerate to the situation," Olivier concluded before walking away, he always left when a woman would want to have a physical confrontation with him. It was what he was used to from a young man, but Vivienne was going so far in it that he was contemplating walking away from the marriage.

It was either that or he would put himself in danger of striking her back. Olivier knew that he wasn't completely innocent, but he would retaliate to his wife hitting him in the usual manner. She wouldn't get allowance because he would say that he was broke, but she would know it's because she hit him. He wouldn't speak to her until she apologized and even if she didn't then he would continue to tighten his financial belt. There would be no fuel in her car, he wouldn't pay the television bill, and he wouldn't get credit for her phone and would attend all his social events alone. This was the only way that he could punish her for physical abuse until he figured out a more permanent solution.

Olivier always showered with freezing cold water, regardless of what the temperature was like outside. It made him feel much fresher and helped him to think clearly. This habit was developed when he was struggling in life and there was no hot water in his neighborhood. He went on like this for six months and when he moved out going back to a warm shower or bath didn't quite feel the same. He learnt several survival skills during his hardships when he just moved to Congo that was why he hated to see financial waste in his home. He remembered how much he used to pray for success when he was in the townships that he knew couldn't take it for granted.

The President knew that Olivier was back in the country; he really wasn't sure what would come next. He hoped that calmer heads would prevail. So far, he had maintained his story that he left for a trip to aid in the Ebola epidemic, but the relevant Congolese government stakeholders all knew the bitter truth. It reminded him of an expression. "What happens when an unstoppable force collides with an unmovable object?" This statement almost described his situation perfectly, he thought to himself while the freezing cold water splashed against his chest.

When Olivier was done in the shower, he picked up his cellphone to make a call.

"Jean-Claude, I need you to pick up my sister tomorrow morning and take her to work. Start her from the very bottom and let her climb in the company at a slow pace, but I want her to be exposed to different things. I also want her to do some studies so let her schedule allow for that," Olivier explained calmly as the shower relaxed him after his encounter with Vivienne. He was feeling much better now and was thinking clearly.

Jean-Claude didn't even ask how he found her or whether he was sure she was the one. He just agreed and congratulated him on finding her at long last. He knew how hard Olivier had tried over the years and could only fathom how happy he must have been. They went on to chat about the progress that the company was making, but not in too much detail. Olivier was under the impression that his cellphone had been bugged, he believed that to be true now more than ever before.

After his call he changed into casual clothes before embarking on the short journey to the cottage via the living room, but his wife wasn't where he had left her. She had relocated to the kitchen to help the chef set the table for dinner. He was happy that she understood the need to make their guest feel comfortable. Today they would sit together at the table and she wouldn't leave out food and go to bed like she would usually do whenever they fought. When they had a really bad argument then she wouldn't cook after releasing the chef early so that Olivier would starve.

As he strolled to the cottage, he began to appreciate how fortunate he was. In that moment he acknowledged how far he had come in life. He lived in a big beautiful house which was reminiscent of an Italian villa. He was a self-made millionaire in a country that had the poorest citizens in the world with regards to GDP per capita. So, for his sister to see all of this, when she had a terrible life showed him just how blessed he really was.

As Olivier reached the door, he knocked gently on it and waited for a response. He was told to enter in-between his sister's sobs. He knew that she was weeping and feared that she had heard the argument that took place a little earlier. If so, he was more than prepared to push all the blame Vivienne's way. He had already caught her up to speed on the version of how they meet which he would tell people. She knew that any mention of the truth would be determent to his career.

"What is the matter? Is there anything that isn't to your liking?" Olivier asked as he slid the door open. She was seated on the edge of her bed wiping her tears. She didn't want him to see her crying which was the opposite of his wife who only cried when he was around.

"Everything is perfect; you just don't know how much this all means to me. It's as if it isn't real if you know what I mean. I feel like I am dreaming and when I wake up, I will be back in shanty town," she explained in a stammer, but she was trying her best to smile. He knew that she was being genuine and this change in scenery must have been a huge shock for her. If he hadn't been rising gradually like he did then it would have been a big change for him also.

"This is reality; now let's get something to eat. You must be very hungry, I know that I am," he said as he placed his hand on her shoulder. He knew that he couldn't be so soft that he turned her into a dependent but was so tempted to expose her to all the great things that this life had to offer.

As they walked towards the house, he informed her that she would be going to work the next day at 6:30 in the morning. Then in the afternoon she would be expected to enroll at the tuition center. She hadn't finished grade twelve yet, so the priority was for her to prepare for that. She did admit that it would be a bit embarrassing for her to be in class with teenagers, but Olivier remained adamant that she had to complete school. Now more than ever he didn't want him or his businesses to be heavily relied on. Anything could happen so he was determined to push her up to diploma level. After that he would try to get her a job outside of his enterprise before letting her move out on her own, at least that was his plan.

His wife rolled her eyes when greeting Sunshine and the dinner table was completely silent. The only noise was the sound of cutlery clinking against the plates. They all had wine with their supper, and he noticed how quickly Sunshine consumed hers. This worried him, but the fact that he also drank would make for him mentioning it to be highly hypocritical. Instead, he knew that some habits would take time to ween her off.

The television was on in the background and news broadcasted that at the latest United Nations conference it was concluded that there would be a deployment of medical soldiers into West Africa. Their mandate would be to build temporary medical facilities and fill the vacuum for medical staff which was lacking in the region. The international community hoped that these medical officers would restrict the spread of the Ebola virus.

Chapter 32

The Recruits

JERRY MACDONALD HAD JUST CELEBRATED his thirtieth birthday however it wasn't much of a celebration. His wife, Betty, organized an afternoon get together with his friends from the army. They spent the afternoon discussing their past war efforts, which were events he would have much rather forgotten. He had joined the army shortly after his grandfather's funeral, back in those days Jerry was as strong as a horse. Nowadays he would find more satisfaction taking walks to gather his thoughts then pumping iron.

His granddad was an army veteran and so was his father and now he felt that it was his turn to carry the baton. The only difference between him and his forefathers was that they all went forward to fight human beings, Jerry on the other hand fought disease. Yet now he was facing one of the deadliest viruses that the world had ever seen. The party ended with farewells from his friends and concerned stares from his wife. She couldn't hide her emotions. As soon as the last guest left, he walked into his daughter's room.

She was fast asleep so he kissed her on the forehead, knowing that he wouldn't be there in the morning. The medical soldiers needed to be at the base at zero, five hundred hours on the dot. Tardiness was unacceptable in his line of work. As he left his daughter's room, he remembered why he was going to West Africa. Ebola was spreading rapidly, and it wouldn't be long before the virus entered the United States. Containing it in Africa would protect American children from it. It was the same way that his forefathers went to Europe to contain the war and thereby secure his own future.

He had read the safety manual several times. The biggest point that couldn't have been stressed enough was to avoid any physical contact with any individuals there without protective gear on. This policy was not to be broken whether individuals looked sick or healthy. The medical soldiers were expected to treat everyone, including their colleagues, the same.

He returned to his bedroom and found his wife who had been arguing with him for weeks with regards to his decision. Every day when she put on the news, she would inform Jerry about how rapidly the Ebola virus was spreading. However, when reports returned that a foreign medical staff member had caught it then the disputes in their home escalated. She argued that a man who loved his family wouldn't voluntarily go half way around the world to the most infectious area in the world to fight the deadliest Ebola outbreak known to man. He in turn argued that if he didn't go and fight then the virus would not be contained and it could reach the U.S. border, at which point it couldn't be contained.

He placed his hand on her shoulder as she turned away from him. It was the night before he was due to leave, and he couldn't leave things like this. She had barely uttered a word to him since he told her about confirmation of his deployment. Now at this late hour he questioned whether or not sticking to his principles was worth destroying his marriage.

"Do you remember when I came back from Afghanistan and you told me about how difficult it was here alone. I went on to tell you about how many soldiers' lives that I saved. Then one day we received visitors. It was a soldier, called Karl, who was in a wheelchair. He came to see us with his family because doctors had explained that even though the bullet was lodged into his spinal cord and he couldn't walk, if I hadn't acted then he would've been killed. You made snacks for our children and his wife broke down in tears thanking me. I only have one talent in life and that is to save lives. I have gone about applying my skills in the military because even though my grandfather and father served America using guns my skills do not lie there. It is my duty to serve humanity," he tried to remind her, but Betty clearly wasn't having any of it. He had done this before but reassured her that medical staff weren't placed near the battlefield however this time round he would be going straight to the front line of this battlefield. Even though he tried to convince her time and time again that this was the same, they both knew that it was completely different.

"It is your duty to serve your family, yet for a second time you are going to leave me here." She snapped before pushing off his arms from her shoulders. She appreciated that he wanted to serve but questioned why it had to be him yet again. In her eyes they had already sacrificed to the national cause. Not to mention the fact that she had asked him time and time again to take up a job in a hospital rather than being a medical staff member in the military. In her opinion he thought that he was being a tough guy, but he was actually just being careless with his life. Not to mention the stress that he caused her.

"The United States of America is our country and I will always serve it when my nation calls for its bravest and brightest," he announced as he went to his wardrobe and started to pack. This made her cry, just like it did last time and just what he was trying to avoid. He carried his medals of valor and knew that she was proud of him deep down. Betty knew that MacDonald men were passionate about serving their country in whichever capacity they deemed fit. They could brag that they fought Nazis, Communism, Jihadists and now Ebola. If that wasn't dedication to America, then they weren't far off.

"When you are away every time that the doorbell rings, I envision that it will be soldiers here to tell me that you are dead. Do you even care about how that makes me feel?" she finally blurted out. He didn't comment, anything he said now would only make it worse. She went on to tell him to sleep on the couch and he nodded to let her know that he understood her instructions. He carried his suitcase out of the room and told her that she didn't have to wake up; he would ask a colleague to pick him up on the way.

While in the living room he twisted and turned until he realized that he wasn't falling asleep. He opted to turn on the lights and read through the pamphlet once more. They were headed to West Africa and there were several safety procedures that all staff needed to be familiar with. Most of them were initiatives to avoid infection but some were precautions on topics such as physical aggression from desperate locals. He needed to brace himself because anything was possible in West Africa. Put impoverished citizens, an epidemic, limited resources with westerners who would appear to be their only hope and you're bound to have one hell of a fiasco.

Chapter 33

Trouble in Paradise

JAMAL AND SHAHAD had finally rekindled their relationship. Jamal remembered how much he loved his wife and all the time that they had spent together. Shahad told him how much she appreciated the change in him his rendition of that statement was that she was referring to the marital problems they had faced as a result of his infidelity. He reassured her that he was a new man and issues of that nature were in the past. Jamal didn't want any more drama and was working towards transforming his life.

They spent the evening cuddled up by the television while they chatted about general events in their past to the event that Jamal was confident that he had fully overcome the memory loss. He could remember every single thing. There was not one remark made by his wife that he couldn't recall, he felt like a student who was passing his exams with flying colors. Further to that the debility that he previously had succumb to had also faded. He felt strong and was back to body building in the gym.

At the end of their movie Shahad walked towards the bedroom as Jamal checked on the guards before locking up the house. He also redeveloped the habit of checking that all of his firearms were in the strategic areas of the house that he left them in. Once satisfied, he made his way to the main bedroom. He had been sharing the bed with his wife for the past couple of days. His wife was delighted about the fact that everything was not only returning back to normal but was also getting better than before. Jamal also felt at peace, even though there was a civil war, in his personal life things had become extremely stable after a prolonged period of uncertainty.

He walked into the room and immediately entered into an embrace with his wife before he made promises to take her on holiday after he managed to catch up on his work. Shahad explained that she just wanted to see all of her children; she missed them dearly and knew that they would never return to Syria, not that she wanted them to.

After they made love Shahad fell asleep while Jamal twisted and turned in the bed until he realized that he couldn't sleep. He sat up and turned on the lamp. He walked to the bookshelf and chose a novel entitled "The Zambian Saint". He always enjoyed fictional books because they tended to be more truthful than non-fiction and he loved political thrillers.

He had only gotten to page three when his phone rang. He thought this to be odd because of the hour of the night. When he lifted it up, he noted that the call came from a private number. He didn't think twice about picking it up even though it was very late at night. He was even about to turn his cellphone off as he was reading in bed so he thought that his caller was very fortunate to catch him. He just hoped that it wasn't the type of call that would force him to get out of bed.

"General Jamal, this is the Raven," an unknown voice announced very excitedly. Jamal raked his brain trying to figure out who this person was. At this stage he had thought his memory was fully restored so was surprised that there were still people who eluded his memory. He questioned for the first time whether he would ever fully remember everything again.

He needed to speak softly because Shahad was fast asleep however the signal was bad so he was forced to raise his voice somewhat more than he would have wanted to. It was possible that it was some kind of prank call, so he didn't want to awake Shahad for no good reason.

"You are who?" Jamal responded; he was worried about such phone calls. He could feel his heart racing; he already knew that there was a problem to deal with. The tone of this so-called Raven suggested that there was something to panic about. Jamal had taken enough risks already since his recovery from the hospital bed to justify him having restless nights.

"I am the Raven sir; I am calling to inform you that state police are on their way to arrest you. The President has been informed by the Party Secretary that you informed the international community about the chemical weapons. You and your wife need to get out of there immediately; the evidence against you is substantial. May Inshallah protect you my old friend, you will need his grace now more than ever," at that statement The Raven cut the line and left Jamal bamboozled, he tried to return the call three times as he needed further clarification yet he couldn't do so with the call coming from a private number. He questioned why things would go bad just when everything had become so stable.

A part of him thought that the phone call could have been some sort of trick devised by the Party Secretary to see if Jamal would indeed flee. However, he quickly denounced this notion because if he ran then he could always say that he did so out of fear of being arrested rather than the actual allegations. He knew that the Party Secretary wouldn't come up with a scheme that could be debated. That man would pursue Jamal only when he was confident that he could take him, like the Raven said it would need to be substantial evidence.

Jamal hadn't told a single soul that he had been the one to alert the Western journalist. The fact that the Raven was so confident that it was him was very convincing. However, when The Raven said that the Party Secretary was the one to find the evidence that almost put the icing on the cake. That gentleman had not hidden his distaste for Jamal and he knew that he was the most likely to approach the President with such news. Something within him told him to trust that the unknown caller was telling the truth, but the individual only hid their identity because the warning that they had just given would have placed him in deep trouble.

Jamal suspected that his phone had been bugged by the intelligence agency many weeks before that. If this was the case then The Raven's warning whether it was true or false would mean that it would be transmitted to the country's leaders. That fact alone was enough for him to make a final decision. Jamal and his wife needed to run and they needed to do it with immediate effect.

Jamal shook Shahad until she woke up; she was a light sleeper, so this made the process short lived. He told her that they needed to get out of Syria and without hesitation she got up and started packing. He was taken aback, somewhat, because the normal reaction would have been to question the need for an evacuation in the middle of night, but this woman didn't. Shahad responded as if she had been mentally prepared for such a moment for a very long time.

"Shahad I was being told to facilitate the use of chemical weapons that were meant to be released in ISIS strongholds. I couldn't care less about the brutal jihadists but imagine the number of woman and children who would've died. With guns the soldiers can aim them at each other and women and children can still be caught in the crossfire, but with chemical weapons they would all die together because they cannot be aimed," Jamal explained while his wife continued to pack obediently. She agreed with him and said that he did the right thing because he was a good man.

"I have no idea where we can go or what we should do. Would you have any clue on a place where we could go to lay low until this thing blows over?" he enquired desperately. The fact that he reached the stage of not having an exit strategy in place disappointed him. Shahad realized that he didn't remember their evacuation plan so stopped what she was doing to educate him.

She informed her husband that he instructed her on exactly what needed to be done if this day ever came. Shahad concluded by telling Jamal to follow her lead. This revelation brought him a lot of relief, because he hadn't a clue where they would run to and who to trust in this situation. For the time being they packed clothing and essential items, but Shahad said no when he asked about his suits and cologne.

Shahad led the way downstairs towards the car while Jamal carried the bags. Once they were out of the house, he locked everything up and put the security alarm on. When he turned around, he noticed that Shahad had jumped into the driver's seat. This was rather peculiar because women seldom did the driving in his country yet Jamal was in no position to question the evacuation process.

As they drove out the guard looked at them in amazement. Jamal told him that they were going on a trip and that he should watch the house until he received further instructions. Shahad concurred with this before speeding off. Jamal found himself in a position where he was relying on his wife's judgment and was glad that he married a capable individual. As she drove into the distance he didn't bother to ask where they were headed. Instead, he used his mobile banking to increase his daily withdraw limit. They needed to carry as much cash as possible in case his Syrian bank accounts were frozen. He didn't know how long they would need to be on the run, but knew that the leadership would not forgive his disloyalty.

When he looked up, he realized exactly where they were. Shahad had driven him to his office and was pulling into the car park. The security guard saluted him before Shahad proceeded into Jamal's reserved parking spot. Jamal looked at his spouse for further instruction and it came almost instantaneously.

"Go and get everything from your safe, I am meant to stay here and watch out. You said that if I see anyone approaching the building then I should drive off and leave you here," Shahad explained robotically before her natural voice took over and she whispered that she would never leave him. She turned off the car and the lights to show that she was staying put.

"How did I know to tell you all of this, did I know that I wouldn't be able to remember?" Jamal asked as he couldn't decipher any reason why a committed former army general who had turned politician would tell his wife how he and she should escape from the government. Such planning would have been more appropriate for the leaders of the opposition parties.

"No, you told me about this in a manner that you would be leading the evacuation. However, there were other evacuation routines for situations where I would be alone. You said that if you needed to escape it would be because of the ruling party. Your attitude towards your colleagues had been worsening leading up to the assassination attempt," Shahad expressed her doubts for the first time. Before that she had been leading him to believe that there was great unity amongst the party. He felt no tension whenever he was visited during his recovery and only the Secretary General seemed to be his only enemy.

Jamal hurried up the stairs and noticed that his hand was shaking frantically when he attempted to open the door. Even though his nerves slowed him down he was soon in the building and dashed to his office at rocket speed. Once inside he was soon on the ground typing the combination on his safe. Once again, he managed without thinking about what he was pressing. He found bank cards, cash and the fake Zambian passports. He thought about whether or not he was overreacting to that anonymous tip. However, the person spoke to him with a coded name and it would have been sensible for him to leave a trusted individual in the state house to report things to him.

Jamal also pulled out a pistol. As he held it, he had another flashback. His mind went back to the day when he was officially leaving the house after University. His mother had helped him pack and even given him blankets and other household items. When the car was parked his father took a walk with him into the back garden.

They had a chat and Jamal was told how proud he had made his family. His father told him to work hard and not get distracted when he began his new life before giving him a pistol. He was told to only use guns for self-defense and not to settle personal scores. His father explained that a young man with a job can easily become a target for bandits. Jamal immediately came out of the memory because there was a loud noise.

He blinked several times to try and relieve himself of his headache. Once he completed this exercise, he noticed that his cellphone rang once more. He lifted it hesitantly however was relieved to find that it was from a number saved in his phonebook. It was the security guard in his home asking when he and his wife would return because they had some visitors. Jamal told him that they were on their way back before he turned his cellphone off. He now knew that it was true, The Raven had saved his life.

He quickly locked up the building before making his way back to the car park with his duffle bags. He found Shahad where he left her, she hadn't moved a muscle. As soon as he re-entered the vehicle she stepped hard onto the accelerator and raced past the guard.

"Where are we going to now?" Jamal asked his wife with her eyes firmly on the road. There was nothing that was going to distract Shahad and he realized that he needed to limit his questions for her.

"You gave me a map with a location that I have put into the GPS. I do not know what is there or who, but you said that the people will help us to finalize our evacuation. This map was given to me about a week before you were shot. You had become very different, spending more time at home and constantly communicating with the kids. You spoke about our escape constantly, which is why when you were shot, I thought that it was done by the state. I never left you alone with anyone from the government because of this reason," Shahad explained and while doing so Jamal was immediately filled with regret with how he treated her in the hospital. He wanted to be left alone in the hospital but she didn't leave his side.

Jamal thanked her for protecting his life. When she explained that it would be a two-hour drive to the destination, he decided to close his eyes and get some rest. He didn't know what to expect from the people who they were going to see. He started to wonder if he wasn't the man that he had thought he was. Only someone with enemies in the state would plan to leave without informing any of his colleagues.

Chapter 34

More Kidnappings

AFTER THE SUCCESSFUL KIDNAPPING of the school children Abaeze knew that his group had to be prepared to do whatever it took to get money. The militia needed to be able to afford to buy weapons, feed their families and work towards emancipating Nigeria from the corrupt imperialists who would sell their country's resources cheaply so that they could feed their greed. The politicians who would do anything so that they could continue to buy expensive American cars and European wine all the while millions of their citizens suffered.

Abaeze could no longer stand back and watch this happen, that was why he didn't care if Boko Haram were referred to as a terrorist organization. He knew the truth and was so focused on establishing a Caliphate in Nigeria. He knew that it could take several years to achieve but they were making so much progress. He felt no ill will towards the methods that were used to obtain finance because they seldom troubled dedicated Muslims. They focused on expatriates, rich non-Muslim Nigerians and western influenced Nigerian Muslims.

The Boko Haram militants stayed in the vehicles outside the Chinese owned gemstone mine. They had sent a young boy to scout and report to them the situation in the mine using a walkie-talkie. The boy explained that he could see that there were still works being done in the night. Abaeze smiled and thought that was a good thing about most Chinese, they worked very late into the night.

Abaeze decided that entering the mine was feasible, but very risky. There were guards throughout the place and with panic buttons it wouldn't be long until reinforcements were brought in to combat any threat. A lot of Boko Haram militants were rotting in jail because of attempting such operations. Even though they were well armed they needed to be smarter than those who led the struggle before them.

Therefore, they intended to follow the first three vehicles that came out of the mine. The Chinese expatriates' movements had been tracked for the last few weeks. The trend was that these guys usually went straight to the casino so it would be easier to snatch them along the way than to go into the mine all guns blazing. It was a priority to minimize casualties, it had always been his main goal whenever embarking on any mission. He cherished his men and that was why he was always willing to exchange hostages for Boko Haram prisoners whenever they got hold of a government soldier or police officer.

Abaeze's plan was for them to demand fifty thousand dollars for each of the expatriates that they managed to capture. The ransom would be payable in cash by the end of the week otherwise the Chinese miners would be beheaded and their headless bodies would be sent back to the mine. He didn't give people too much time to find the money because the longer they kept them, the more things that could go wrong.

The boy informed them on the walkie-talkie that he had seen Asian men leaving the mine at the same time. He also alerted to the fact that each of them was driving themselves. Abaeze was delighted to hear this; it meant that they wouldn't have to deal with any overzealous drivers who might have wanted to go out of their way to protect their employers.

Just like clockwork the five Chinese employees drove away from the mine. Abaeze's car remained hidden in the bush and he joined the trail after the last four-by-four raced passed them. The militants kept a safe distance and once they were five minutes before the main road the other militants who had stayed by the main road used their cars to block the exit to the road. As the Chinese tried to reverse, they found that Abaeze's group was blocking them from doing so. They hooted and raved their cars aggressively, it was possible that at that point they were not fully aware that their lives were in serious danger.

Abaeze and two others of his militias came out of their respective cars and pointed their weapons at the china-men. Each was forced out of their cars until it was established that they had collected five expatriates. The five Chinese miners screamed and yelled. They even tried to fight off the militias but were beaten with the guns until they stopped resisting. Abaeze decided that they would take four and leave one of them. Once this was done, he told some of his men to take the five new cars. They would be taken to garages, get spray painted and then sold on the black market. The lucky china man who was spared started running back towards the mine as Abaeze and his men cruised off into different directions.

They wanted the fifth china man to go and relay what had happened to his supervisors and the police. Abaeze sat in the car with one of the Chinese men and this individual started to urinate in his pants. He knew who he was dealing with and couldn't control himself. They already informed the fifth expatriate that the price was fifty thousand dollars per individual if he wanted to see his friends again. They would be told where to take the money and when. For now, they needed to simply collect the funds because Abaeze wouldn't allow for any delays.

The Chinese workers were all held at different locations in solitary confinement. They would be deprived of food and water for two days then they would be recorded and told to beg their colleagues to find the money. This recording would be couriered to the mine however there would be no instruction on where to send the money. The request for funds would come on the third day with a new video of them being beaten.

One of the soldiers would wait at the mine, take and count the fifty thousand dollars before leaving. After an hour one of their colleagues would be dropped and this process would be repeated until all four men were returned. The local police would be given five thousand dollars as a token for not being overzealous; the money would be dropped anonymously but they knew the drill. Kidnappings of this nature were performed on a weekly basis. They needed cash and it was a low-cost business that brought about big returns. Abaeze knew that Nigeria was filled with wealthy people, both local and foreign. All they had to do was be careful and the needed cash would always be there to fund their missions.

Chapter 35

Darkness before the Dawn

OLIVIER'S MORNING BEGAN at four am; he always woke up without his alarm. He got up and his wife grunted when he turned on the lamp. He ignored her complaints about the light because she was just going to go back to sleep after he left. Vivienne would stay in their bed until eleven, at which point she would have breakfast in bed. He knew her daily schedule and was disgusted by it. He literally became squeamish on the days he worked from home and was forced to observe it. Ever since the children grew up and she was no longer required to prepare them for school Vivienne no longer saw the point in getting out of bed early.

When the children left the house, Olivier felt like his wife had lost the will to live. She didn't have energy to do anything productive and complained about every little thing. She could go on for hours about something as simple as the grass not being cut. Fortunately for him he only had to listen to her complaints at the end of his day. His mind had become numb to them a long time ago. He would sit and block out her words and think about how work was going while she rambled on and on in a semi-hysterical manner. All she required was for him to say "I agree" at the end of whatever it is she had to say.

Vivienne would only get dressed before noon if she was due to have lunch with one of her friends or relatives. If she had no lunch plans, then she would walk around the house giving advice to the gardeners in her dressing gown. If she was feeling lonely then she would drive up to see her parents. Vivienne had put on a lot of weight during their marriage, especially after she gave birth to a boy. It was as if having a son was her surety that Olivier would never leave her so she no longer had to put in much effort. She would constantly complain about her weight yet took no effort to deal with it. On the rare occasion that she would attempt to take a diet, it would never last more than a month. Olivier made as much noise as possible when he got up to run, in the hope that he would inspire his spouse.

After the realization that he would be exercising alone, yet again, Olivier put on his running shoes and turned off the lamp before making his way downstairs. At a young age he had realized the importance of regular exercise; it not only helped to fight off illnesses, but also was when he practiced making speeches. He thought of different scenarios and would practice what he would say, not only to the public but in response to political opponents and to the media. During his running he would also conduct business planning in his head. He was constantly balancing the state affairs of Katanga and his business interests simultaneously because both were equally important and required an effort to maintain their rapport. Politics required money to sustain oneself through the expensive campaign process. Business in Congo required political affiliation if one was to excel all the way to the top. The business was good for his political career and politics was good for his business prospects.

He made his way out of the main house, but stopped in his stride when he noticed that the cottage lights were on suggesting that Sunshine was awake. He thought about ignoring her and proceeding on his route but couldn't move. It was peculiar that his sister would be awake at four in the morning because even his guards were snoring in the guard house. His curiosity led him to go and knock on the door to find out. He hoped that something wasn't the matter and assumed that it was some sort of health matter that awoke his sister

The door was unlocked, and Sunshine announced that he could enter. When he entered the room, he realized that his sister was not only awake, but also fully dressed for work. She was sitting on the desk and reading through some of his business textbooks while she took notes in a booklet. He asked her what she was doing up because she hadn't even started school yet, he couldn't imagine that anything had been assigned to her via email.

She said that if he was able to achieve all of his success through books then she would keep reading and studying until she did the same because she knew that they were both village children. Sunshine told him that she used to think that only people with rich parents or white skin could become successful, but he had proved that theory incorrect. She also showed admiration for the fact that he exercised, he could decipher in her questions about his routine that she would soon follow his example. Olivier knew that when a person had admiration for another, then they would do whatever their hero did so that they could also have the things that their hero had. At first Olivier was cautious that Sunshine would experience dystopia but the determination that he saw indicated to him that she didn't harbour any resentment towards their different life journeys.

He smiled at her before saying that if she worked hard then there would be nothing that she couldn't achieve. Olivier retreated out of the door because he didn't want to disturb her any longer. He felt that he had found a driven woman in his life that he could mentor; Sunshine was determined not to be his dependent for long. Her seeing Olivier as a steppingstone was exactly the very attitude that he hoped to instill in her.

He left that room, elated, before embarking on an hour long run. After only a few minutes into his run something felt different, Olivier realized that he was extremely nervous. This time round he jogged with fear in his heart because he was out in the open. Since the assassination attempt, he had tried his best to move around with protection, either a firearm on him or an armed guard close by. Anyone could attack him with ease and his schedule was well known throughout Katanga. He constantly mentioned the importance of regular exercise whenever asked about his lifestyle. During his campaigns he would invite citizens to run with him before providing water at the end of the course. These small marathons were an opportunity for him to show off how fit he was to the public.

He didn't practice any speeches during this particular run and only stopped looking over his shoulder when he diverted from his usual course. His stomach was churning throughout it all.

After his run he reached home as the sun was beginning to rise. He walked towards the gym that was next to the cottages and could see that his sister was still at work with the books. In the gym he wasn't as focused on weightlifting as he was on general fitness. He ensured that he did a complete workout, exercising his back, shoulders, triceps, abs and legs as much as he did for his triceps.

He put the news on the television and the headline was that the international community would be deploying an army of health workers into Liberia, Guinea and Sierra Leone. The initiative was being led by the United States. This pleased him. He had barely done any Ebola related work while he was there since his focus was on his sister. When the clock reached six, he decided to cut his workout short. He wanted to start bright and early because he could only imagine how the work had piled up on his desk.

After his cold shower he made himself a vegetarian breakfast. Tomatoes, onions, lettuce, brown bread and mangoes were on his menu. While he munched, he wondered why he couldn't completely commit to this healthy lifestyle. The rest of his meals were with a lot of meat and alcohol. He knew that the older he got, the more committed he would be to the health regime. He had a lot to live for and hoped to contribute his part to lengthening his life whilst knowing that ultimately his future was in God's hands.

His driver was waiting next to his car when he walked out. The driver went on to check the car for any bombs or tracking devices. Olivier had ordered some new bomb detecting equipment from Japan that had arrived two days before he returned home. The new protocol would be for the car to be screened every time that Olivier was about to jump in, even if he just stopped at a gas station. He and his driver were also going to be armed at all times. He was comforted by the fact that he was in his stronghold, but knew better then to become complacent because of this. People could be bought and almost anyone could be used to betray him.

Jean Claude drove in and was surprised that he was being forced to stop at the gate. The guards would inspect everyone and their vehicles before allowing them into his house, even the familiar faces. He didn't apologize to his colleague when he was finally let in and guided the man to his sister's cottage. Sunshine was very enthusiastic and Jean Claude was joking with her quite a lot. It seemed like they were both determined to make this work for Olivier's benefit. He told Jean Claude and Sunshine to go inside and have some breakfast as he was already on his way out.

The car ride was quite fast, the benefit of leaving the house early was that you got to beat most of the traffic. Olivier received a warm reception from his staff members when he entered the office. He was pleased that they were on time and they must have been grateful that they didn't slack off while the boss was away. As expected, his desk was full of files and documents that needed his approval, however it was much less than if the Deputy hadn't stepped in.

Only twenty minutes after Olivier reached his government office, his receptionist busted through his door. The lady was out of breath but eventually informed him that the police were there to arrest him. Olivier looked up at her in horror but had to think fast. He got onto the phone to inform the Deputy Governor that he would need to do his work for him until he sorted out the problem. His Deputy was home as he was meant to embark on his leave of absence since he had been working hard while Olivier was away.

His Deputy was extremely loyal and obedient; he seldom spoke and was almost the complete opposite to Olivier. His Deputy lived off politics and didn't have any other major business interests. However, this man lived a simple life and wasn't about the glamor which led Olivier to believe that the man's lack of entrepreneurship wouldn't lead him to pilfering public funds. After the call Olivier could hear loud voices just outside his office door.

Without hesitation the police burst into his office authoritatively and he knew that their orders came from the very top. It was unlikely that they could be so arrogant on their own initiative. He also noticed that there were a few officers from the anti-corruption agency. The gentlemen stood still in his office as if they were waiting for someone and they refused to answer questions when Olivier's staff asked them why they were there. Olivier stood up, not for any particular reason but just so that he could not only see who was coming in through the reception but also how his staff members were being treated during this impromptu visit from the police.

The idea that they were waiting for someone was completely justified when the journalists came through his door with the cameramen. "Is the President really going to embarrass me on national television?" he thought to himself. Olivier hadn't instigated any conflict with regards to the assassination attempt yet this level of tomfoolery was definitely a game changer. The senior officer stepped forward as the cameras were rolling. "Mr.

Olivier Katanga, I am here to arrest you pending suspicions that there has been mass abuse of office by yourself since your appointment as Governor of the Katanga region," the officer issued him with the summons while the cameras ensured that the nation saw everything.

Olivier didn't try to fight the process and was prepared to descend into the car quietly until the officer insisted on placing handcuffs on him. This made him extremely angry. Before being sent into the vehicle he told the cameras that his arrest had been politically motivated because he refused to agree to a change in the constitution that will allow the President to run for yet another term.

He also told the media that he had left Congo after an assassination attempt in Kinshasa. The car that exploded was meant to have him sitting in it. The police officer kept shoving him from the media and journalists however he had gotten everything out in the open.

While he sat in the police car, he heard some of the other officers telling the journalists that they needed to cut out Olivier's comments when they air the footage. The senior police officer took a moment in front of the cameras to explain that no one is above the law and that the President was committed to fighting corruption without sparing anyone in his government. He let the public know that the anti-corruption members were in the office exercising their right to search Olivier's office for the incriminating evidence that they knew was residing in there. The police told the public that they had a warrant to search his office and businesses.

Olivier sat silently as he was driven to the police station for questioning. When he arrived, he found another five party members who were suffering the same fate as he was. It was somewhat comforting to know that he wasn't alone.

"President Mbuyi has made it official. He was going to re-contest the Presidency. His first move today was to dictate an injunction banning any party members from contesting the party presidency in anticipation of the upcoming election. Anyone who supports or endorses other candidates will be suspended from the party with immediate effect," Herve informed Olivier as soon as they passed each other in the corridor.

Olivier was impressed with the pace to which Mbuyi was disposing of his enemies. Here in the police station, he was simply pushing party members towards Olivier as they showed growing allegiance by sticking to their principles. Other party members walked into the police station and requested that they should be arrested for supporting Olivier. After an hour of keeping him and his colleagues in a holding cell, Olivier's supporters began to assemble outside of the police station and the protest began.

He was the popular Governor of Katanga, whose surname was changed to Katanga, and he was in a prison in Katanga. The police were straining themselves to dispose of his supporters, but the numbers were ever increasing until it became evident that the police couldn't control the crowd. Some of his supporters began throwing stones at the impounded cars which were parked.

The same senior police officer that had arrested Olivier now looked very worried as he picked up his cellphone and made a call that Olivier couldn't quite hear. When the officer was done, he made his way to the holding cell and told Olivier that he was free to go, but the other party members had to stay. Olivier responded by telling him that he wasn't leaving the police station without all of the party members who had been also arrested without cause. The senior police officer went to make another phone call and Olivier knew that his stance had exalted his status with the members who stood side by side with him in that prison.

The senior police officer returned with four other men who forced Olivier out of the building however he had the opportunity to tell his party members that he would not leave the station until all of them were released.

As Olivier stepped out of the station his supporters began to chant his initials "O. K.,   O. K., We say Yes to OK! All will be OK with O. K.", He walked towards a van and stood on the back of it while his supporters looked on excitedly. They were anticipating instructions from their leader. Olivier asked for a megaphone and realized that his arrest was an opportunity for a free rally. Usually during a rally, he would need to spend money providing transport for his many followers, but this time they were already assembled. There were about two hundred people in the crowd, mixed ages and sexes. He cleared his voice to speak and in the corners of his eyes he could see cameras filming him, but he remained focused on the crowd.

"When I was in Kinshasa, I met with President Mbuyi who told me that he wanted to run for another illegal term in office. I reminded the President that the Democratic Republic of Congo not only had the word democratic in its name, but was also a real democracy. I refused to support his decision and told him that the party needed to go to a convention to choose a new party president. The President went on to threaten me. By the grace of God, I left my car moments before a bomb was set off. This was a deliberate attempt on my life. I carried on to West Africa to contribute my brainpower to the fight against Ebola that our brothers and sisters are struggling with. I returned to Congo yesterday and this morning I have been arrested without cause. Now we cannot leave this place until all of the party members who were arrested for supporting democracy are also freed. There are strong, intelligent men and women in that police station whose only crime is that they respect the wishes of the Congolese people and refuse to follow that dictator on his path of destruction!"

There was an almighty roar from the crowd as his supporters responded with enthusiasm to his impromptu speech. The journalists who came to his office would have cut out his negative comments when he spoke out against the President, but the ones who were in attendance at the police station were independent. He also saw a number of cellphones in the air filming him during his address.

While Olivier continued making speeches on the platform his bodyguard asked him to come off the platform as the crowd began to get rowdy. As he came down, his bodyguard pulled him aside and informed him that the president of ADD, Congo's largest opposition party, had been killed. The official report that came from Kinshasa was that there was a carjacking. Only Pierre was killed, but his driver and the man's family was spared. President Mbuyi had just conveyed his condolences on radio, but large numbers of ADD supporters were said to be moving towards Kinshasa.

The news travelled quickly throughout the crowd who now felt that they needed to force their way into the police station so as to prevent political assassinations from happening to the members that were still being held inside. Suddenly there was a surge of one hundred supporters who were running into the police station through all of the entry points. Police officers were being beaten and the senior officer quickly opened the cell that was holding the political prisoners. Once they were out the senior officer locked himself in the cell for protection from the mob.

The party members were carried towards Olivier and he waved to thank his supporters. His personal vehicles came into view and he entered one of them before they all went to his home. The party members had a working lunch there as they discussed their strategy.

Chapter 36

Help is on the Way

JERRY MACDONALD and the other medical soldiers, as they were calling themselves, attended a lengthy debriefing. The initial point that was stressed at great lengths was the need for them to prioritize their own safety upon arrival in West Africa. They were told to wear gloves throughout their time there and to wash their hands with disinfectant whenever they were forced to remove them.

Another point was that there was mistrust between the local people and foreign health workers because some factions in the communities believed that the Westerners were the ones who brought the virus to Africa. They were informed of the procedure that they should take if they felt any of the symptoms. Basically, isolation was the only remedy and any infection would mark the end of the trip for that individual.

Interestingly enough there was mention on the fact that they would be stigmatized when they got back by their friends and neighbors. People would be highly reluctant to interact with them and this shouldn't be a surprise when they did return. If they needed to talk about the negatives then a list of qualified psychiatrists would be passed along to help them through public rejection at the end of their tenure.

Jerry was disappointed that the "medical soldiers" were banned from taking alcohol or products that had caffeine during their time in West Africa. They were expected to rest whenever they were tired instead of using products to stimulate their energy. Jerry walked away with the pamphlets and brochures as he made his way to the plane. He was going to be deployed to Sierra Leone. The only thing that he knew about that country was that diamonds came from there and there had been a civil war that surrounded that same commodity. The fighting had come to a halt as far as Jerry was concerned, but this Ebola epidemic would worsen their economic woes for years to come.

He didn't know anyone on the same route as his. Many of his other colleagues would be deployed whenever they were called, but he was the first of his peers to be summoned. On the flight he found himself chatting with a middle-aged lady, she wasn't going to be on the field, but would be a medical consultant for the local government.

She explained that she would only be there for two weeks before returning, he wondered whether or not such consultants were a waste of resources. He thought that video conferencing was the cheaper option yet appreciated everyone's bravery. They had all been instructed to put their affairs in order prior to departure and most had said goodbye to their families as if they would never see them again. Despite Jerry's commitment to serving his country and fellow man he did wonder about the logic of leaving his wife. Was his embarking on this mission truly worth the risk of leaving behind his loved ones? He decided there and then that this mission would be his last, he would never leave his family again.

Chapter 37

The Escape

JAMAL'S WIFE SLOWED THE CAR as they approached a building that was several miles off the main road. She didn't question the GPS even though they were in a secluded area and this worried her. She parked next to the complex as they both realized why they were guided to that location. There was a makeshift airstrip and a huge hut that was probably storing an airplane or helicopter. Both of them were extremely relieved to know that they would be flying out of the country.

Shahad admitted that she wasn't sure what to do next, getting to the site was the last stage in Jamal's previous explanation. Jamal opened his duffle bag and searched through the items one by one, hoping that something would come to mind. He was nervous about entering that building because he didn't know who was inside. During a civil war friends and enemies were ever changing.

He found himself holding up the fake Zambian passport and wondered why this country was chosen. He closed his eyes and was immediately confronted by another flashback. He could remember going to Zambia and this time he remembered the timeframe. It was a few months before he was shot. Jamal had gone there to meet his son, who had settled temporarily in that country.

His son was on a contract in the Zambian capital city of Lusaka. He was flying charter planes for big mining executives, politicians and the wealthiest tier of the business community. Jamal remembered one afternoon when he ventured into the Matero district, which wasn't the best neighborhood, and paid a man, named Isaac Mwaanga, to create the passports for himself and his wife. Isaac had a connection in the Home Affairs department who could produce the passports within a day. Jamal had encouraged the urgency by only paying Isaac twenty percent of the agreed fee when they met with the promise to pay the balance upon completion.

When the passports were in his possession Jamal went on to transfer money to his son's Zambian bank account to be kept in savings in case of any emergency. Jamal knew how responsible his offspring was and had full confidence that the money wouldn't be misused or even withdrawn at all.

Finally, he recalled instructing his son to use some of the money to buy a house on his behalf. Jamal realized that everything was in place as he opened his eyes once more, but this time to his surprise he didn't have a headache. There was a fury of memories that rushed into his head all at once and the last was that Jamal had met with the major opposition in Syria. He had secret talks with them and was working behind the scenes to betray the incumbent regime.

Jamal now knew that he had been to that facility before. It was where the opposition was camped, and he had held many a meeting there in the past. He opened his mouth to inform Shahad of all that he now knew but before he had the chance, he looked through her window and realized that there were armed men who were surrounding the car.

They were told to exit the vehicle by a man Jamal recognized, Khalid El Faziz, who was the figurehead leader of the Democratic Movement. He looked at Shahad and told her that it was okay because he knew who those men were. This comment did little to ease her nerves. She wasn't completely confident in her husband's military abilities since the memory loss; before she would never doubt his decision making.

The armed men brushed them off and checked the baggage for weapons. Jamal's gun was immediately confiscated, but while they searched, he began to explain himself to his comrade. He knew that it would be difficult to confess to these people that his memory of them had only just returned but he had to try; if not for him, then to just secure Shahad's safety.

"Khalid, I have come to you because my wife and I need to evacuate Syria and travel to Zambia. It has to happen tonight because the President knows that I betrayed him to a Western journalist, we cannot stay here!" Jamal responded aggressively while he was thrust against the car and handcuffed by the armed guards who wore balaclavas. Khalid scratched his chin for a few seconds as if he was contemplating what to do next before he cleared his voice and responded.

"General Jamal, your wife will leave but you are staying here with us. A leader doesn't abandon his followers. We have sacrificed a lot for you," Khalid responded coldly as if he had a lot of resentment. He ordered one of the guards to awaken the pilot who was fast asleep inside the hostel. Shahad began to cry and kept refusing to leave without him.

Jamal was flattered but noticed Khalid shaking his head from side to side to show that his mind was set. The General was relieved because all of his family would be far away from the fighting. Now he could focus his energies on fulfilling his obligations to the opposition before he too would take a one-way ticket away from his beloved country. He knew that in that moment Khalid's stance was made more out of frustration out of being ignored over the weeks than because Jamal truly needed to stay. But nonetheless Jamal was not in a position to negotiate.

When the pilot eventually came, he walked straight to the small plane and turned it on. Shahad kept trying to push off the guards until Jamal walked up to her. He gave his wife a tender kiss before telling her that she should not disobey him.

"You need to leave and be safe. I will join you when the right opportunity comes but for now give me peace of mind by cooperating. We will be together again soon my dear," he whispered in her ear in case the soldiers expected him to stay in Syria for good. His wife wept loudly but obeyed him. Her luggage and documentation were carried by one of the soldiers.

Jamal's eyes remained fixed on the plane until it took off. When he felt certain that she was safe he turned around to face the music. There was complete silence as the guard removed his handcuffs and all the men walked into the building.

Chapter 38

The Business of Terrorism

ABAEZE'S PLAN had worked perfectly. He had received the money and had shared some of the spoils among his devoted comrades. They were not to live materialistic lives but due to their courage he wanted to reward them. The rest of the money was going to the important activities that would allow the organization to not only survive but also grow.

He was deep in the bush at the site where the American businessman, Mark Thomson, would drop his airplane and sell them state of the art weapons. He hated everything about Mark from his white skin to the smug look on his face whenever he received money. If there was any other way, then Abaeze would take it but there wasn't. Mark was the most efficient gun-runner he knew and the man didn't care about who he was supplying.

This man was very busy. Abaeze knew that his ISIS colleagues in Syria also bought their weapons through Mark not to mention Hezbollah and the Free Syrian army. When the plane landed Mark walked out coolly with dark sunglasses on. He nodded at Abaeze and he returned the gesture before stepping into the plane to analyze the stock.

Mark had only brought two types of guns, he had AK-47s and M16s, that was it. This disappointed Abaeze because he wanted some pistols for the guys to carry around when they walked the towns in civilian clothing. Nonetheless he knew that Mark's guns seldom got jammed and were state of the art so he reserved his complaints.

The box of AK-47's had sizes along them that were not for weapons. The descriptions showed the sizes for clothing and when Abaeze opened the top one, he had to remove the packaged clothing before he could view the inventory that he really came to see. Mark was very careful and hid his weapons deep in the boxes in case of issues with customs when he was flying in the various air zones.

The M16's were lighter guns which he thought the child soldiers could use whilst the AK-47's were over four kilograms so he knew that the bigger boys and the men could carry them. The M16 could fire more rounds so he knew that in a battle he would send the child soldiers in first to cause maximum damage before the men went in.

He stepped back out to see Mark and to hear the prices before he placed his order. Mark informed him that this time the prices were non-negotiable because he had a big order to fulfill on his next stop to the Middle East. The AK-47s were 160 dollars per unit and the M16's were 700 dollars per unit. Abaeze would have definitely negotiated because these weapons were not brand new, yet he knew that Mark would go on about his transport costs and paying bribes to state officials in all of the countries that he visited.

Abaeze had forty-five thousand dollars remaining from the ransom and didn't mind spending all of it. They were planning another kidnapping of a wealthy Nigerian businessman for the end of the week. This effort would require a lot of firepower so the guns were an investment for a quick return.

"I will take 150 AK-47's and 25 M16's. This will put my bill at 41,500 dollars, with the remaining five thousand dollars I would like to buy bullets," Abaeze instructed him as he gave Mark the briefcase with the money. Mark's smug look returned to his face before he handed the briefcase to the pilot who would go and count it in the cockpit with their machine.

Abaeze's soldiers removed the boxes and Mark gave him a huge discount on the bullets. After a few minutes the pilot returned and gave Mark thumbs up before Abaeze parted ways with the gun runner. The militia raced back into the bush, delighted with their new stock of weapons.

Chapter 39

Calm Before the Storm

JERRY MACDONALD SPENT his first night in the boarding hostel. He had already been familiarized with his schedule for the next day, but for now he was told to rest, but he couldn't sleep. He battled with insomnia for an hour, at first, he tried to read but got frustrated with his novel after twenty minutes. He listened to music on his MP3 player, but found himself skipping through the tracks until he had gone through all of the songs. He decided that rather than taking sleeping pills, that would make him drowsy the next day, the better option was for him to find a way to pass time.

He found himself climbing down his bunk bed before putting on his tracksuit bottoms. He was surprised that no one else was disturbed by the amount of snoring in the room however the snoring probably drowned out the noise of his movements. He laughed to think that the snoring served some purpose. He exited the room before embarking on his aimless journey into the unfamiliar Sierra Leone streets. He wasn't sure where he was going to go, and this was definitely against the rules as it was way past their curfew. However just like in high school, he was never one to follow all the rules.

He hadn't gone far from the hostel when he was attracted to a construction site because of the floodlights and noise. He strutted towards there as he would have much rather had some human interactions instead of walking along a makeshift road in Sierra Leone. Even a tough guy like him knew better than to go out looking for trouble.

As he approached the site, he realized that the guys who were undertaking the construction were some of his colleagues from the flight. There were also many local builders roaming around also. Nobody stopped Jerry as they must have thought that he belonged, so he acted the part. He grabbed a helmet from the basket and got closer to the main structure.

"What are ya'll building over here?" Jerry quizzed the American builder who stood next to him. It was obvious that Jerry was from the deep south, but this man had a distinct New Yorker accent. Jerry didn't think that this particular man had been on his flight because he was very good at remembering faces and hadn't seen this gentleman before.

"We are building a temporary clinic, let me show you around," the New Yorker responded before he took a large sip of what smelt like coffee. It turned out that Jerry wasn't the only one who wasn't following protocol as caffeine was a red flag. Individuals were meant to rest when they were tired, but this wasn't the American way. Even John F. Kennedy once said, when he was promoting the space mission, that their country was not built by those who rested and waited. This clinic would not have been completed by those who rested and waited either.

Everyone who stepped off that plane to help came with energy to give their very all.

"Over here is where we will store the medicine, everything that is required to counter the effects of the virus obviously because there's no cure. The items that have been stored will just serve to prevent headaches, flu and sore stomachs," the New Yorker said, who at this point revealed that his name was Michael, before he turned on the light bulb. Even though the light was very dim Jerry was able to move around and take it all in. There were shelves stacked with medication for all of the symptoms that Michael had spoken about, however the majority of storage was taken up by the protective suits.

Jerry wondered how he would be able to properly examine a sick person whilst in a suit and goggles. When this question was poised to Michael his response was that it would be suicidal to attend to the patients in any other way. Michael reminded him that this was the fastest spreading Ebola virus in world history, part of the solution was keeping himself safe. Jerry felt like that answer was straight out of the handbook because the reality for medical staff was very different. He didn't want to engage in an argument and neither did Michael as he carried on with the tour.

"Here we have the wards; we expect them to get full pretty fast at daybreak so we also have mattresses that will be laid on the floor. We work with the government to alert the citizens to the fact that there is a new facility so people will know about this place within moments of it being complete." Jerry didn't respond to this but simply gazed around the ward. This room would not have been opened to the public in the States, but due to the time constraint it would have to do.

There was no proper rest room but a basin had been installed where he assumed people could wash their hands. Those who needed the toilet would be taken to the pit latrines; the place was bound to get messy very quickly considering the type of virus that they were dealing with. Ebola caused diarrhea and bleeding which needed to be dealt with using a proper rest room and washing facilities. Jerry was starting to get nervous about what would come the next day.

Michael on the other hand was oblivious to this and continued the tour. As they walked along the wooden floor his tour guide kept telling him that they weren't finished and it would look much better when it was all done. Jerry looked at the time and wondered how drastic a turnaround could take place before daybreak yet said nothing. He was by no means an expert builder so wanted the professional to talk without much interruption.

"Next we have the isolation quarters. We will be separating the patients from each other with the use of curtains however patients will be told not to move from their beds. Individuals who would be in isolation would be extremely infectious. The medical staff on duty is going to have to be very firm about patients remaining on their beds. Finally at the end of the hall is the changing room that is reserved for medical staff.

They can change in and out of their protective equipment with the opportunity to leave their clothing to soak in the disinfecting detergent that will be brought in first thing in the morning. Even when changing you guys will be expected to keep your gloves on throughout it all," Michael concluded as he stood very happy with his team's progress on the construction. The two men began to walk towards the entrance thus ending the tour.

"You guys have gone so far, when are you hoping to complete?" Jerry finally commented as they left the building block and Michael continued to walk towards the exit of the site as if he was now ushering Jerry off of the premises. Jerry had hoped that he could have been allowed to hang around for a bit more because he still wasn't tired. Jerry was more than prepared to offer himself to Michael as extra hands on the project.

"The structure should be completed by five this morning so that it can be opened to the public by six. Then we go off and sleep before starting on another temporary facility about thirty minutes from here. We have to work like the assembly line, that's why you should really be resting before you start your twelve-hour shift." Michael concluded before patting Jerry on the back and requesting that he render his hard hat back. Jerry obliged, but rattled his brain for one last question before departing back to his barracks.

"Why do you build in the night?" Jerry asked as he attempted to prolong their discussion. He dug his shoe into ground and tried to write his initials in the sand. He had developed this habit as a child and just couldn't shake it. Whenever he was about to leave a place, he wrote his signature somewhere like a dog that marked its territory.

"The situation here in Sierra Leone is extremely severe, so if people are not accommodated in our temporary clinics or state hospitals, they may disturb our building process by trying to use our facilities before we are completely finished. Now march back to your barracks soldier, get some rest before tomorrow. You will need it."

As Jerry walked back to the hostel, he looked at his watch once again and counted backwards. His daughter would have been home from school so he pulled his cellphone out of his pocket and began to dial his wife's number. He was nervous about calling his wife because of how he had left things, but knew that maintaining silence would only allow the hostility to perpetuate.

"Hello Betty, I hope that I am not calling at a bad time," Jerry said all at once, his wife responded by explaining that she was so happy to hear from him. She had been worried when he didn't call to let her know that he had arrived safely. He apologized before she allowed him the opportunity to describe how things were. He downplayed everything that was taking place on the ground.

He told her that they were very comfortable in the room and he was sharing with another few people. Jerry went on to say that the medical facilities were of a very high standard and they would only be acting as a vacuum for patients who the hospitals didn't have enough room for. He murmured during his account as he tried to depict his trip to Sierra Leone as a holiday however, he knew that she wasn't totally convinced. They both knew that he was going to say whatever he could to make things better and she did appreciate it. Betty knew that her husband loved his family and his country so she could start to understand the honor behind what he was doing.

When the discussion reached the point of her talking about work, he knew that things had been patched up so he asked to speak to their daughter. Betty went through the house looking for his little girl while the hostel came into Jerry's view. He had left the area via the playground at the back so used it to go back in. He didn't want to be caught breaking the rules on his first night.

He sat on the swings and began to rock back and forth until he heard his daughter's voice.

"Hi Daddy, I already miss you," Amanda said as she usually did whenever he was away. Even though he had heard it before, it always broke his heart to be away from his little girl. He promised himself that he would only spend time away from his family for a meaningful cause, and fighting one of the deadliest viruses of recent times certainly qualified. He told her that he missed her more then she could ever imagine.

"When are you coming home?" She asked innocently. Jerry was taken aback by this because in actual fact he didn't know the answer. Their mandate was to be there until the outbreak was brought under control; there was no timeframe or roadmap for this objective.

"I'll be back as soon as I can sweetheart," Jerry whispered back at her.

Chapter 40

The Cards are on the Table

OLIVIER WAS CONFRONTED by news that he had been temporarily suspended from the ruling party when he lifted up his morning paper. He had received some warnings that this was going to occur from some of his close colleagues; however, he was confident that he was too popular for the central committee to actually do it. This was a bold move and he knew all of the people in that committee. The newspaper article detailed that it was a unanimous decision so Olivier intended on holding a grudge against all of them.

The reason that was cited in the newspaper was that Olivier was suspended pending investigations into misuse of government funds and unethical business practices. The article went on to mention that government contracts in Katanga were awarded based on personal friendships with Olivier and firms were being forced to pay him to be allowed to carry on with their operations. Olivier dropped the paper and picked up his phone to call his lawyer.

The firm that represented him was Aurelie and Company. As soon as he was put through to Aurelie by his receptionist his lawyer informed him that he was up to speed with the newspaper article. He suggested a number of defenses that Olivier could use to fight his suspension. Olivier didn't want to be too impetuous in his decision making however they both agreed on two initial actions. The first thing was for Olivier to deny all of the allegations using the other media houses. The state newspaper published the article so Aurelie would start the legal process of suing them for defamation of character.

Aurelie concluded by telling him not to worry too much and that he would be updated once the papers were served in the courts. Olivier felt better after this chat, his lawyer had gotten him out of a few tight messes in the past, but this time it was different. He was going head-to-head with the country's President in a country where the judiciary was highly flawed. He remained seated in his chair for a few minutes as he reflected on the situation. No more procrastination and picked up his phone once more to make another call. This call was directed to his Chief Executive Officer who had left several messages requesting that they needed to talk immediately.

After only one ring the phone was answered; it was as if his CEO was sitting in the office just waiting to receive the call. Jean Claude didn't waste time with meaningless chit chat and immediately embarked on a series of complaints on their new circumstances. Jean Claude was deeply concerned by the anti-corruption agents who were hounding all of the different companies in the conglomerate. These same agents were also conducting spot checks and audits of compliance to tax laws. Armed policemen were walking around his businesses hovering around workers and the staff members were all very nervous. President Mbuyi's plot was ubiquitous, nothing was spared.

Olivier put the phone down and wondered if the police would do much more. In Katanga province they were constantly requesting donations from him, yet if they were prepared to harass him then they would directly feel the financial implications. He couldn't say all of this to Jean Claude on the phone but there was a good chance that all of this was an opportunity for the parsimonious President, and nothing would materialize. He wanted his Chief Executive Officer and staff to be extra careful until it indeed blew over. From what he knew his companies contributed heavily to the tax base in Katanga, removing them from the economy would directly and indirectly affect thousands of people.

The night before the article was released Jean Claude had spent hours at Olivier's house to discuss the sudden drastic changes to the business. Several things that had often been so easy suddenly became extremely difficult while Olivier was on his West Africa trip. He realized that this would have been very strange for Jean Claude who was unaware of the assassination attempt; Olivier on the other hand had been expecting it from the moment that he reached loggerheads with the President in Kinshasa. Olivier told Jean Claude to carry on as usual, even though he kept stressing that thirty percent of their business had been lost through the cancellation of government contracts.

After his experience at the police station a few days before that Olivier had to spend a lot of time consoling his wife who was devastated to know that there had been an attempt on his life. Vivienne had no idea of the extent to which trouble was brewing because her husband had always preferred to struggle through difficulties alone. His wife demanded that their children should not return and Olivier actually concurred.

His son had been on the phone in tears when he told his father that his peers kept discussing the assassination attempt and the staff members would always break into silence whenever he entered a room. Olivier initially thought that in Europe it would be unlikely that these issues would be in his son's face every day. He had wanted the young man to have space to focus on his academics.

With the death of the main opposition leader and the party suspensions that were being dished out Olivier knew that if Mbuyi won the general election then there would be a lot of uncertainty ahead of him. The intimidation and harassment of his businesses would intensify if the factions knew that Mbuyi would protect them for another term. It was now in Olivier's best interest to ensure that the President was not re-elected, meaning that he needed his own party to lose the election.

Jean Claude decided to leave the office during the raid by state agents and even though Olivier was extremely annoyed by this he was grateful that his CEO chose to hideout with him. Olivier ushered Jean Claude to the lounge room, and they shut the door to indicate to Vivienne and the workers that they didn't want to be disturbed.

He sat with a long-faced Jean Claude while he turned on the television. There was a parliamentary session in process. The speaker announced that the topic would be the installation of an amendment to the constitution, allowing for a fourth term to the position of President. Olivier sat in his robe and stared on in fear. He knew that they had a majority in parliament and suspensions of key players such as himself would ensure that the MP's who were in attendance would be inclined to follow out of fear.

The President had achieved a majority in parliament by appointing opposition members to ministerial positions so that they crossed the floor. Those who accepted these postings would have to change their party membership. He had weeded out those non-dedicated opposition members by offering jobs and the incentives that came with them. The opposition members of parliament who weren't offered jobs would have been threatened, bribed or both to ensure that this amendment passed in the house by a two thirds majority.

Olivier stayed glued to the screen throughout the parliamentary session until the amendment passed, as he knew it would, but hoped that it wouldn't throughout the process. President Mbuyi's plan had worked, and Olivier knew that the man would win the national election.

With the opposition left without much time to promote a new candidate and his internal rivals squashed the odds were in Mbuyi's favor and this saddened Olivier. The television was turned off and both men sat in silence until his friend tried to break the ice. Jean Claude explained that Olivier's sister was working very hard in the spare parts shop as if to tell his friend that not all had been lost. They discussed the hardships that would come during the next seven years if Mbuyi won the election and looked at focusing more on their businesses that were outside of Congo.

Olivier said that there was an urgent need to move their heavy machinery and cash to Zambia, Botswana and South Africa. He also concluded by saying that their business headquarters would have to move to Nigeria after the election so Jean Claude needed to prepare his family to move. Olivier would find a manager to control what was left of their local business, which wouldn't be much.

After a few minutes Olivier's cellphone began to ring and this immediately interrupted his chain of thought. His anonymous caller alerted him to the fact that there were protests that were sparking on a nationwide scale following the installation of the fourth term. Different stakeholders were mobilizing themselves to go out and protest against Mbuyi. This movement was going to be massive from the information that he had on the ground.

Olivier was also told that a large group of over a thousand people were headed to his home where they would demand that he contests for the party Presidency. After this statement the unknown caller hung up his phone without allowing Olivier a chance to ask any questions.

Olivier knew better then to doubt such information because his private number wasn't publicly available. Whoever had it in such short notice was probably in a good position to be a credible source. He told Jean Claude about the call in short detail before instructing him to go back to the office. As his CEO grabbed his keys and dashed out of the house Olivier moved just as fast when he ran up the stairs and into the shower. Vivienne followed him up and asked what all of the commotion was about as she entered the bathroom but left shortly after he told her to get dressed before the press arrived.

He took time to shower and shave. He wanted to look his best for the media that were on their way to his home. If there was really going to be adrenaline against the President, then he had to be in the best light and all signs of his hangover needed to be eradicated. Politics was a fascinating game. He went to bed feeling unhappy with his life, after breakfast he was miserable and now as it approached lunch, he was excited for what would come next.

Chapter 41

Life of a Prisoner

MOHAMMAD WALKED onto the grounds staring at the brick fence. He hadn't been allowed to leave the premises since his declaration that he wanted to resign. His boss spoke to him extremely harshly whenever rendering instruction. Throughout the day Mohammad slipped into a deep depression and had lost the will to live. He constantly contemplated different ways to escape.

Tariq dropped off some textbooks and took the risk of confiding in him. "What you need to do Mohammad is self-educate yourself. You will only be allowed to leave the compound to write examinations. You were not very smart in how you talked to the boss." Mohammad couldn't help but release a large sigh, "Tariq. What am I going to do? I am not even allowed to interact with the maids. I am not even allowed to speak to any of the females on the property. The male staff members won't even associate with me. It is like the word of my dispute has travelled to all sections of the compound.

It was clear to everyone that Mohammad's boss wanted to make an example of him to everyone. He wanted his workers to become more grateful for the comfortable conditions and to let them know that no one would be leaving. They were a family and only Mr. Hussein would decide who stayed and who got to leave.

Mohammad rubbed his tired face. "Tariq. Have you seen Yasmina?" Mohammad suspected that she had been handed over to be one of the wives to the man who raped her. But he had hoped that this wasn't the case, he naively still had ambitions to marry her. Tariq responded to his question with a hard stare which suggested that their conversation was over.

Mohammad's duties had also been increased from being a houseboy to now being a gardener as well as handyman. His work schedule ran throughout the day and the only break he had was at night when he was also expected to be studying. As he swept the lawn and looked to the sky, he thought about Azmina.

His biggest regret was not resisting her charms because before that at least he was in control of his life. He could go to work and had the option to leave. He had friends in the compound where he lived before moving into Omar's house and even though they were very poor he had fond memories. When there was no fighting in the streets Mohammad and his friends would use plastic bags to create a football that they would kick around for a few minutes on the weekends.

He and his friends also cooked food on the fire at night and chatted about stories. Some of the tales were funny, some were sad but at least he wasn't lonely. Now he wondered if he would ever be happy again. He continued to sweep by the fence while he sang quietly to himself. He dropped the broom as he noticed unevenness on the wall. Something didn't seem quite right, and his heart was racing as he thought about whether or not to investigate it.

He looked around to see if anyone was watching him and when it became evident that the coast was clear he knelt down on his knees and touched the bricks. Six bricks were loose and could be removed. He knew that this had been done deliberately because if the loose bricks were removed then an adult's body could be sneaked in and out of the grounds.

Mohammad stood up, lifted the broom, and walked back towards the servant's quarters as he whistled. "How long had the bricks been loose? Who else knows about them? Was this an opportunity or some sort of a trap?" His mind swirled with fear and anticipation.

Chapter 42

Zambian Refuge

JAMAL'S WIFE SHAHAD was met at Lusaka's International Airport by her son, Karim, who was her last born. Karim waved with a huge grin from behind the fence as his mother walked along the gravel strip. Karim was given special permission to be there as other passengers would only be received in the arrivals section. Even though his mother smiled at him she did not look well. Shahad had been thinking about Jamal's wellbeing throughout her journey, not to mention the fear that she had whenever the airport's officers would look through her passport at all of the various stops along the way.

She had gone relatively unnoticed and as she filled in her immigration form, she ticked the box that wrote returning citizen. The home address that she filled in was on the piece of paper that her husband put into the passport before he was hospitalized. The wait for her bag was frustrating her, but Karim was allowed into the terminal. She watched as all of the staff greeted her son as he made his way towards her.

He gave her a long hug, "Mother, I haven't seen you for so long. You look so exhausted." He whispered as he held her tightly. He could feel her shivering with emotional exhaustion. "I have decided against returning to Syria until the darn Civil War is over."

Karim had been encouraging his parents to leave the country, yet with his father's high position it meant that his hopes were very unrealistic. He celebrated in his own heart that his mother was now here. He hoped to show her what her life could be like in Zambia so that she would consider staying permanently. He didn't want to separate his parents but had sleepless nights whenever he saw photographs of the situation back in Syria.

"Tell me mother, where is father and what is the media not telling us?"

"Son, your father's life is in the hands of Allah" she whispered under her breath as she waited for the luggage.

Her bag eventually came, and the customs officers didn't bother to stop them. This was probably because it was wrapped and had padlocks on all the zippers. His mother went through the Ebola checks before she could leave. She was baffled by this because there were no known Ebola cases in Syria.

When they stepped out a gentleman asked to trolley her luggage, when the bags were placed the man hurried towards the designated staff parking area as he was familiar with Karim. As they strolled to the car Karim noticed how his mother was shaking frantically yet it was such a sunny day.

"The children are in school as well as my wife so you will see everyone only in the evening. Dad bought the house next to mine and there is only a small fence separating the two so you will have your privacy yet can walk in and out of my house," Karim mentioned to try and spread some joy yet he knew that a lot more was required for her to cheer up.

"Thank you, Karim, I don't want you to think that I don't appreciate all that you did to ensure that we could come here. I am just worried about your father; he was kidnapped before we left yet the captors allowed me to proceed. They could be torturing him or he could be dead for all that I know," she said as the tears rolled down her face. Karim didn't respond right away. He gave the man some change for assisting him and once they were in the car and buckled up, he held her hand and looked into her eyes sympathetically.

"One thing that we both know about the man is that General Jamal Ahmed is a soldier. He is indestructible and always thinks several moves beyond his opponents. He always finds a way out," Karim responded before driving out.

As they left the airport grounds there was traffic build up in Avondale, which is the first major suburb after the airport. His mother seemed oblivious to this as she stared out of the window. When they passed the Nkholoma Stadium Karim decided that he would take her for lunch in Longacres, which was about ten minutes from where they lived in Ibex. The restaurant he decided on served gourmet Indian food and he thought that this would be as close to Syrian food as she would get for a while.

Chapter 43

Memory Fully Restored

ONCE INSIDE a light was turned on. Most of the men were sleeping on the floor and they were awoken in a respectful manner. This led General Jamal to believe that they were prominent individuals but for the moment he only remembered Khalid's name; the rest were on the tip of his tongue, but he couldn't quite get them over the line. A seat was placed for him to sit on as all eyes were on him. Khalid looked furious before he opened the discussion.

"What type of leader are you? We have not been given any further instructions since the assassination attempt. We have been left in the cold and I have kept things going without you. We assumed that you would communicate with us when you recovered, yet you are only doing your work with that wicked regime. Many of our members are questioning whether or not you are still with us or you have now defected back. I have been defending you, but now you come here and try to use the evacuation plan without any explanation. We are risking our lives for you!" Khalid yelled at the top of his voice. Most of the members had been caught up to speed as whispers circulated the room. They unanimously agreed with Khalid and his anger was shared throughout the room.

"Khalid, I remember your face and your name, but haven't a clue where from or even what you are talking about," this response from General Jamal caused a lot of murmuring by those who were seated there and he could see the horror on the faces of the gentlemen. Jamal tried to reassure the group that he was suffering from memory loss and his recollection came at an irregular, sluggish pace.

A gentleman rose and introduced himself to Jamal as Nadir. As soon as Jamal heard this name, he was hit with a recollection that only increased the more that Nadir spoke. This time his eyes remained open as his mind connected dots rapidly. The only negative effect was that his right eye kept twitching.

Nadir stepped in front of Jamal, "You are the leader of the Movement for Democracy; our intention is to overthrow the government via a political coup because all other dialogue has been exhausted. We were weeks away from commencing our plan to kidnap President Abd al-Uzza and replacing him with you to hold the position until a general election could take place. You have been protecting us from government attacks. However, to many of us it seems like you are pretending to have suffered from memory loss because you are now afraid of carrying out the operation." As soon as Nadir finished giving his account the final pieces of Jamal's memory returned.

He had started the Movement for Democracy when the President refused to concede defeat and the civil war began. He placed Khalid as the figurehead, yet he was the real leader of the party. Khalid was building national support and Jamal stayed in the government to not only protect them but to also divert state resources to sustain them. They had lost comrades along the way, but their casualties were much less than other opposition groups.

The Secretary General hated Jamal because he had slept with the man's wife over ten years ago. The President told him to forgive Jamal and instructed them to shake hands. The fact that the President knew about their conflict meant he disregarded everything that the Secretary General said against Jamal and this worked in Jamal's favor over the years.

Jamal was a philanthropist before the civil war began yet everyone's pockets had been squeezed since. He intended to overthrow the government, facilitate the general election, but had no intention to stay. He would ask Khalid to run as their Presidential candidate and when the votes were counted Jamal would hand over the instruments of power before moving to Zambia with his wife to live with their children and grandchildren. Even though he loved his country he would not have peace of mind if he remained there. After a civil war there is blood on everyone's hands.

He would retire to Africa and live a low-key life with Shahad and the rest of his family, at least that was the plan. By the time that Jamal's recollection ended he was filled with the biggest headache that he had ever had. The pain was so severe that he collapsed off the chair and fell to the ground.

When he eventually awoke, he was informed by Khalid that he had been unconscious for the last ten minutes. He arose and immediately knew what he needed to do. He was finally restored to the man that he was, and his vision was clear once again. He was finally certain that every memory leading up to the assassination was restored.

"My comrades, my memory loss was very real. In the hospital I didn't even know who my wife was, I was asking for my parent's because my last memory was graduating from University. However, things started to come back to me at a sluggish pace. Eventually I recognized my children, I was able to perform my job and, in the process, I uncovered that the current regime was going to conduct a mass genocide in the Ar-Raqqah region. Their aim was to attack ISIS, however with the use of chemical weapons then more civilians would get caught up in the crossfire than in a gun battle. I couldn't allow this so intervened and leaked information to the international community. I think you all recall the UN envoy that came to destroy the chemical weapons. My intervention in the process has been revealed to the state, however our friend inside the state house warned me in good time. Raven has proven yet again to be a selfless ally and as long as his identity inside is protected then we still have a lot to be optimistic about. Now that the state is against me, I can come out of the shadows and present myself to the community as the leader of the Movement for Democracy, we can let the people know about the planned attack on Ar-Raqqah and stress that we are not in support of extremist groups. After this last memory recollection, I can see clearly yet again. I now know all your faces and your roles and commend you on holding the fort during my absence; you also did not harm me when you thought that I had defected. Men of your integrity will be integral to the success of the new Syria."

The men cheered and clapped with the same enthusiasm as they would normally do when their leader addressed them. One by one they walked up to him and embraced him as their brother. Jamal was delighted that Shahad was safe, and his children were far away. He hovered over a table and began to discuss the President's usual routine as well as the moments when the man was least protected. The head of their militant wing began to strategize on ways that they could capture the head of state. The revelation that Jamal was a traitor now meant that access to weapons was restricted however their plan was not made with the intention to cause mass bloodshed.

Jamal cleared his throat as he took charge, "The President is well protected during the week, but his security decreases by almost half on Saturday and one third on Sunday. We are going to have to get him on Sunday whether this contradicts some of our religious beliefs or not. He spends the day with his family at their resort which is an hour outside of the capital. The place is spacious with several entry points. The entire area is fenced and there are security cameras however I have identified a blind spot. There is an area where the camera is blocked by a tree and I have marked it on the map. There are dogs on site, but when the family is there the most vicious of these beasts will be locked away. The dogs that will be there will be vicious so will also need to be killed using poison or we will have to shoot them with silencer caps on our guns so that we aren't heard. We can cut through the fence, but this will be detected by the security alarm system. This means that whether we like it or not our presence will be felt, and this will turn into an armed struggle. There is a bunker inside the house where the President and his family will surely run to when the fighting begins. I know the code to the bunker and will go with a team to get the man. Our numbers should overwhelm the security at the resort. Once the President is in our midst, we will try to get him to hand over the instruments of power at gunpoint. Knowing how stubborn Abd al-Uzza is, he will probably refuse. Especially because his father held onto power for thirty years before handing it over to him. At this point he will be killed; I will pull the trigger. We will parade his body in the streets to build momentum until we march on towards the Secretary General who gains presidential powers after the death of the leader. We will arrest all senior government officials and the Syrian people can carry the day," Jamal explained enthusiastically, the words almost floated off his tongue which led him to believe that he had been thinking of the plan for a long time.

Khalid had a worried look on his face. "Killing him had never been discussed before, we are meant to be different from them by sticking to our non-violent ways. If we reach the stage of plotting death on a head of state, then where will this end and if you pull the trigger then it is unlikely that you will go on to become President. You can be convicted for murder or treason," Khalid expressed with great concern, but there were mixed reactions in that room. Most supported Jamal's plans yet there were still a few who were as cautious as Khalid.

Jamal stood with his hands on the table. "If the President hands over the instruments of power when I have him in the bunker with a gun to his head then I will lead this party to a Presidential election. If not then I will kill him and flee Syria, never to be seen or heard from again. Khalid will carry the party, but when a dictator falls then democratic elections follow, this has been the case throughout the region. We have seen this happen several times over, but it took courage from our neighbors and their leaders for what became the Arab spring uprising. It is now our time to be brave, negotiations and dialogue have failed. If it requires me killing one man to save thousands of Syrian lives, then I'd gladly do it and deal with any consequences that will follow."

Jamal looked around the room and saw faces. The men were proud of him and nodded their heads with confidence.

Chapter 44

The Fate of the Raven

THE MAN WHO ALERTED JAMAL of the danger was the President's chef. The chef had been converted to support the Movement for Democracy after attending one of their rallies in his township. The chef deciphered that this group was not extremist nor were they preaching violence. They bore arms to protect themselves from the state and extremist groups. The Raven's real name was Ismail and he had been working in the kitchen for many years, the President and his colleagues would barely notice Ismail's presence which made him an ideal spy.

This night he returned to work to bring food for the Secretary General and the President. He was surprised that all members of staff were being forced to render their cellphones. He knew that he should have called Jamal from a payphone, but there wasn't enough time. He smiled and told the guard that he wasn't even on duty, but the gentleman simply reached into his pocket and retrieved the cellphone.

The staff were told to remain in the quarters while their phones were searched. Ismail knew that it was only a matter of time until he was caught so asked for permission to use the toilet. When he was refused, he forced himself to wet his pants and the guard allowed him. Ten minutes after Ismail went to the toilet the senior officer walked into the servant's quarters requesting for him. When told that he had gone to the toilet there was panic as the guards hurried there.

The senior officer's fears were justified when they uncovered that the toilet was empty. He grabbed his walkie-talkie and asked the gatemen to close up only to find that they had already allowed Ismail to leave a few minutes before that. The police were immediately alerted and the manhunt for the spy began.

Ismail avoided the main roads; he could hear the sirens in the city and his only aim was to get to his home as soon as possible. He pushed an old man off of his bicycle and began to race off as quickly as his legs could carry him. The police sirens seemed to be getting louder, but fortunately he didn't live far from his workplace.

As he neared his home, he saw that the front door was open. He hesitantly walked in there and saw his wife next to the senior guards from the state house. He knew that the jig was up so surrendered himself peacefully. One of the guards informed him that his wife would also be going for questioning because he ran away. If he had faced his punishment like a man then she would have been spared.

Ismail was overwhelmed with regret because he knew exactly what questioning by the state truly meant in Syria. The fact that his innocent wife was going to face the same torture as he was the most devastating part of the entire ordeal. Whether he confessed or kept quiet Ismail knew that his life was over.

When they reached the interrogation center Ismail was stripped naked before he was tied from the ceiling. The guards started to whip him while they yelled that his wife was being raped and beaten in the next room. Ismail began to weep because he believed them. He yelled out in pain as they whipped deeper and deeper into his back. They were beating him senselessly without asking any questions. Eventually the door opened and a man in a sharp suit began to speak to him.

"Ismail, if you want you and your wife to be set free then you will answer my questions correctly. If you try to be strong then we will remove a finger, one at a time. If you lie, then we will remove an eye. If you hesitate to answer a question for too long, then your private parts will be taken from you. I almost forgot, anything that is done to you will also be done to your wife. Is there anything that you would like to say before we begin the questioning?" the man asked rhetorically. Ismail wasn't prepared to take any chances and test this man's resolve. All he could hope for was that she was indeed released because he was dead either way.

"Yes Sir, please release my wife she is completely innocent, and I am the guilty one. I attended a political rally for the Movement for Democracy and became a spy for that organization. I have been leaking information to them for the last eight months," he blurted out while the stinging feeling in his back began to cease. The guards had finally stopped beating him and he knew it was just a break for him to confess.

"Now, what is your connection to General Jamal?" the sharply dressed man probed on. Ismail explained that General Jamal was the true leader of this organization. This caused a lot of murmuring in the room. The men couldn't believe what they were hearing.

"This is simply impossible; the General's disloyalty only started after his accident. The assassination attempt is what changed the man. Before that he was one of the most dedicated individuals in the Syrian leadership. Are you lying, Ismail?" the man pressed as he looked ready to remove Ismail's eye as he had promised to do earlier.

"No Sir, he may not have founded the party, but even before his accident I had been informed that he is the unofficial leader of that party. The overall plan is for the party to kidnap the president, then force him to surrender the instruments of power to General Jamal who will become the president of Syria. General Jamal will then be the custodian for a democratic election that will take place sixty days after the political coup. Your party will be banned from politics as well as Islamic State and other extremist groups," Ismail explained. The gentleman stepped aside and pulled out his cellphone to pass on this information. Ismail was afraid that the guards would start to beat him again during this short interval, but they didn't. The man returned and asked for General Jamal's exact whereabouts.

"Be fair to me, I know that after I tell you I will be killed or imprisoned. Release my wife, let me see her exit this facility then we can sit in a car and I will drive you and your troops to the Movement for Democracy headquarters where General Jamal and all of the other leaders are camped. We must be quick lest the General flees Syria," Ismail introduced the element of a shortage of time as his only bargaining tool. If the men kept his wife and tortured him then they could risk losing the chance to apprehend Jamal. Even an hour wasted on torture could be a detriment to the overall goal of crushing the Movement for Democracy party.

The gentleman in the suit didn't waste any time in ordering the guards to untie Ismail. He was handcuffed as well as having chains to his legs. A blanket was placed over him to cover his naked body. They helped him along until he was in the open field. One of the barracks opened and his wife walked out and there was blood on what used to be her white dress. She was told to run out of there before they changed their minds. Ismail watched as she exited the center and disappeared into the night through the gates. Once he saw this happen, he was reminded that his wife could be found and killed if he misled them.

Ismail was carried into the car and sat next to the interrogator. The gentleman was on the phone requesting military assistance. They waited for thirty minutes until the tanks and trucks arrived. Ismail began to lead what must have been over a hundred troops to a group that was probably only protected by a tenth of that firepower. He knew that even though his wife had been released, if he led them astray then they would simply find her again or go for his children. Even though he was at pains that he was betraying his brethren he knew that there was nothing else that he could do.

Chapter 45

Beautiful Chaos

THE NATIONWIDE RIOTING took a turn for the worse; at least it did from the President's perspective. The minister without portfolio was pulled from his house and violently beaten to death before he was lit ablaze by a group of thugs. Videos of this event were leaked online, and it was truly gruesome to watch the skin dissolve as the gentleman shook frantically on the ground. The video went viral on social media and it wasn't long before it had over a hundred thousand views.

Olivier was extremely concerned because if there were vigilantes who were taking the law into their own hands then it was very possible that if any of them felt that he was also liable then his life could be at risk yet again. He thought that he could face death, but not like that. Burning to death was one of the worst ways to die in his opinion and after watching the video over and over again it reaffirmed his notion.

President Mbuyi responded to this video by releasing a public statement saying that protestors of the new constitution would be shot on site. He declared a state of emergency where any opposition to the fourth term would be imprisoned without trial. The police were given permission to kill protestors whether they were violent or peaceful. No one was allowed to take to the streets for any marching. Mbuyi made several other threats to the public which were direct violations of human rights.

Olivier knew that the fight against Mbuyi was completely out of his hands, either the public would be beaten into submission or they would beat the government right back. He was filled with fear even though he knew that the reaction from those vigilantes showed that members of the public agreed with the position that he took from the very beginning. Olivier hoped that no one would forget that he was against this amendment and so wasn't part of those who allowed it to pass in parliament.

Shortly after he viewed the video for the fifth time Olivier was contacted by his counterparts from outside of Congo who were worried that a civil war was eminent. His callers were from Western countries and he knew that his African friends wouldn't call as they wouldn't be certain if his phone had been bugged or not. Olivier decided to mute his voice with regards to what his next move would be, the people of Congo had taken over, they knew his stance and now he had to see how far they would go. Whatever the case was he was prepared to move in the direction that he was blown to.

The international community always had a keen eye on the political environment in Congo. The number of mineral resources available meant that everyone was hoping to benefit, whether they admitted this or not. Olivier didn't particularly care what people's overall intentions really were. All he knew was that in that moment he needed all the friends that he could get.

When he was done with his calls Olivier decided to turn off his phone and focus on the news channels. The bulletins were almost in real time and the stories were changing so rapidly that he found it difficult to keep up. He switched between local and international news to get an enhanced picture of what was going down. It was so difficult for him to keep up with everything, so he turned on the radio as well.

An hour after the president's announcement of retaliation, over a hundred thousand protestors were seen marching towards Parliament. The western news reporter said that the protestors had organized themselves mainly through social media, but some had bravely decided to go from house-to-house rallying support in the townships.

The suggestion was that the mass protestors were willing to use violence to ensure that the President was not only forbidden from having an extra term, but that he should step down with immediate effect. They carried banners and posters with the overwhelming message being "Mbuyi out now". This was the complete opposite from what the man was hoping to achieve and a slap in the face after his stern warning.

Olivier knew that the secret police could arrest a few hundred people when they were operating at full capacity. The fact that tens of thousands of angry Congolese men and women were mobilizing themselves at once meant that they would not be able to contain them. Olivier's initial suspicions were validated when the media broadcasted that the army and police were being transported to provide a human shield for the parliament building.

Olivier increased the volume on his radio as army generals were telling the public that the President and state property would be protected by all the military firepower in both human and material resources. They promised the public that the soldiers would have real ammunition and rubber bullets were no longer on the table of discussion. The Generals spoke aggressively during the radio session and Olivier wondered why these brave men were safely in a studio instead of being a part of the human shield that they boasted about. He knew deep down that even the Generals were too scared of the masses.

During Olivier's political career he knew that freedom of speech and freedom of assembly had been squashed by the regime with directives coming from the very top. The frustration that the people were airing came after many years of being bullied by the State, but finally they had had enough. He knew that he had to bring all of these liberties back with immediate effort. Mbuyi was probably going to meet his demise on the path that he had set out to avoid it.

The media was in full swing and the international media were providing satellite images of the masses as they neared the parliament. Olivier felt like he was watching an action movie, he was so grateful for technology because the whole world was on the edge of their seats. He rose and locked the living room door; he didn't want to be disturbed. Olivier could barely breathe and the mob which was estimated to be over five hundred people inched closer and closer to the manmade barrier between themselves and the parliamentary building.

The army and police were greatly outnumbered, and you could see them dropping their weapons. Many of them had refused to fire upon the masses and this would be shown to their superiors. Some of them decided to obey these orders but were quickly struck down by the mob and the officers who had defected. Olivier thought about the army generals who were probably still in the studio thinking of ways to flee Congo. Their broadcasts had done little to motivate their soldiers to kill their fellow brethren. The President had always taken great care of the army generals and their soldiers, but this task was too big.

Members of the crowd were also bearing arms and police officers eventually decided to remove their uniforms and join the movement, it was a decision that their supervisors would have concurred with after seeing their officers brutally attacked. The human shield that was being boasted about on the radio was completely dismantled within moments of the crowd arriving. Now there was nothing in the way of the people and the parliamentary building, Olivier wasn't sure what they intended to do but his eyes were glued to the screen.

The mob kept pressing against the gates to Parliament until they were crushed to the ground. This was the moment when it was clear that there was no rule of law. Olivier could see barrels of gasoline being poured on the premises and their objective finally became clear. They wanted to bring down the parliament, that allowed the President to amend the constitution, to the ground. The rest of the crowd stood back and cheered while the gentlemen who had been pouring the gasoline on site began to light matches and set the scene ablaze. The mob continued to cheer and celebrate until someone grabbed the megaphone and told them that they needed to do the same at the state house, but the individual went on to announce that the President should burn inside.

The crowd began to march towards the state house and when they were out of sight fire fighters were called in to minimize the damage. They were unable to save the building, but prevented it from spreading. The effort from the firefighters was shown on state media however the helicopters from the international news crew followed the mob. Olivier realized that the President was faced with two options either he went to the public and declared that he had stepped down or he would face the wrath of the mob. After a few moments Olivier realized that there was a third option and from his interaction with the man he thought it to be the most likely of the President's moves. President Mbuyi could flee, then reverse the amendment to the constitution and ask the people to allow him to finish his term.

Word eventually reached the President that the mob was on their way and he was made aware that the army could not stop the insurgency. Mbuyi and his family were told that it was safer if they departed in two different cars. His head of security made this decision for them before explaining the evacuation plan. There were two private jets that were prepared to take him overseas where they would be reunited. Mbuyi tried to reject this but was told that it was protocol and with the element of limited time there was no time to debate the matter.

Mbuyi thought that it would have made more sense for him to use the secret tunnels that had been built for such occasions. He would have much rather used the tunnels than the open road but knew that it would take time to go through the tunnels and he would still be in Congo. The option that was presented by the head of security allowed him to leave the country.

The President, his bodyguard and driver left first however Mbuyi had left his family packing up in their vehicle. Once out of the gate the driver locked the door and Mbuyi realized that they were moving towards the angry crowd. He tried to protest, but his bodyguard pointed a pistol to his head. He realized that he had been betrayed and only his family would be safe.

"You have caused a lot of suffering in this country. People have lost their parents because of your secret police who refused them to express their grievances and now everything that has been bottled up is being aired in this violence. I lost my best friend because he posted negative comments about you on social media; now you will feel what he felt," the driver stopped the car when the mob appeared at the top of the road. They pushed the President out of the car and raced off in the opposite direction. President Mbuyi tried to run but after a few minutes the mob descended on him and he was beaten to death. The crowd chanted around his dead body. Carrying his limp corpse over their heads they rose to the top of the stairs of the building.

Chapter 46

Ugly Chaos

THINGS WERE HECTIC at the hospital and Jerry had been on his feet the entire day. They were terribly understaffed, and Jerry had worked through his lunch break. It was his shift in the isolation room. A middle-aged man was screaming in pain while he lay on the ground. Jerry knelt down before he jabbed him with a pain killer. The man regurgitated blood.

The vomit made it impossible for Jerry to see as his goggles were completely stained. He used his gloves to try and wipe the blood, but this only served to stain the glass. The man yelled out desperately and Jerry couldn't inject a man that he couldn't see. Jerry called back for assistance, but no one came to his aid.

Protocol dictated that he should return to the disinfectant room and change into new protective equipment, but he couldn't see. Jerry rose up and used the curtain to guide him away from the bed, the man was crying and praying aloud. "Oh my dear God, please release me from this pain. Please God release me now" The man's prayers turned to sobbing. Jerry was left with no option but to remove his goggles.

He could now see the man looking worse than before. He looked to the door and thought about how long it would take him to go, disinfect and then return. The man pleaded with Jerry for the painkiller and his heart was racing as he stood frozen. He couldn't leave this man suffering as every second in pain was agony.

Jerry moved to the man, knelt down and jabbed the man in the right arm. The man's body shook frantically and before Jerry could move the patient vomited blood in his face once again, this time with nothing to protect him. His eyes stung and Jerry struggled to open them. He rubbed them with his gloves before racing towards the treatment room.

The other medical officers saw him and tried to restrain him as Jerry told them that they were wasting time and he needed to treat his eyes before the virus entered his bloodstream. While fighting off his colleagues Jerry felt a sharp pain in his heart and realized that he was having a panic attack before he went crashing down to the floor.

Chapter 47

Pieces in Play

BOKO HARAM not only had its members in the bush fighting government troops, but also had some members who were dressed in business suits that were fighting battles of strategic purpose. Those at the helm of the organization's power realized that in order for them to actually grow they needed to expand into the very system that they were trying to destroy. Abu Okafor as a commander of Boko Haram had strategically placed Boko Haram members in positions where they could masquerade as general members of the public.

The most important department that needed infiltration was the military. Hassan Adeyemi, who had once been a schoolboy whose village was raided by Boko Haram, was used to enter the army. Hassan had shown great commitment to the cause and was a well-spoken young man who was prolific with a rifle. Hassan had also become great at one-on-one combat with a knife or his bare hands. At eighteen years of age Hassan was a killing machine. This was what led Abu Okafor to send the young man to conduct a private mission. Hassan went to the army barracks for the Nigerian army on registration day and showed great agility. He was liked by those who were training him so Abu hoped that Hassan would rise quickly in the armed forces.

A few days, after induction Hassan was officially a part of the Nigerian army. He would be camped in Lagos because of all his ability not only in fighting, but tactical analysis. Abu was delighted with this; Hassan would leak information to them but was expected to stay under the radar. He was a long-term investment with the hope that he could rise to the top of the Nigerian army and then instruct the troops to turn on the state and allow Boko Haram to govern Nigeria.

Abu's other pawn was, Ayobamidele Eze who was going to run for Member of Parliament. This man converted to Boko Haram willingly after pursuing his own studies to uncover just what the group was about. Abu found that Ayobamidele was a book worm and promoted this. The only restriction that he placed on him was that he should only read Islamic literature and academic textbooks. Ayobamidele mixed well in society and had recently completed a degree in Economics. He had asked to continue studying, but Abu felt that he had gone far enough to start contributing.

Abu instructed Ayobamidele to run as an independent candidate for Member of Parliament. He didn't care which seat he represented, only that he would win. If Ayobamidele won, his seat then the government would try to get him to join them so as to increase their parliamentary power. This was a result that Abu was hoping for, he wanted Ayobamidele to rise as much as possible in the government so that if the armed struggle failed than they could achieve power through having policy makers on their side.

Ayobamidele could also be used to convince party members to support the policies that the organization was promoting. He hoped that this would allow for an easy transition when Boko Haram took over political power either through the system or the armed struggle. Abu wanted to hedge his bets either way.

His last major asset was Olawale Adebayo who was a businessman in Borno. Abu wasn't completely sure about this gentleman's affiliation. He was a shop keeper who also had some trucks. Olawale came to Abu and his colleagues suggesting that he wanted to support Boko Haram shortly after the raids on the government schools. Olawale's only request was that his home and his family would be protected. He claimed to be a Muslim and that he was a strong supporter of the organization, but Abu wasn't sure.

When he looked at Olawale he saw a man who was so scared of Boko Haram that he was willing to pay them and pretend to be a Muslim just so that they would leave him alone. Abu actually didn't mind this and more and more businessmen emerged after Olawale. Abu knew that they needed the money, so these individuals were completely protected, and their businesses were treated as sacred by the militia. Most of the finance that was needed to keep all of his troops fed came from these businesspeople, so Abu wasn't too strict on whether or not they actually went for prayers at the mosque. Abu collected the money in person, not because he couldn't delegate this duty, but simply because he wanted to look at these people's faces. They always smiled and none acted disgruntled. If they missed a payment, then he wanted to make sure that the apologies were sincere and hear for himself exactly when they intended to make up for them.

Chapter 48

Winds of Change Have Blown

AFTER THE DEATH of President Mbuyi, the instruments of power were immediately passed onto Vice President Luteka. The masses were still unhappy about this and were openly expressing their dissent.

Protests ensued during the national mourning that was declared for Mbuyi. His funeral was a façade as a mob hounded the day. All the anxiety led to the absence of prominent political figures at the funeral. It was now as if everyone was distancing themselves from Mbuyi's legacy. No one travelled to Congo from the international community which further exhibited that few people were willing to sink with this ship.

Mbuyi's funeral was a sham. His body had been so badly disfigured that his corpse was not displayed. His family decided to bury him on their farm and the event was closed to the public. The Congolese people were meant to pay their respects at church services that were held in the football stadiums around the country. Vice President Luteka attended the one in Kinshasa and was booed while he gave the life history. The Vice President abandoned the platform when the mob decided to throw rotten fruit at him, a clear sign that he was despised almost as much as Mbuyi. They wanted him to know that any diversion from the democratic process by him would be greeted with the same fervor.

Olivier watched the entire proceedings from the comfort of his living room where there was complete silence. None of his guests were brave enough to even whisper a word, he was glued to the television and there was the very realistic feeling that the winds of change were blowing. He analyzed everything that was being broadcast and made mental notes. He thought about those who were there and all those who were absent and what that represented.

A journalist gave the Vice president a short interview before the man entered his vehicle to flee the service as the protesting began to intensify. The Vice president did take the time to inform the nation that he had no intention of contesting for the presidency and that the party would go to a convention to pick a candidate that would contest for the Presidency.

There were smiles around the room and Olivier couldn't help but release his own smirk. The convention was finally a chance for everyone to test their popularity on a fair scale. Olivier's phone rang and to his surprise it was the Vice President who had announced that he was catching a helicopter to Katanga to meet with Olivier. He was being escorted by Mr. Odia who was the head of national intelligence.

The meeting was meant to be private, so Olivier suggested that they come straight to his home. When he put his phone down, he asked his wife to prepare for their guests. This was really her peak period with the household being a meeting point.

The movements of the top tier party members were being hounded and even though it was obvious that any meeting between them was political they could disguise it as social, if need be, when it took place at the household.

After a few hours his guests arrived, and Olivier was dressed very casually. Before the President embarked on his campaign to prolong his stay at the top, information had been leaked to Olivier that he was the most popular candidate in the party. His sources within the intelligence agency were highly credible but protecting their identities had always been of the outmost importance.

Olivier was greeted passionately by Vice President Luteka and the Intelligence Chief, Mr. Odia. These gentlemen's smiles were wider than a child on Christmas Day, yet Olivier could also sense their nerves. Luteka's hand was shaking during and after exchanging a handshake with Olivier. If he wasn't certain before, he was now sure that they had travelled all the way to plead with him to become the party's presidential candidate. Over the years he developed the ability to look a person in the eyes and hear their thoughts. This man's thoughts were engulfed in embarrassment.

Even though the Vice President only mentioned the two of them another car pulled up to the gate. Mr. Luteka explained that senior government officials, Moses Nlele and Fabrice Mpuka, also wanted to attend this discussion. Olivier was furious that those two would even think to go to his house after the ambush in Kinshasa. They sided with the President during the meeting and he believed that they would have known all about the car explosion.

He swallowed his saliva and it seemed to take a long time to go down his throat. He decided that he couldn't shake Nlele and Mpuka's hands or pretend to like them like he planned on doing with his other former enemies. These two old men would know that their political careers were finished from the moment that they would see the venom in Olivier's eyes.

They walked in and were guided to the dining room by Vivienne. The chef had prepared a large buffet. By the time that Nlele and Mpuka surfaced in the room Olivier was already seated at the table with his hands holding cutlery. He nodded at them to acknowledge their presence but ensured that a distinct frown remained firmly plastered on his face.

Both Nlele and Mpuka saw Olivier's face and were immediately filled with fear. Like a child who was going to sit with their father after failing their examinations. They nodded back before proceeding to the buffet where they both helped themselves to incredibly small portions of food. To Olivier's immediate left was the Vice President and the Chief of intelligence was on his immediate right.

They all thanked him for the hospitality, but no time was spent on meaningless chit chat. The reason for their visit was brought to the table by Odia after only a few moments when Olivier finished praying for the meal aloud. While he chewed his first bite, he was approached with a question that he expected to come near the end of the discussion.

"Governor Olivier Katanga, we need to have an idea of whether or not you intend to run as our candidate in the general election that will be held in three months. We realize that we cannot pressure anyone, but our reports have found that you are the most popular candidate and the only individual who will obtain a landslide victory. All of those who supported the President's amendment to the constitution are known in the community and will not be able to win. We beg you to take up this role and lead us Sir. If you do not stand then this party may not survive and we will all be ruined if the ADD or any other party comes into power," Odia said as all four of the men looked at Olivier to interpret his reaction.

He didn't give them what they wanted. Instead, he continued to chew his food while he focused all of his attention on his plate. He put his cutlery down and took a large sip of his wine. He could tell that the suspense was killing them, especially the riffraff like Nlele and Mpuka who were political prostitutes.

"I thought that I was suspended from the party?" he asked almost in a whisper before taking another large bite of his steak. Olivier was definitely in the driver's seat and he was going to savor this moment as much as the bloody steak that stared back at him from his gold rimmed plate. They were all going to get a telling off before he eased their concerns and informed them that he had full intention of not only leading the party, but also winning the national vote.

Odia was lost for words, but it was the highly unpopular Vice President's turn to try and get an answer out of Olivier, none of them were leaving until they knew for sure exactly what his thoughts were. "The central committee is meeting as we speak to reverse all of the suspensions. Yours will be the most publicized because it was the most unjust. Young man, your nation wants you to be its leader not to mention the fact that your party needs you."

Olivier felt like clapping sarcastically at that patriotic speech. All that Luteka and Odia cared about was whether or not they would have jobs over the next seven years and Nlele and Mpuka only wanted to apologize so that if Olivier became President, he wouldn't exercise retribution on the grudge that they both knew that he was holding. These men had made so many speeches over the year about their commitment to the Congolese citizens, but Olivier knew very few politicians who actually meant it. The majority were there to eat from the profits of their country's resources and nothing else.

"What was being done to me and my close colleagues who stood by me was unacceptable. I will contest for the party's presidency, but we must respect the party manifesto. We cannot go down Mbuyi's dark road and I will be criticizing him heavily during my campaign. As a party we are distancing ourselves from his amendment to the constitution. I will only become the Party President if I win the most votes at a convention where all delegates can have the opportunity to choose." Olivier spoke more loudly than he had that entire day. He finally barked instructions at these men who now worked for him. One by one they pledged loyalty to him, starting with Odia and ending with Nlele.

The entire group agreed with Olivier that a convention should be held in accordance with the party manifesto. Olivier knew that they just did this because they needed him. That was probably the same group that encouraged the late Mbuyi to manipulate the constitution. He took their compliments with a pinch of salt; he was just their best chance of remaining in power and they were going to respect his wishes because if he won then he would be able to fire them.

Olivier showed no grudges, but knew that several of them had the potential to hinder progress with regards to his national agenda. It was unlikely that the senior members would have any new ideas yet some could contribute valuable advice due to their experience. However, you, can't teach an old dog new tricks so, he didn't think that the ones who had been embezzling state funds year after year could be taught to behave otherwise. Olivier would take time to carefully vet each and every individual before appointing them in his new administration.

After the meal all of his visitors left at the same time and Olivier offered Odia and Luteka hugs before giving handshakes to Mpuka and Nlele. The two old men were very worried about the hostile treatment especially since he had been so close to both of them before that. He knew that they would both go out of their ways to be loyal to him so as to retain that friendship that had since disappeared.

Within the same day, the government contracts that had been taken away from his businesses had been returned. Jean Claude was elated when he was on the phone telling Olivier the good news; they had even been compensated for the loss of business. The compensation actually exceeded their average sales over that same period. He knew that everyone would be in a hurry to repair the damage that was caused.

Things were on the rise yet again and Olivier always felt that this was the easy part. The true test was how they had carried themselves during that short period of facing financial pressure. There were even provisions in place for them to take on more pressure and this made him incredibly proud. Jean Claude's loyalty had also been tested and he passed with flying colors.

Not one item of Olivier's private files was leaked and Jean Claude would have felt the heat.

Since the man had been there during the difficult time then he was definitely going to be in the forefront when it was time to share the spoils and there would be plenty. The President's business interests both locally and in the surrounding countries always flourished. He wouldn't have to do anything except leave the door open because customers would be flowing in at a rapid pace.

By the time that night fell the evening news announced that there was a unanimous decision by the central committee to lift his suspension and that the charges by the state had been dropped due to lack of evidence. His lawyer Aurelie called him shortly after that announcement and he told him to continue with suing the print media with regards to the defamation of character charges. There was no reason that he should stop until the newspaper issued a public apology. If he made an example of them then it would make others think twice in the future. He would drop other charges; there was no point in taking a government that he could be running to court.

Olivier decided that he would not tell his wife that he was more than likely the new President of his party. He wanted to manage expectations in his home and businesses by being prudent with his words, but extremely aggressive with his actions. Even though he had endeavored to keep his intent to himself within a few days the nation knew about his intent.

His face was in the paper as a contender at the party's convention, yet it was in vain because no other party member bothered to contest. He put in his nomination on the first day, but no one else came forward during the week when they were to be put in.

He knew that Nlele, Luteka and Mpuka were all campaigning hard within the party structures to get everyone behind him. He hoped that this was the only reason why others hadn't come forward and there had been no intimidation. He couldn't stand political violence and was more than prepared to punish anyone who used it; whether they were with or against him.

The convention was conveniently hosted in Katanga and Olivier knew that this was done to give him a huge advantage if there had been another candidate. The absence of competition meant that the convention was just a formality; he didn't want to cancel it because that would appear undemocratic. He wanted to follow all of the rules leading up to the election, all the while leaving no stone unturned.

With the event in Katanga his office basically had the responsibility of hosting all of the party members that were travelling from around the country. It was a highly costly event, and he did question its importance when he constantly told people to minimize the costs. There was accommodation for all of the members not to mention feeding them on the day. Olivier was presented to the crowd when he arrived at the field and was welcomed with a huge roar, the momentum was with him within the party, and no one wanted to be left out.

The convention turned out to be a social gathering for party members with everyone going to great lengths to congratulate Olivier. He was declared the party President within the first ten minutes of him arriving and this brought him great satisfaction. He was taken back to when he left that Yambuku village all of those years ago, he would never have dreamt that he would have gotten to where he was. The Vice president closed the function by explaining that his role was simply to facilitate the general election in his capacity as acting president.

The fact that there were no succession wrangles ensured that immediately after the convention he could sit down with his campaign team and start to establish their short-term plans. The first issue that he discussed with his team was the mobilization of campaign funds. During the discussion Luteka and Nlele were gently guiding him towards using state funds but Olivier shut this idea down instantly. He was resolute that they would get campaign money from donors as the opposition had to.

He really wanted to uphold high moral standards from the very beginning. Often when he was rising in the political arena, he had to keep his mouth shut even during moments when he saw mass misappropriation of funds or extreme corruption. Now he was the top dog and could hammer this behavior on the head. None of these senior men felt confident enough to press him about the use of public funds. There were each trying to recreate a friendship with him by laughing at all of his jokes and agreeing with his stance on following the rules.

At the close of their meeting Olivier presented a roadmap for how he intended on improving the business environment, once he sold his ideas to his members then he hoped that they would go out to different stakeholders in the community to mobilize funds. An election was meant to be entirely financed by local interests however this was seldom the case. He and his opponents would have colleagues out of Congo who would want to put money towards it.

While his senior members were going around asking for donations from businesses, Olivier would take some time to request for contributions from his friends in Nigeria, Zambia and Zimbabwe. He had also made some meaningful friendships with expatriates in his country, especially those from China. There were a select number of Asian businessmen who would donate without him having to ask, however these individuals would probably be donating just as much money to his opponents.

Within the days that followed the convention Olivier's face was on posters and shirts that were being distributed throughout the land. He was receiving endorsements from some opposition party leaders who didn't intend on running for the election due to the time constraint. He invited these opposition leaders to follow on his nationwide campaign and urged his supporters to remove violence from politics because the opposition and the ruling party members were all part of the same family. The Democratic Republic of Congo was their family.

Chapter 49

The Great General Jamal

JAMAL WAS SUDDENLY AWOKEN in the middle of the night. The safe house was far away from town so he wondered why he could hear vehicles roaring in the distance. The cars must have been approaching them because the sounds of the engines were only getting louder. Jamal got up and shook Khalid, who was sleeping on the mattress next to him.

"Are we expecting anyone?" Jamal shouted as he could hear the distinct sound of a tank.

Before Khalid had the opportunity to respond they heard gunfire. Jamal dropped to the ground and everyone in the living room woke up. The guard who was on night duty ran inside and alerted them to the fact that they were under attack by the state forces.

This guard explained that they were greatly outnumbered, and the others had already been killed. Khalid and the others marched to the attic and Jamal followed them without any knowledge of what they would do. Bullets shot through the windows and they realized that it wouldn't be long before they were inside the building.

There was a dim light in the attic, but Jamal could see a large cache of firearms and each of the men grabbed a weapon before running back to face the intruders. Jamal was very nervous; he knew that bullets could do very little to defeat tanks and they needed something stronger like a bazooka.

Jamal picked up a rifle, there was nothing else that they could do. At least the guns gave them a chance, even if the odds were stacked against them. With the rifle in his grip Jamal was ready to make his way into the firing zone but Khalid placed a hand on his shoulder to stop him.

"General, you will use the back door. Run east through the field until you see a small farm. Inside the barn is a car and the keys are in the glove compartment. I will see you again General, in this life or the next," Khalid explained before repeating that the organization would continue to survive through him.

Jamal decided against protesting as Khalid was adamant. He was relieved that there was an evacuation plan in place for him however he was very concerned for the others. From the screams coming from outside he knew that he wanted to be going in the opposite direction. Jamal and Khalid took a moment to shake hands before he made his way through the backdoor with his rifle hanging from his shoulder.

He took a deep breath before using the back door. The night was crisp, and he was really exposed. He heard screams in the building and realized that the soldiers had penetrated the safe house. Jamal saw a lone soldier and crept towards him slowly before slamming the back of his gun against the man's head and knocking him out.

He did this not only because he was reluctant to kill but also so that he could avoid firing the gun, which would only serve to attract unwanted attention. He leaned against the buildings wall and looked back before it became clear that there was no one on that side of the house. He held the rifle tightly as he galloped through the side gate. He could see the barn in the direction that Khalid had pointed to and ran faster than he had ever done in the past. A part of him felt that if he could get assistance then he could save those of them who surrendered.

Jamal felt nervous when he reached the doors of the barn as they were open. He slid in and turned on the light.

As soon as he did this, he found four soldiers with rifles pointed directly at him. The Raven was also standing there next to a sharply dressed man. Jamal realized that the Raven had given up all of them including information on the exit strategy for the organization's leader. Jamal knew that he was quick with the gun, but this would be an impossible situation to come out of.

The gunshots continued to fire in the background and Jamal thought of how he would talk his way out of this. He had to compromise with them so immediately placed his rifle on the ground to indicate that he wouldn't resist arrest. He thought that he needed to put himself in a position so that he could just go to jail and receive minimum physical abuse. He knew within himself that he had reached the end of the line.

He opened his mouth but before he could speak the man in a suit walked up to him and placed his pistol against Jamal's head. The General's heart was racing as he felt the cold sensation of the pistol on his forehead. Jamal hoped that this was just an intimidation technique as the state would probably want to interrogate him so as to find out what he knew.

"No one wants to hear what you have to say," the man said before pulling the trigger. Jamal fell to the ground and received another three gunshots to the head just so that they were sure he was dead. The fact that he had survived in the past made him want to guarantee that the man wouldn't live to see another day. Jamal's body was carried out by two of the soldiers. The Raven stood stone still. Paralyzed for a moment he fought back a tear of respect for the General. The man in the suit was who the state would use when they need a special elimination to take place. He never spoke to those assigned to help him nor did he have a name. He lifted his weapon before shooting the Raven in the head, they couldn't have any loose ends. This case was closed; the state had managed to destroy one of the biggest threats in one night.

Chapter 50

Ebola

JERRY SLOWLY OPENED HIS EYES squinting at a shining light. It took him a moment to realize exactly where he was. He sat up from the bed and looked around the room, while rubbing his eyes, until it was evident that he was in the clinic's isolation room. He rose from the bed and stumbled towards the door and started to frantically knock calling for someone's attention. Eventually one of his colleagues heard the sound and came to his rescue.

The door was opened and the lady, whose name eluded him, advised that he should continue to rest. The lady went on to explain that he had passed out due to the shock after his encounter with his patient. She spoke in a tone that Jerry was very familiar with. It was the type of tone that suggested that bad news was coming.

The medical officer was dressed in protective clothing and this immediately sent alarm bells ringing in Jerry's mind. He knew that the blood from the infected patient had entered his eyes which had caused him to enter a panic in the first place. He knew enough about Ebola to conclude that he had more than likely been infected. After a few minutes the medical officer confirmed his suspicions and declared that he had been tested and the Ebola virus had entered his blood stream yet was very much in its infancy.

Jerry's heart was racing, each time he blinked he thought about the amount of pain that his patients were going through when he was treating them. Many of them had died which made him doubt that he would survive for much longer. Jerry took a deep breath before asking what would happen next even though he was aware of the procedure; he had come to the end of his journey.

The officer told him that he would be flown back to the States to be treated in an American hospital. He wouldn't be allowed to visit his family or friends until he was fully recovered. He would be placed in isolation throughout until he fully recovered. Jerry nodded; he had reached the end of the line. It was time for him to go back; he had served the world and saved enough lives. Now Jerry had to wait for when his body would begin to deteriorate and pray that he would survive.

He asked for his cellphone as he needed to speak to his wife. He thought deeply about what he would say until the medical officer returned before telling him to take as much time as he needed. The phone rang and a part of him wished that she wouldn't pick up so that he could have just left a voicemail.

"Hi Betty, I need to inform you that I am coming back to the States, but protocol has changed. I will be in isolation for a while before I can reenter the community," Jerry lied as he couldn't bring himself to let his wife know what was really going on. He hoped that the media wouldn't publicize his illness as he knew how much the epidemic was receiving media coverage.

"I'm just glad that you are coming home. I know I didn't support you before but you are a great man and we are so proud of you," Betty responded with a sign of relief. She felt bad for the way that they left things and since he had now achieved what he wanted she wondered why she had opposed his decision so much before that.

"Thank you, baby, it means the world to me that you would say that. I think that I am now ready to do what you asked. After my isolation period I will start to look for a local job so that I can give you the life that you want and deserve," he concluded before ending the call. He meant what he said, he had done his time and served his nation. He was now ready to move on and be a normal family man, all the while knowing that he had done his patriotic duty.

Jerry was treated like a delicate object from that moment onwards. His bags were packed for him and he had to wear the protective gear during his flight back to the States, he was taken to Boston at Saint John's hospital which was the first to respond to the call out and announced that they were prepared to take him on. Jerry didn't realize how hard it was for a hospital to agree to take on an Ebola patient in the States. However, he was educated to the fact that it was not only a risk to the staff but the hospital also had to be big enough to facilitate him as he needed to be isolated from the other patients. Jerry braced himself for what was to come.

Chapter 51

The Presidential Race

OLIVIER WAS STRONGLY ADVISED against hosting a debate on national television. His actions were worrying the senior party members. During his first week in charge, he had completely disbanded the party's militia group which was very useful at intimidating the opposition. The head of the secret police had been relieved of his duties after a decade of commitment, the party members were also now in the dark with regards to what the public were saying about them.

Olivier insisted that if they reintroduced autonomy then the public would respond by supporting them at the ballots. He was nervous about his reforms however he hated corruption in his country and wanted to use his opportunity to crack down on it. He had also changed the way that business would be done within his own company so as to avoid bias and hypocrisy.

This evening's debate was going to be between the four individuals who were looking to contest for the country's presidency. It was going to be televised and was the platform for the public to find out more about the individuals. They had some snacks before it began as Olivier wanted the opposition to know that this election would be conducted without the intimidation and violence that the opposition had been suffering from for many years.

There was hostility towards him by the President of the Young Empowerment party (YE), however the others appreciated the gestures shown by him. They waited nervously in the backstage until the announcer called them out one at a time ending with Olivier.

The announcer explained that each participant would have two minutes with which to answer a question. He went on to say that most of the questions were posed from the general public with the use of social media however the audience would be allowed to throw in random questions towards the end of the proceedings.

The first question was what each candidate would do with regards to the constitution that now allowed for four terms in the office of the president. Each candidate criticized Mbuyi for his undemocratic move they all said that they would reverse it. Olivier did the same but went further to say that he would change it to two terms and reminded the public that this was his position from the start, that was why Mbuyi suspended him and tried to have him assassinated. The audience clapped, showing that they were fully aware of his position and the risks that came with it.

The next question was what new ideas each candidate had, this brought out different suggestions. The YE president spoke about reducing the retirement age to fifty so that young people could have opportunities in the workplace. He also spoke about the government working with commercial banks to provide finance for young entrepreneurs with the government providing the surety as many young people had the ideas but not the collateral that the banks required.

The ADD president spoke about the problems with the federal systems and how to maximize government revenues they needed to centralize. He said that the federal system meant that national goals were being restricted. This remark didn't sit well with the audience and Olivier already knew that it wouldn't be a popular policy.

Olivier took a different approach to answering this question. He was the only candidate who could speak about what he was actually doing. It was risky to confess party flaws but all of the blame was placed on Mbuyi. He said that his first order of business was to dismantle the government militia and secret police that were harassing opposition and general citizens. He said that Mbuyi crushed journalist autonomy and freedom of speech which he reversed by inviting opposition to this debate. He said that he would strengthen institutions to prevent corruption and this would increase the actual revenue.

He said with more money to pump into education, health and the private sector then the standard of living would increase and Congo could become the bread basket of Africa. He said he needed more than two minutes to explain exactly how he would do it but promised to release an hour-long podcast explaining his vision in greater detail.

Eventually there was a period when all candidates were allowed an opportunity to make general remarks. Each presidential aspirant used this opportunity to criticize the current regime, especially Olivier. They said that even though there was statistical evidence that Katanga had improved under him each aspirant mentioned how much money Olivier had made as a result of being Governor.

His only defense was that it wasn't illegal to make money and made reference to questionable deals that the other candidates were involved in. He knew that he was the wealthiest presidential aspirant but to survive in opposition all of the others needed money and they sometimes took it from criminals.

Olivier did mention that the playing field hadn't been fair and he would allow all opposition to campaign freely so that they wouldn't have an excuse to deal with criminals in the future. The rest of the debate went well from his viewpoint and they ended by taking pictures with each other as they held hands. This moment was quite significant as opposition was not usually embraced in his country's history.

Chapter 52

Mourning in a State of Confusion

THE HEADLINE IN THE STATE PAPER read, "General Jamal Shot Dead" Shadad wept as she read of her husband's death. The article wrote that General Jamal had been kidnapped by the Movement for Democracy's violent guerilla group. The state forces had gone to their hideout to rescue General Jamal but Jamal was killed in the crossfire. The article went on to talk about Jamal's courage and that they considered the Movement for Democracy to be a terrorist organization. Finally, the article closed by informing the public that the Party Secretary would also add the Defense Ministry to his portfolio. He was chosen because he choreographed the rescue operation using his personal initiative.

Shahad was baffled by this account, her husband had claimed to recognize those men however he could have just said that to convince her to board that plane and leave. The fact that his party tried to rescue him was also hard to believe as Jamal told her that he had betrayed them. She was confused about the entire conspiracy but only one thing was for certain, her beloved husband was dead and nothing could change that fact.

She placed her tablet on the bed and screamed out at the top of her voice. She couldn't stop shouting out in agony as she realized that she would never see her husband again. She fell to the ground and yelled out as her emotional pain physically drained her. Karim ran into the room as he heard his mother from his house. When he saw her, he immediately tried to help her up but she hit him and told her son to read the tablet. Karim was shell-shocked but obeyed her instructions and picked it up. After a few seconds he understood that his father was dead, and he wasn't sure what to do. Karim had always thought his father to be indestructible, so this news was something that he had never prepared himself mentally for.

Karim walked out of the room as his mother wanted to be left alone; he couldn't stop scratching his head. His wife had already taken the kids to school so he was alone with her and this suited him. He called his siblings and alerted them to the death, each asked about the funeral proceedings and there seemed to be no answer. Karim went on to make a call to a few family friends until he was directed to a contact in the Syrian government. The gentleman on the other line was quick to inform Karim that there was not going to be a public funeral with an open casket since the body was disfigured from the bullets.

A funeral was also not going to take place because they couldn't have state officials in an open area as the terrorists could use it as an opportunity. Karim was told that his father's cremation would be televised in the next two hours on the national television channel. The man on the line conveyed his deepest condolences and told him to call again if they had any further queries.

The gentleman also took the opportunity to inform Karim that the house in Syria would be handed over to the new Minister of Defense so Karim provided them with his mailing address for his parent's personal items to be sent. The speed at which they were trying to erase his father's memory sounded like they were in a hurry to close his chapter. Karim decided that he would never make contact with them again; something seemed suspicious about his father's death.

That was it; there was no more Syria for the Ahmed family. Now he had to tell his mother that she couldn't even return to bury him, he wasn't sure how she would react to this. He knocked gently on the door and found that his mother was weeping more quietly than before. Karim held her hand and updated her on the situation. He told her that she would stay with them in Zambia as there was nothing left for her abroad. She seemed to be okay with this as she simply nodded.

Later on, in the day they watched the cremation on the internet to bring some closure before they sat on the porch and shared fond memories that they had with the great General Jamal Ahmed

Chapter 53

Destiny Fulfilled

OLIVIER KATANGA'S LANDSLIDE VICTORY was first announced on local news before international broadcasters also aired the results. The congratulatory messages began rolling in from presidents from all around Africa and abroad. A few Nigerian, so called, prophets were announcing that they predicted his victory, however most people did. The majority of the opposition leaders opted to stay out of the election. They only wanted to contest in the general election that was in a year's time because they didn't have adequate time to mobilize campaign funds.

The first thing that Olivier needed to do after his inauguration was to appoint cabinet ministers. He decided to retain the health, youth, sports and agriculture ministers. Ever other ministry was completely revamped with him making changes also the deputies. The previous cabinet was full of relatives of the former president, many of whom he did not deem properly qualified. He was not going to tolerate Mbuyi's nepotism, which he had despised for many years. He also used the opportunity to combine certain ministries as he felt that several had been created so as to create more government jobs and not to propel efficiency. An example was him combining the finance and commerce ministries.

The second thing that he did was to copy the Nelson Mandela style of truth and reconciliation sessions. He realized before he disbanded the secret police that there were several people who had suffered from politically motivated brutality. The victims needed some closure even though he didn't want to promote an unproductive series of revenge. These sessions were mainly held in opposition strongholds, so he had a panel of five individuals from different political parties as well as the government spokesperson who chaired these sessions.

The testimonies that came out of those sessions was truly devastating, the secret police would kidnap opposition supporters and torture them for several months so as to convert them. The ones who would refuse to change their political preference would not be seen again. Women had lost husbands, mothers had lost children and families had been displaced. The world now knew the full extent of Mbuyi's legacy. Information was leaked during these sessions that there were mass graves around the country where opposition supporters had been buried.

The fact that he not only added new faces to the party, but also completely rebranded it allowed his new cabinet to judge all of the atrocities that were committed by the Mbuyi adminis-tration. This was very useful during these sessions as women came forward saying that their husbands went missing shortly after they were heard criticizing the President. People in opposition strongholds came out to talk about how medicine and other essentials were not delivered to their hospitals as Mbuyi wanted to teach them a lesson for not giving him support. This was also the case with farming fertilizers and infrastructure development; there had been a lot of neglect.

Everything revealed at these gatherings was documented and recorded on national television. The government spokesperson would end each session in the same manner, ensuring the public that the new President was not only open to criticism from all factions of the public, he was also prepared to work with opposition leaders to address the problems in their strongholds which had been deserted. This was well received both locally and abroad. Olivier wanted to create a new Congolese image, not the usual story of corruption, conflict and misused resources.

The state also opened up a case against the late President where his overseas assets were being handed over to the Congolese government. Olivier wasn't too concerned with this as his focus was more on the forward then the back however the assets were considerable and the public were adamant about recovering what they could. Olivier wasn't going to spend too much time worrying about settling old scores; he was more vested in the current state of affairs, being that the Congolese people were the poorest in the world in terms of per capita GDP. He intended turning this around by installing harsh repercussions for corruption and strengthening their institutions. There was certainly enough mineral wealth for this to be achieved.

His third major move was to meet with opposition members to discuss the needs of the people in their strongholds after the nationwide sessions. There were very few convictions that followed the truth and reconciliation campaign as amnesty was granted to individuals who came through to apologize to the families that they affected and the individual would also be required to prove that their actions were politically motivated and not due to their own violent psychological state. The next assurance from Olivier was to change the political climate so that such behavior never returned to the country. The concept of political cadres was banned as these individuals were being used to cause lawlessness.

After these initial problems were addressed, Olivier took a world tour to rebuild Congo's image so as to attract foreign investment in sectors other than mining. He started his tour in China as he met with prominent statesmen at a China-Africa convention which was held in Beijing. After that he proceeded to the European Union where he attempted to woo the various leaders so they too would consider long term investment in Congo. He guaranteed that their investments would be safe as well as boasting of the reforms that would ensure that this was achieved.

The first three months as president flew by at an intense pace and he realized how high the mountain was to achieve his vision. Olivier sat in the garden with his sister, Jean Claude, Vivienne and his two children. He prayed aloud before they started to eat the food. He held Vivienne's hand during the meal and felt at peace. He knew that there was a long road ahead however in that moment he was delighted with his life and how everything ended up.

Chapter 54

A Returning Soldier

WHILE IN ISOLATION information leaked to the media that Jerry MacDonald had contracted the Ebola virus. His wife and family were panicking especially since they were not allowed to see him. Jerry himself was panicking, he had seen people die from this virus and he was infected. He wasn't feeling the full extent of the symptoms and at the end of a long month his doctor informed him that he was cured. The only thing that he combated with during the thirty days was a stomach-ache as food was failing to stay in his system. He had lost a lot of weight but his last couple of meals had digested properly and he felt much better.

When he heard that he was cured his mind raced back to when he contracted that deadly virus. He had just been doing his job and the very thing that he feared most had come to be. He was relieved that it was all over, and he could now be with his family. Aside from the fear of dying the worst part of isolation was fighting off boredom and severe anxiety.

Once changed into his own clothes he felt like a prisoner who had just been set free. There was an indescribable air of relief that engulfed him as he walked away from the isolation unit and into the general ward. He could see his family waiting for him as he walked out of the hospital doors and into the sunshine. His wife ran up to him and without any hesitation smothered him with kisses that lasted over a minute. Betty wasn't angry that he had lied about his condition. This had bothered him during his isolation. Behind her were his parents and little girl who were just as excited to see him.

His father told him that he had done a brave thing going to fight Ebola and now the MacDonald men could be satisfied that they had given a part of their lives to the global case. Jerry agreed wholeheartedly as he reiterated that he was now going to stay put as he was at peace with his contribution. His daughter took the floor after that and never let it go as she updated her father on every single event from her class field trip to how the dog was sick and she went on and on but Jerry didn't care. He was just delighted to be there.

During the days that followed Jerry came to realize that not everyone was happy to have close contact with him even close neighbors waved from a distance but didn't dare come near him. His friends spoke to him by Zoom and on the phone but always claimed to be too busy whenever he asked to meet them. The sad truth is that he basically moved from one isolation center to another, but at least he had family.

Jerry now felt firsthand the stigma that an Ebola survivor went through. After a few weeks some medical staff that he worked with in Congo also returned. They were the first non-family members to come close to him. This was incredibly enjoyable as he sorely missed other human interaction. One by one he hugged them as they entered the house.

The visitors all informed him that they shared the same plight as the stigmatization from the public was towards any health worker, regardless of their safe quarantined condition. As long as they came from Africa. The returning health workers knew that they needed to hold on to one another until the public forgot about Ebola and accepted them back into the community.

After sitting for a few minutes one of his visitors reached into their pocket and pulled out an envelope with Jerry's name on it – Corporal Jerry MacDonald. Part of the reason that we all came for a visit was to give you this letter. We all got one. Jerry read the official gold seal from the government of Congo signed by the new President Oliver Katanga. The President gave a heartfelt thank you to Jerry for risking his life to fight the virus. It spoke of bravery and universal love for his fellow man. Jerry passed the letter to his wife as the tears started to roll down his face. In the past few weeks, he questioned why he had gone to the front line, but that day he got his answer.

Chapter 55

Freedom from the Caliphate

MOHAMMAD WAITED FOR MIDNIGHT before he commenced his escape. He returned to the spot where he had discovered the loose bricks during the day. The guards didn't notice him at all as they were busy watching the small television in the guardhouse. Mohammad's body fit through the gap perfectly. He was finally free. He took a deep breath because he hadn't thought of any sensational plan. His aim was to leave the compound and make up the rest of his escape plan as he went along.

He jogged towards the border. He couldn't be too fast because it wasn't too close and he didn't want to run out of steam. However, he couldn't be too slow because once his absence was uncovered, he didn't know what would happen next. He knew that Hussein would try to bring him back and if he did then Mohammad would've been worse off than he was before.

After an hour of running at a controlled jog he finally neared the border. He approached it cautiously as there were floodlights that were shining at all angles. He wondered if the guards were awake or not. He had to take a risk and get closer to the fence. He was only a few feet away from his salvation when he heard shouting. He had been spotted. He rose up and thought about running but that was suicide because guns were pointed at him.

He was told to enter the office and was immediately locked inside the holding cell. He was checked for arms before he was locked inside, and the questioning began.

"Who are you and why are you running on the streets at this time of night?" he was asked by the soldier aggressively. He hoped that this man would sympathize with him as he had no money to bribe him with. Mohammad didn't have to act sad; he really was and this could be seen on his face.

"Please I just want to escape, things are so hard for me. I respect ISIS but I will die from depression. Please allow me to leave, I am a nobody with no money to pay the exit fee. Have mercy on me," Mohammad pleaded, and he could see the sympathy in the soldier's eyes. The militia opened the cell and told Mohammad never to return once out through the gates. As soon as Mohammad walked out another ISIS soldier walked in and he immediately recognized him. It was one of the guys who had raped the maid and beaten him up

"Wait, you are the one who reported us to Mr. Hussein. Now you will learn a lesson," the soldier said as he also remembered Mohammad.

At that pronouncement tanks burst through the border's fences. The tanks fired on the ISIS soldiers who ran out to try and prevent them from entering the city. The soldiers that were in the office picked up their guns before running out. Mohammad knew that it was a good time to escape but those in the tanks wouldn't be able to differentiate between him and ISIS, so he went under the table and prayed for the very best.

If he left that office, then he could be fired upon by anyone.

After a few minutes that felt like a lifetime Mohammad was pulled from under the table by government soldiers. Before he was asked anything, he burst out that he had been held prisoner in Ar-Raqqah and just wanted to leave. He told them about the atrocities that were taking place and his appearance supported his claim that he was simply an abused worker and not an ISIS militia who was posing as a civilian. The fact that handcuffs were on his wrists confirmed his argument as being true.

The soldiers told him that it was his lucky day and that he should flee the city because chemical bombs would be dropped around the town. Mohammad did not wait on ceremony and ran out of the gates. He was finally free. He could hear the helicopters in the distance and knew that the bombs were on their way. He ran away relieved that he had chosen tonight of all nights to escape before ar-Raqqah came crashing to the ground.

Little did Mohammad know of General Jamal and his death. Little did he know that the General's plan to stop the chemical bombing was thwarted. All he knew was that he escaped his own private hell while the world of politics and war raged around him. All he knew was that Allah showed him favor. A favorite citation from the Quran swelled in his mind from his childhood. "Never will we be struck except by what Allah has decreed for us; He is our protector." His mind filled with gratitude. How could he have survived all of what was inflicted on him if it was not for the protection of Allah.

Chapter 56

The End of One Chapter is the Beginning of a New

THE YEAR WAS 2019. President Olivier Katanga had been in power for four years and his hair had already gone completely grey. He sat in a large black leather office chair with his feet crossed on his mahogany desk watching the news. He kept a keen eye on the happenings around the African continent, following the general election in Nigeria the new President was leading the charge on Boko Haram. African Union members pledged troops to the fight against Boko Haram. President Olivier Katanga from the Democratic Republic of Congo was adamant about the need to finally stop the insurgence. The New Nigerian president was told to address the needs of his people that Boko Haram was providing for while the AU troops were being assembled. The Nigerian President was proud to announce that 300 schoolgirls were rescued after his first month and more rescue missions were underway before there would be a full military onslaught on Boko Haram.

The television news reader went on to talk about the promises from the Republican party presidential aspirant to send

American troops into Syria to end the civil war. The next story was that a scientist in Yugoslavia claimed to have found the cure for the Ebola virus. Finally, the reporter began to highlight that there was an outbreak of a disease known as coronavirus in the Chinese city of Wuhan in the Hubei Province. At this story he turned off the television. He had enough on his plate. Rebel forces were causing trouble in the south of Congo, in the north a group of secessionists had risen in Katanga. Within his party, his fight against corruption had created an endless number of enemies. Olivier decided then that he wouldn't worry about a disease in a Chinese city so far away.

Olivier sat back in his chair and thought about his father Doctor Clancy. He had shared the faith with his son, yet Olivier could never claim to be a great Christian. He did however know that God had always been protecting him. He thought about that moment when his car exploded while he was a safe distance away. Olivier reached across the desk and placed his hand on his bible. "Thank you, Lord," mumbled from his almost silent lips. He remembered the last time he ever solicited a prostitute that led him to his sister and had suddenly fueled his fight against human trafficking and prostitution. With greater conviction, hand still on the Bible, he said out loud. "Thank you, Lord, for bringing my sister back to me."

A tear rolled down his face as he thought about all of the things he had gained undeservedly and yet had lost so much. After his divorce with Vivienne, his son turned away from him completely. He would not pick up his phone calls, only respond via official emails. It wasn't until he got remarried that he lost his daughter. She had hoped that her parent's separation was temporary, and was therefore devastated at the pace at which her father was able to move on.

He tried to compensate for lost time with his children by giving them generous gifts of money and material things even though they had never been materialistic. As he slumped back into his chair he mumbled, "Thank you Lord for keeping my children safe."

Olivier was fulfilled politically, but deep within felt an emptiness that he could not share his journey with the people he loved the most. He stared out of the window, took in a large sigh, and rose to face the world. He looked at his desk, his receptionist had brought him a cup of tea but every time he reached for it, he felt that childhood sensation of fear. He asked himself "Could it be poisoned?

A Short Autobiography

My name is Darrell Nkholoma Phiri. I was born May 30 1992 in Ashford, Middlesex, United Kingdom. I lived there with my parents until I was just under the age of two when we moved to Zambia. When I was around eight years old my father prompted me to take up reading. He often gave me the novels which he himself had just completed. It soon became a steadfast hobby of mine to read and have my imagination carry me away. I was often a sickly child, mainly bedridden with asthma, so a good book would often allow my mind to escape from the confines of my hospital bed.

It was not until I was eighteen when my mother was diagnosed with breast cancer that I took up writing; this time not as a bed-ridden patient but as a caregiver. I found solace with writing in-between my caring duties. I told my mother that if she would survive the cancer then I would finish writing a book. Joyously I can say that we both kept up our ends of the deal.

Yet another decade came to pass when the publishing contract for "The Epidemic" was signed. I was fortunate enough to have been in New Zealand for work during the pandemic, joining Grant Thornton, an audit, tax and accounting firm as I entered my second year in the country.

The isolation, created by the pandemic lockdown and loss of many loved ones during 2020, was the fuel I needed to revisit my epidemic, dream-inspired, novel I had finished in 2016. My beloved grandmother, Mary Chifunda Kalikeka, passed two days after I received the publishing contract and therefore my novel is dedicated to her memory.

Reading and writing has helped to get me through many difficult moments. I would like to encourage anyone reading this that when life gives you lemons make lemonade. Turn adversity into creativity but hold onto your career because it can take many years for writing to bear fruit, if it does at all. My advice is to follow the advice of John F. Kennedy as he highlighted in his inauguration speech "Let us encourage the arts and commerce". I believe that the two-walk hand in hand.

All in all, it is my wish that through my writing I can inspire many Zambian children and those around the world to take up the culture of reading. It will lead to greater articulation, diversity in thought and if nothing else it will allow your imagination to take you places outside of your current reality.

Thank you

Darrell N. Phiri